TELL ME WHY

DARK HEARTS BOOK 1

TELL ME WHY

MIA O'SULLIVAN

STAY IN TOUCH WITH MIA

Follow Mia on Facebook

https://www.facebook.com/Mia-OSullivan-101473111481021/

Join my mailing list and get your FREE book, plus all the latest updates, news, freebies, fun, and new book releases!

https://BookHip.com/MATKVC

ONE

Monterey, California

A CLOUD OF DUST, along with the desiccated corpses of several spiders, billowed out from the wooden shutter, and Romy held back a shriek as a very much alive bug skittered out and across her hand.

She stepped back, shaking her hand and coughing as the dust caught in her throat. *Maybe this wasn't such a good idea.* Romy looked around the large room. Now that the shutters were open, light flooded in and she could see the potential of the small building at the corner of the block, the same potential her father had seen when he'd opened his bookstore there three decades ago. No one had been inside for ten years before Romy had opened it up four days ago, and it showed. Debris and dust. That was the sum of her parents' bookstore now.

October in Monterey was rarely warm, but this fall had been colder than normal, and after Romy had been working for just an hour in the unheated building, her hands were frozen. Even her legs, clad in her usual uniform of blue jeans, were cold. She shoved a heap of torn, faded wallpaper to a corner and dusted herself off.

There was a coffee shop at the end of the block, and a cup of latte sounded more than tempting. Romy went to the small ballroom and grimaced at her reflection in the mirror. Her long, dark hair was gray with dust, and her face was smudged with dirt and grime.

She scrubbed at it as best she could and piled her hair up in a loose bun at the nape of her neck. Her clothes, she couldn't do much about. Stepping out of the gallery, she locked the door and headed along the sidewalk. The stores along the block were all decorated for Halloween, and despite the cold and damp air, Romy's spirits lifted. The fall colors were warm and inviting, and as she pushed her way into the coffeehouse, a wave of noise hit her. She ordered her pumpkin spice latte and found a table by the window.

People watching had always been one of Romy's guilty pleasures. Out on the street, late season tourists mingled with the locals. Romy felt as if she were a tourist, too. Even though Monterey was her birthplace, she had been away too long.

At twenty-nine, Romy had been living and working in Manhattan for a decade. Six months ago, when her beloved grandmother, Nari, had died, Romy told her younger cousin that she was moving back to the West Coast to care for him.

Nineteen-year-old Jae had rolled his eyes. "Ro, I'm at Berkeley most of the year, and me and Moon are thinking of renting an apartment with some other guys next year. You don't need to put your career on hold for me."

But the truth was, Romy had tired of the New York lifestyle. Her career as an art curator was shaped there and supported by her mentor, Sebastien, but when she went to him earlier that summer and told him she was opening her own gallery back west, he understood. "You should. There's only so far you can go here, Romy, and you're way too talented to be my assistant forever."

Sebastien, an astute Englishman with a dry sense of humor

and easy manner, had promised her he would help her in any way he could, but Romy knew that most galleries folded within the first year. She had a plan, however, and that plan's name was Milo Keys. Romy had been a fan of the artist since she was a teenager, with one painting in particular speaking to her.

Antigone was a portrait of the artist's wife, standing at a window, staring out over the ocean view. Romy couldn't put her finger on why the artwork meant so much for her—maybe it was the look in the subject's eyes. Somehow the painter had imbued so many different emotions in her eyes: love, peace, regret... confusion. *Conflict.*

It had been the last painting Milo Keys exhibited, over a decade ago now. He had simply stopped being in the public eye, and throughout her college career and her career as first an intern, then assistant curator, Romy had always tried to find out more about the reclusive artist.

But Milo Keys was exceptional, she found, at something other than painting. *Disappearing.* His artwork was quietly withdrawn from galleries all over the world, and there was scant information on the internet about him. He'd had most of it scrubbed. All Romy had been able to find was an obituary for Sarah Keys dated three years prior. Romy had known instinctively that wherever Sarah was laid to rest, Milo would want to be near her.

Sebastien and Romy's best friend, Autumn, had both looked at her askance, but she shrugged. "Call it a hunch, but a man who loses a woman he painted like that—" She nodded at the faded print she had on her office wall. She knew it in her soul—Sarah Keys was interred at the San Carlos Cemetery... which meant Milo Keys was probably in Monterey.

Romy sipped at her coffee, lost in her thoughts. She had been right—the private detective, whom she'd eventually given in to and hired after a lot of soul searching, had confirmed it.

3

"Dude's doing very nicely for himself, thank you," the detective had said after handing her a folder. "Cliffside home in Big Sur. Secluded and very, very private. Ocean views."

Romy had looked through the portfolio of images. The P.I. was right. Milo Key's home was huge, especially for one man. She wondered if all his money came from art. She pushed that thought aside. It wasn't any of her business, but clearly, he didn't need money, and he wasn't all that keen to be back in the public eye.

Which kind of screwed her, if she wanted to persuade him to exhibit with her newbie gallery.

Romy sighed, shaking her head. A second later, she almost jumped out of her seat as she felt a light touch on her shoulder.

A petite blonde woman behind her became startled, too, then held her hands up apologetically. "Oh, gosh, I'm sorry, I didn't mean to make you... Romy?"

Her heartbeat returning to normal, Romy blinked at the newcomer. "Nan? Nan Sommers?"

The blonde grinned widely, a cheeky grin that took her face from beautiful to playful in a flash. "*Romeo, Romeo...*"

"*Where for art thou fine ass,*" they both finished with a laugh, and Romy stood and gathered her old friend in a huge bear hug. "God, Nan... it's been too long."

They sat down at the table, and Romy ordered them more coffee. Nan grinned at her, then glared. "Too long, Ms. Park. I know you were dabbling with those high falutin' folks in NYC."

Romy chocked on a sip of coffee. "*High falutin'*?"

Nan grinned. "Forgive the patois, I've been watching a lot of old movies lately."

"Uh-oh. Man trouble?"

Nan grimaced. "Well, not anymore. Huck's gone to Los Angeles now, and good riddance."

Romy felt a pang of sadness. Nan and Huck had been

together since they were in high school, and although Romy had never much cared for the guy, she knew he had loved Nan. At least until the urge had hit to become an actor—"and a self-confessed *poon hound*," Nan told her now with a roll of her eyes. "Can you believe he actually used those words?"

Romy could, but she politely shook her head. She was glad that Nan looked happy, however, and asked her friend about her life. "Quiet. Just me and the dog, and that's fine by me. How about you? Are you back for good?"

Romy nodded and filled Nan in on the gallery. Nan's eyebrows shot up. "You sneak! You could have told me you were coming back. I had no idea you even still owned that building."

"I wasn't sure I was even going to use it. Too many memories, you know?" Romy swallowed the lump in her throat.

Nan patted her hand sympathetically. "I could have found you another space if you had told me you were coming home."

"You handle gallery spaces?"

"I handle *everything*," Nan said a little sniffily, then laughed. "But seriously, are you happy with the space? I'm just asking because I'm angling for an invite."

Romy laughed. "You are welcome, anytime... why don't we head down there now if you have a moment?"

"For you, anything."

As they walked down the block to the gallery, Romy felt warm. Why hadn't she contacted Nan to tell her she was coming home? Being with her childhood friend right now was so easy, so comfortable. So... right.

Nan walked through the few rooms of the gallery, hmm-ing and hawing and Romy grinned at her. "I know it's small, but I'm hoping for quality over quantity at my shows."

Nan nodded, but she frowned. "Ro... will it give you a steady income?"

A jolt of pain shot through Romy, but she kept her expression steady. "I still... Jae and I... the compensation from..."

"Ah, got it." Nan looked at her in sympathy, putting a hand on her arm. "I heard about it, of course, but it's none of my business."

"We invested it. My grandmother wasn't a modern woman, but with money, she was a genius. Jae takes after her. He invested, hasn't even touch the capital, just uses the interest to live on. I have to use some of my nest egg for this place, but... I'm lucky enough to be able to call this my passion, not my source of income."

"Like I said, none of my business. You know if you need anything, I'm right here. Where are you living?"

"A rented condo for the moment, then, when I've renovated this place, upstairs here, I think."

Nan looked doubtful and Romy grinned. "Oh, ye of little faith. Come upstairs. It's actually in better condition than the downstairs."

An hour later, Romy said goodbye to Nan, having promised her friend they would get together the following evening. She looked around the gallery and decided she had had enough of working today. She drove back to her small condo and went inside. The condo was probably overpriced for how small it was— one bed and two baths, but the tiny balcony and ocean view was worth it.

Romy took a shower and made herself a bowl of soup for supper, taking it out onto the balcony to eat. The cold evening rolled in from the water, and she pulled her sweater tighter around her, but didn't go inside for a while. It was quiet up here, and she found the peace of it intoxicating, despite the frigid air. In an hour or so, Jae would call, checking up on her as if she were the younger cousin, and then she would spend the rest of the evening reading.

Romy hugged her knees up to her chest, looking out to the lights of Monterey and to the sailboats in the bay, bobbing gently in the water. Yeah, this place was wildly overpriced—and worth every single cent. This was the closest she had felt to contentment... maybe ever.

A new life, a quiet life. Work hard and chill out in equal measure. That was her plan right now. Romy got up, gathered her stuff and went inside to read.

He watched her from the car, parked discreetly in the street below her balcony. So, Romy Park had come home at last. He'd kept an eye on her career over the years, and even as late as last year, he had made plans to follow her to New York. Of course, his commitments here in California would have made that difficult, and when he'd discovered she was coming home to Monterey, that problem went away.

And, thank god. Soon, she would remember his name, and the wrongs of years ago would be corrected. Whether she knew it or not, Romy's life belonged to him, and so she would be his.

That she might disobey him never even crossed his mind.

TWO

ROMY ONLY HEARD THEM enter the bedroom at the last moment—
she didn't even have time to brace herself before they both leaped
on top of the bed and began to bounce, yelling their hellos.

"Oh, you absolute demon spawns," she grumbled as Jae and
Moon grinned at her. "Don't you know it's rude to jump a lady?"

"You're no lady," Jae, her junior by a decade and more of a
little brother than her cousin, threw back at her with a withering
look. She swatted at him and grinned in satisfaction when she
connected with bare flesh. "Ouch, vandal."

"You deserve it. Hey, Moonie."

Moon kissed her cheek. "Hey, Ro. This was Jae's idea. I tried
to talk him out of it, promise."

She would almost believe the young man if he didn't wear the
most outrageously faux-innocent look on his beautiful face. Moon
had been Jae's best friend since the young Korean American had
moved to Monterey back in sixth grade. The two of them shared
an oddball sense of humor, and Moon's inherent kindness had
helped Jae through losing his parents. Moon was also the biggest
flirt Romy had ever known, yielding an abundance of charm and
ethereally good looks as his biggest weapons in life.

Romy smiled at them both, then glanced at the clock and groaned. "What the hell, guys? It's *six* a.m. What the hell kind of time did you leave Berkeley to get here?"

"An all-night party at Pebble Beach."

"So, you haven't slept?"

"Nope."

Romy waved them away from her bed so she could get up. Thankfully, she had slept in her long t-shirt and was decent, because neither seemed in a hurry to leave her room. "How you have the energy," she grumbled at them as she padded into her bathroom.

By the time she'd showered and brushed her teeth, Jae and Moon were in her small galley kitchen, cooking breakfast. Despite herself, the smell of the pancakes and the eggs made her mouth water, and she scarfed down the plate of food Jae set in front of her, burning her mouth in the process.

Jae watched her fondly. "Hungry?"

"Only had soup last night."

"Jeez, Ro. Would it kill you to learn to cook?" Jae shook his head. He had never been able to understand that Ro found cooking unbearably dull, even though she loved food. He himself adored being in the kitchen, and he and Moon had found a love of fine cuisine that had often led to dreams of owning their own restaurant, despite neither being a trained chef. "At least get one of those subscription services. You just have to follow a recipe then."

Romy shrugged. To her, as long as she got a balanced diet, it didn't matter if she dined on soup or cereal. "So, are you two going to tell me why you pitched up today? And why you're not in class?"

Moon grinned at her. "It's Saturday, doofus. We said we'd come help out at the gallery, remember?"

Ah, right. Romy finished her breakfast and drained her orange juice. "My contractor is coming to meet us later this morning, so at least we'll get some clue as to when the heavy work will start."

Why, Romy wondered an hour later, did the gallery always seem less habitable than how she remembered leaving it the previous day? She, Jae, and Moon picked their way through the trash on the floor of the restrooms and began to clear it.

By noon, they were exhausted.

"I'll go grab us some coffee and sandwiches," Romy said. "You two take a break."

Romy washed her hands then went out into the street. The day was overcast, and a faint drizzle of rain hung in the air. There was a snarl-up of traffic as Romy crossed the street, and she had to duck and weave among the cars to get to the coffeehouse.

When she was leaving the sandwich bar a few minutes later, the traffic was still at a standstill, and as Romy moved to cross the street, she stopped.

The woman in the car in front of her was crying. *No, not crying,* Romy thought with a pang. *Sobbing.* A heart was breaking, right in front of her.

The woman looked up, sensing Romy's scrutiny, and with a shock, Romy recognized her. *Harper Van Warren.* The woman who had, a decade before, married the love of Romy's life, Connor Small. The last time Romy had seen her was the day of the accident, too…

Harper dashed away her tears and looked away. Romy felt awkward and began to cross the road, but then she heard the window of Harper's car slide down. "Romy?"

Romy sighed. This was a confrontation she didn't want right now, but neither did she want to be rude. "Hey, Harper."

"I didn't know that you were back in Monterey."

"Yeah... just a couple of weeks so far." Romy decided to bite the bullet. "Are you okay?"

She saw a myriad of emotions flash over Harper's lovely face. The other woman was only a couple of years older than Romy, but Romy had always felt like an awkward teenager next to the sophisticated Harper.

The Van Warrens were old, *old* money. Old Frederick Van Warren, Harper's great-grandfather had practically owned half the town at the beginning of the twentieth century, and although most of it had been sold off, the Van Warrens were still at the top of Monterey society. Connor had certainly thought so, Romy thought now, then checked herself. No time for bitterness right now.

Harper forced a smile. "I'm fine. Hormones."

"Ah." Romy knew she was lying but went along with it. She hesitated, then looked at Harper, glancing at the standstill traffic in front of the car. "You know what's good for that? Hot chocolate. Can I buy you a cup?"

Harper looked as surprised as Romy felt with herself, but a second later, Harper had pulled the car out of the traffic and to the sidewalk. "Actually, that sounds great." She got out of the car, then nodded to the cups in Romy's hands. "But..."

"Oh, yeah. Can you give me a sec, I just have to drop these off, and then I'm all yours."

"Sure."

To Romy's surprise, Harper walked with her back to the gallery, saying hello to a bemused Jae and Moon, who gave Romy a curious stare. She didn't explain, just told them she would be back in time to meet the contractor.

At the coffeehouse, she and Harper found a table. *This wasn't the way I thought this day would go.* Romy shot a look at her companion. Now that she had stopped crying, Harper looked more like the young debutante she had been back then—because apparently, debutantes were still a thing for some people, even in the 21st century.

Harper smiled wryly. "I know. This is weird." She sighed heavily. "But it doesn't have to be, and to be honest, it's a relief to be with someone who's not impressed with my family's money."

Romy blinked. "I'm not sure—"

"Romy, I know we were never friends back then, but I always like you. I respected your parents. I would see you all at your dad's place..." She trailed off, flushing.

Romy sighed. It was like this whenever she ran into someone who had known her parents before they died. Jin and Giovanna Park had run the local bookstore, a warm, friendly store with huge squashy couches and an open-door policy. All ages would gather there to chat to the sedate and erudite Jin or to argue politics with the fiery, feminist Giovanna. Jin was a second-generation Korean American. He had met Giovanni, an overseas student from Rome, at college, and they'd married the day after graduation. Romy had followed after three miscarriages, and the Parks had felt no need to add to their brood.

They doted on their daughter but instilled a good work ethic in her, along with both confidence and humility, too. Romy had the happiest childhood she could have imagined—which made it all the more agonizing when it was all ripped away in the blink of an eye.

"And how about you, Harper? How's...married life?" Romy changed the subject. *Let's just the address the elephant in the room, right?* But then she regretted the question as Harper's face creased with pain, and Romy cursed herself. "Oh, Harper, I'm sorry."

"It's okay." Harper drew in a deep breath. "Connor and I are getting divorced. It's been a long time coming, really." She fiddled with the label of the tea bag in her drink. "We were wrong from the start."

Romy shifted uncomfortably in her seat. The *last* thing she wanted to talk about was Connor, but then again, he was the one thing they had in common. Harper seemed to sense her discomfort and half-smiled. "Sorry. It's just… it's fresh, you know. We split maybe three months ago, and it's still strange for me to wake up without Connor in bed beside me."

"What happened?" Romy didn't want to ask the obvious question, but it fell out of her mouth anyway.

Harper sighed. "Monogamy isn't for everyone. It wasn't for us. We always said we had an open relationship, but…" She trailed off, her eyes searching Romy's, and Romy felt her face burn, although she didn't know why. It wasn't like she had seen or spoken to Connor since the day of his wedding.

"Maybe I'm not the right person to talk with about him."

"Maybe. And it's really not fair of me to speak about our problems." Harper shook herself and smiled genuinely for the first time. "It's just a bad day, is all. And… well, I have found, due to the divorce, a lot of my girlfriends were very excited that Connor was single again. Let's just say that."

Romy felt incensed on Harper's behalf. "Then maybe they were never your friends."

There was a ghost of a smile on Harper's face. "You're probably right. I forgot how nice you are."

"We don't really know each other, do we?"

"I guess not. But it is nice to see you. Can we do this again? I find myself in need of female company and conversation that isn't all about the men in our lives."

Romy smiled at her. Despite her unease, she felt for this woman. "Of course. You know where I'll be."

"Ah, yes, the gallery. You'll have some competition."

Romy smiled. "I know, but I'm hoping to specialize, show only one artist at a time."

"Who's the dream get for you?"

Romy felt her face redden again, and she hesitated, but then she decided that Harper had shared with her, and she owed her something back. "Milo Keys."

As expected, Harper's eyebrows shot up in surprise. "Ambitious."

"I know. And, honestly, I don't expect to get him, but that won't stop me trying."

Harper suddenly smiled. "I might be able to help you out there."

Romy's stomach dropped, the adrenalin sending a painful jolt through her. "What?" She was suddenly aware she was gaping at Harper, and Harper grinned back at her.

"Milo is a friend. I could put in a good word, but I have to warn you, he's not likely to say yes to an exhibit. But I can introduce you, at least, so you can work on him."

"You'd do that for me?"

"Of course."

Romy shook her head but smiled. "Thank you, Harper. That means a great deal to me."

For the rest of the conversation, they kept to Romy's plans for her gallery, and Harper seemed to relax as they chatted about the artists they loved.

Romy was floored by the fact that the woman she had always seen as the one who had 'stolen' Romy's love away from her was being so open and friendly. *But then again, I was a kid back then. Harper never stole anything from me. Connor just wanted more prestige and money than my family could ever give him.*

She was glad that Harper had calmed herself now, but it didn't help the uneasiness Romy felt. The way Harper had been crying in the car… that had been more than just mere upset, more than just tears over a divorce. So much more…It was devastation.

THREE

MILO KEYS HID A smile as he opened the door to Harper Van Warren later that day, and she marched in, demanding to know why there was a realtor's board outside his gates.

"I would have thought that was obvious."

Harper gaped at him. "Milo, you *love* this place. You've spent years remodeling. Why would you sell now?"

Milo nodded his head towards the balcony. "Harper, take a breath. Come sit with me. I have a jug of mimosas with your name on it."

Harper, who had taken an Uber out to Big Sur, relaxed a little. As they settled out on the deck, Milo studied her. "Have you been crying again?"

"No."

"Liar."

Harper grinned ruefully at him. Since they had become close friends—after Sarah's death—they had become as close as siblings, Harper being one of the few people Milo could stand in large doses. He was her rock when her marriage to Connor finally imploded—not that he himself mourned the loss of Connor in his life. He loathed the other man, always had, even since before

Sarah died. She had worked with the guy on a few projects at the architect's office in Monterey and had very few good things to say about him, except that she couldn't see what someone like Harper Van Warren saw in the guy. "To say he is vapid would be a kindness," Sarah would say, shaking her head.

After a couple of work barbecues, she had become friends with Harper, and although Milo was a shy man, even back then, he too started to get to know her. It was only after Sarah's suicide that he and Harper became closer. If he were being honest, it didn't hurt that their friendship pissed Connor Small off.

At forty-two, Milo Keys had pretty much written off a romantic life for himself. Sarah's death had desiccated him, making him give up the art career he'd worked so hard for and burying himself out here in what could be described as a Gothic mansion out on the cliffside. It was huge, way too big for a family of ten, let alone a lone widower and his dog, but it had been Sarah's dream house when she grew up here. Ten days after her funeral, Milo had seen it was for sale and didn't even blink. He closed within the week.

Now, three years later... "I cannot believe you want to sell this place," Harper said, shaking her head again as Milo sighed. How could he make her understand that instead of the tribute to Sarah's dream he'd thought the house might be, instead, it turned out to be something quite different.

A mausoleum.

"Look, I need something new. Something smaller." He ruffled the silky ears of his St. Bernard dog, Sailor. Sailor turned his head and licked his hand before sighing heavily and laying down. *Even you're depressed, buddy,* Milo thought.

Harper was studying him. "Nan Sommers might be able to help you out. I can call her."

"Already done. Nan's been understanding."

Harper shifted in her chair. "Speaking of Nan, a friend of hers has come back to town. Romy Park. Do you remember her?"

Milo frowned. "Is that Jin's girl?"

"Yes. She's been in New York since just after she woke up from the coma."

"I didn't know. Didn't her grandmother come over from Korea to take care of her? And the little kid?"

"Jae. He's at Berkeley now."

"Jesus, I feel old."

"It was a decade ago, the accident."

Milo nodded. "You know a lot about them."

"The accident was the same day as my wedding." Harper sighed. "Another car crash. Oh, sorry, that wasn't a great analogy."

"I won't tell." Milo looked at her sympathetically. "Seriously, Harper, did you have a bad day again today?"

She shrugged. "You know how it is."

"Would you honestly want him back?"

"Fuck, *no*," she said a little too fiercely, and they both laughed. "I really don't want to talk about him and, anyway, I had a point."

"That's new."

She glared at him. "Shut it. What was my point? Ah, yes. Romy Park. Guess what she's been doing in New York?"

"Surprise me." The sun was beginning to set now, blazing across the horizon, turning the sky a riot of red, orange, and purple. Milo squinted against the glare. He had to admit—at times like this, he wondered if he'd made the right decision to sell this place.

"Romy Park."

He blinked at Harper. "Huh?"

She flicked his arm. "I said, Romy Park. She was in New York for a decade, training and becoming an art curator."

Something began to nag at the back of Milo's brain. "So?"

"So..." Harper drew out the vowel. "She's opening a small gallery in town, and guess who her dream exhibiter would be?"

Milo felt a jolt of both anger and of fear. "Harper."

"I know, I *know*, and I said you'd probably say no. I made sure she knew that. But she's a sweet girl. Maybe you could just—"

"No, Harper."

"Just come meet her is all I was going to say." Harper grinned at him. "For me. She's a fan. You should hear the way she talked about *Antigone*."

Milo shot her an annoyed look. "Not fair, Harper."

She had the grace to look apologetic. "That's how much I want you to meet her. Just do a drive-by when I meet her for coffee next time."

"You're friends with her now?"

Harper smiled. "You know what? I very much think I will be."

When Harper had left, Milo snapped Sailor's harness on and drove down to Sand Dollar Beach to walk the dog. It was almost dark now, probably too dark to be out walking the dog, but Milo didn't care. The beach was empty, and he could enjoy walking Sailor without the risk of being recognized.

He had been quite the celebrity in the area during the heyday of his art career, and quickly, much to his own dismay, become one of the most recognizable faces on the Monterey art scene. It didn't hurt that he stood almost six feet six inches tall or that he had the face of a Roman God, with his close cropped dark brown hair and sculpted features.

Sarah used to tease him mercilessly that he was every art lover's fantasy man, and certainly he had a hardcore group of fans who hung on his every word the few times he exhibited or was hired to speak at a show.

Milo embraced his introvert nature, and when he met the extroverted Sarah, at first, he had thought they would have nothing in common. Sarah had other ideas, and, in the end, he had to admit she was right. They complemented each other perfectly. Sarah would save him in social situations, and when she needed him—the times her bipolar disorder would mean she lost her 'filter,' Milo was there to save her from any embarrassment. They doted on each other, and on Sailor—their surrogate child. They would have loved to have children naturally, but Sarah's biggest fear was handing her kids the same manic depression she had suffered from her whole life.

So they planned to adopt. The call they had been waiting for had come through… three days after Milo found Sarah's body in their bedroom.

At first, he refused to believe she had killed herself. "Who stabs themselves in the stomach to kill themselves? Why didn't she take pills, or cut her wrists, or…" He argued every which way with the police, with Sarah's family, with the medical examiner.

He even contended that the note she had left—"*I love you, I'm sorry*"—wasn't her handwriting. He was the only one who thought that. After the funeral, he simply shut down. He cut off all communication with virtually everyone on Sarah's side, convinced they blamed him for her death.

For a year, he barely went out. He'd sold the house where Sarah died and bought the clifftop mansion. A ridiculous prospect, but he felt closer to Sarah there.

Had felt closer.

But something had been nagging at him for months. A new life. It was either that or sink. So now he'd put the mansion on the market and was thinking about where he wanted to go next. Seattle. Chicago. Hell, maybe even another country entirely. Italy. France.

Sailor nudged his hand now. The dog was getting older, and he was always a homebody. He'd indulged Milo with a long walk now and again, but tonight wasn't one of those nights.

Sighing, Milo walked back to his truck and loaded the dog in the back. He pulled the car into traffic and then, on a whim, joined the CA-1 and drove to Monterey. The town was busy tonight, and Milo slowed the car to crawl through the streets. Harper had told him where the Park girl was remodeling her gallery, and now, as he turned the corner, he saw it. There were lights on, and through the big picture windows he could see three young people painting the walls and laughing and joking around.

Milo pulled the car over to the opposite curb and sat there, watching the scene for a moment. He didn't recognize any of them, but he supposed one of the younger Korean guys was Jae Park, Romy's cousin.

His eyes slid to the curvy young woman being teased by her companions. Romy Park was certainly beautiful, her dark hair escaping from a messy bun at the nape of her neck and a wide smile on her sweetly rounded face. Even from here, Milo could see her parents in her dark almond eyes and her tan skin. He had known Jin Park reasonably well, having been a regular customer at his bookstore. It had affected the whole community when Jin, Giovanna, and Jin's sister, Hyuna—Jae's mother—had been killed in the accident.

So… Romy Park knew all about grief. That was one thing in her favor, and hopefully why she would understand why he didn't want to exhibit.

Milo checked himself. He realized he was actually considering meeting her… *what*? *When did that happen*? And why was he thinking of excuses for when he told her no?

Sailor harrumphed and lumbered into the passenger seat,

licking Milo's hand. Milo absentmindedly scratched the dog's head. Sailor yawned expansively and settled onto the seat, barely fitting his huge body onto it. "Yeah, I know, buddy. Just so you know, I *do* feel like the world's biggest creeper right now. Let's go home, okay?"

Casting one last glance over to the unfinished gallery, Milo started the car, turned the car around, and headed home.

FOUR

ROMY WALKED BACK TO the gallery. She'd gone out just to grab some food for her 'slaves' as Jae and Moon now referred to themselves, but she'd gotten distracted by the window displays in other art galleries along the streets. Whether that was a good idea or not, she didn't know. They were so professionally run that she wondered if she really knew what she was doing. A couple of the people inside knew who she was and were encouraging—on the surface, that is. She was, after all, their competition, but then again, they were the established ones. Whether they'd be as friendly if they knew she was going to try and land Milo Keys for the gallery, she couldn't guess.

Deep in thought, she was stunned when she got back to the gallery and saw that Jae and Moon had finally cleared the last of the debris away. The two of them had traveled from Berkeley every moment they could spare for the last two weeks, and Romy was incredibly grateful for it. The structure of the gallery was intact—it was just that there was so much broken furniture and fixings and the results of neglect that, some days, Romy wondered if they'd ever get it clean.

"Dudes, are you guys on something?" Romy joked. "You've almost cleared the place."

"Ro, there wasn't much left."

She smiled gratefully at them. "Seriously, I owe you."

Moon put his arm around her shoulders. "Beer is good."

"Beer is always good," Jae added.

Romy chuckled. "You're on."

"Knock, knock."

They all turned to see a tall, dark-haired man with merry blue eyes grinning at them. Romy grinned back at him. "Hey, Nico."

The contractor. Romy switched into her professional mode, and Jae and Moon melted away as she chatted with Nico about her plans for the gallery.

Nico Fleming was a riot, she had discovered a few minutes after they had met, but he was also blessed with vision. He studied Romy's mood boards and listened intently as she expressed her wishes for the space.

"Obviously, there are standard requirements for any gallery— the white walls to show off the art, the lighting, but I kind of wanted a very natural vibe throughout. Nothing too MOMA-ey here."

"Apart from the white."

"Apart from that." Romy grinned at him, noticing the way his eyes crinkled at the edges when he smiled. He couldn't be more than five years older than her, dressed casually in jeans and a flannel shirt, and he had an easy manner that gave her the confidence that she would be able to work with him to get the aesthetic she wanted for her gallery.

Jae had mentioned during last night's dinner that he thought Nico had an eye for Romy, too. Romy had rolled her eyes, shaking her head. "Jae, romance is the *last* thing on my mind."

"*Now* you tell me." Moon quipped and grinned at her. She gave him a mock scowl.

"Just stop that, Moon Kim. I'm old enough to be your—"

"Slightly older lover," Moon finished with a chuckle, and Romy couldn't help but laugh. She had to admit, being flirted with by someone as gorgeous as Moon was one hell of a confidence boost.

Jae was grimacing. "Quit it, the pair of you, it's gross." He snickered a little. "I am curious to know, when was the last time you dated someone, Ro?"

Romy felt uncomfortable, but she hid it from them. "I'm saving myself."

"For whom?"

Romy winked at Moon. "You, obviously, when you get out of short trousers."

Moon laughed, but Jae rolled his eyes. "I'm serious."

"And I'm… *single*. Resolutely so. Now change the subject."

To her relief, he had taken the hint and shut up. But now, as Romy chatted to Nico, she wondered if her young cousin had been right. There was certainly a lot of meaningful eye contact between herself and Nico, but she couldn't tell whether he was just attentive as a colleague or if it was more than that.

She realized she wasn't concentrating on what Nico was saying. "I'm sorry, what was that?"

Nico grinned. "Spacing out? I don't blame you; this part of the process is really dull. But soon we will start the actual remodeling, and you'll be up to see exactly what you want becoming a reality. That's the plan, anyway."

"Hello?"

Romy recognized Harper's sweet voice coming in from the other room. She walked out to meet her friend. "Hey, there, this is a nice surprise."

It was still strange to Romy to greet Harper Van Warren in

such a familiar way, but over the last couple of weeks, the other woman had dropped in a few times to see how she was getting on and to offer any advice about local businesses that might help Romy out. Romy had found Harper easy to talk to and confide in, and she sensed the other woman enjoyed having a close girlfriend again. Harper smiled at her now.

"If I am being a stalker, do tell me."

Romy laughed. "Not at all, it's lovely to see you. Come and meet Nico."

She introduced them, and Nico took Harper through his plans for the place, while Romy listened and nodded along. Nico excused himself and left the two women alone after a few minutes.

Harper looked at Romy. "Handsome, very, very sexy."

Romy chuckled. "All yours, if you want him." Then she realized what she said and grimaced. "Oh, sorry, I didn't mean…"

Harper put her hand on Romy's arm. "Stop tiptoeing around me, I'm good. Actually, I do have an ulterior motive for coming here today. A dinner party—well, that sounds too informal. Call it a potluck dinner without you having to actually bring any pots of anything with you." Romy laughed at her convoluted sentence.

"Sounds interesting."

"You'll come? It'll just be me, you, and," she began grinning widely, pausing for effect, "…Milo Keys."

For a second, Romy couldn't breathe. She stared at Harper in disbelief. "Milo… You're kidding me, right? Just teasing?"

Harper shook her head. "Nope. It'll be fun, the three of us. I told you, Milo and I are quite close."

After a small silence, Romy narrowed her eyes at her new friend. "Does he know I'm coming?"

Harper had the good grace to look sheepish. "Well…"

Romy shook her head. "No, Harper, that's not fair to the

man. He will feel ambushed, and I doubt that will put him in a good mood, nor will it persuade him to come out of retirement."

She felt a strange couple of sadness in her chest at the thought of turning down such an opportunity, but as an introvert herself, she hated when people forced themselves on her, figuratively speaking of course, and so she had every sympathy with Milo Keys' reticence.

"Harper, I know your heart is in the right place, I do, but I can't do that to him."

Harper looked disappointed. "But if he agreed to it, you'd come?"

"But *only* if he agrees to it." Romy gave Harper a stern look, but Harper nodded.

"Fine. I'll call him right now." She took out her phone and flicked through her contacts. Romy felt nervous and turned to give her some privacy, but Harper put a hand on her arm to stop her.

"Milo? Yeah, it's me. Listen, I'm having a few people over for dinner, want to join?"

Romy glared at Harper—she could tell what she was doing, not mentioning Romy's name. Romy sighed. Clearly, Harper was used to getting what she wanted.

And Romy had to admit to herself, there was a strange little thrill in her body now. The thought that she was so close to meeting her hero, the man whose work had inspired her to go into art in the first place.

She could hear his deep voice but couldn't make out the words on the other end of the line, but when Harper smiled widely, she knew Milo had agreed. Romy pointed at herself and mouthed, "Tell him," at Harper, but Harper ignored her. Harper said goodbye to Milo and shut off the phone, giving Romy a victorious smile.

"Done and done." She saw Romy's glare. "Hey, I never said I would mention that you were coming, just that there would be other people there."

Romy knew she wasn't going to win this argument but accepted Harper's invitation anyway; she wasn't a fool, and this was a guaranteed *in* with Milo Keys. She could hardly turn it down, could she?

Later on, having promised Harper she would be there at her dinner party over the weekend, Romy went to find Nico. He was in the unfinished staffroom, measuring the wall where Romy wanted a huge picture window installed. He looked up and smiled as she came in.

"Hey."

"Hey yourself. Sorry about that."

Nico shrugged good-naturedly. "No problem. Listen, I have an appointment to get to right now, but I was wondering if you were free for a late supper? Say around nine o'clock? There's a great little burger place just opened—it's a friend's place. We can talk more about what we can do with this room."

Romy hesitated. She wasn't sure whether she was being asked out on a romantic date or if it was just a work thing. She couldn't read Nico's expression. "Maybe another night," she said carefully. "I have another appointment tonight."

She could feel her face burning at the lie, but Nico nodded and smiled. "Cool beans. Another time."

"Definitely." She was relieved he didn't take the rejection badly, but then again, he may just have meant it as a business thing. She didn't want to question why she always panicked at the thought of any romantic situation.

Nico left soon afterwards. Jae and Moon had gone back to Berkeley late that afternoon, and now Romy was alone. She tidied up as best she could and lugged a couple of huge trash bags out to the dumpsters in the alley at the back of the gallery. There was a sharp nip to the air tonight, and she shivered, tugging her thin coat around her. She really needed to go shopping, get some new clothes. All of her thicker jackets were way too warm for the Californian climate, but she had nothing that could protect her for the damp air coming off the ocean. In Manhattan, that hadn't been a problem.

She went back into the gallery and locked the doors behind her. It was eerie, being here after dark alone. The open spaces of the gallery rang with silence. Romy snagged her bag from the ersatz staffroom and went out to the main room to cut off the lights.

As she moved to lock the door, she shrieked as a dark shadow fell across it and the door opened. It took a moment in the darkness for her eyes to adjust, and when they did, they widened in shock and surprise as she took in the man, that all-too-familiar man, standing in her doorway. He smiled at her.

"Hey, Romy. Long time, no see."

Romy stared at Connor Small in disbelief as he stepped forward and kissed her cheek. He smiled down at her, but the smile did not reach his eyes. He cupped her cheek in his hand and Romy was too shocked to pull away.

"I've missed you so much, baby, so, so much."

And before she could stop him, he pressed his lips against hers.

FIVE

MUCH LATER, ROMY SUPPOSED that other women would have slapped him, or thrown him out, or simply asked him what the hell he was doing.

I should have done all of those things, she said to herself now, *because the one thing I definitely shouldn't have done was invite him back to my place. What the hell was I thinking?* She moved around the kitchen of her condo, making coffee, and feeling Connor's gaze boring into the back of her head. *This isn't how I wanted to see you again,* she thought now, close to tears.

She handed a mug of hot coffee to Connor and was rewarded with one of his smiles. She remembered that smile all too well; it had gotten Connor out of trouble on so many occasions. Out of trouble... and into her pants, on more than one occasion. Not tonight though, not ever again, she thought fiercely, thinking of her new friend. She wondered what Harper would think of her now.

She finally met Connor's gaze. "What are you doing here, Connor? I thought you left town after the divorce."

"Did Harper tell you that?" He grinned at her surprise. "Yeah, I know you and she have gotten close since you came back to town. Don't worry, I'm not stalking you, I just got a lot of friends in the town. And to answer your question, I've got a place out at Salinas. Harper was *good* enough to loan me the money for the rent."

Ugh. Romy ignored the dig at her new friend and fixed Connor with an inquisitive look. "So you're coming to town a lot then?"

"Well, I got a reason now."

"And what might that be?" *Please don't say it,* she thought, *please don't act like there's anything between us after all this time. We don't know each other.*

"Well, to be frank, you."

Romy's heart sank. "Connor, it's been ten years. I was a kid back then. We don't know each other."

"But we do have a history, Romy."

Before she could stop herself, a decade's worth of bitterness came out of her mouth. "That you threw away because you wanted to marry into money, Connor. Remember that? Because I do, I…"

She stopped herself before she could say anymore. She didn't want to give him any satisfaction by thinking he had any sort of hold over her anymore. Connor, to his credit, held up his hands, his eyes serious.

"Look, I didn't mean anything by that except I'd like to be your friend. I'm sorry about the kiss earlier. That was inappropriate and wrong. Just seeing you brought back so many memories, and yes, I do know what I threw away for the money." He seemed to shrink in his seat, all the bravado disappearing. He looked up at her. "I wrecked my life, your life, and Harper's life because I was greedy and stupid."

Romy didn't know what to say to that. She sighed. "Look, Connor, I came back here to start again. A new life, emphasis on the *new*. I do not want to rehash old history. What was between us was nothing, really. A schoolgirl crush."

Connor winced and Romy felt bad for saying it. Because it was a lie; it was more than a crush. She had loved this man with every cell in her body. He had invaded her every waking—and most of her sleeping—thoughts. When she had stood in the congregation at his wedding, it had felt like acid being poured through her veins to hear him give himself to another woman.

She remembered the feeling of that, but Romy couldn't summon up why she had felt so strongly for this man. Maybe it was because he was her first love, maybe because she had given him her virginity.

And maybe because he had said that he adored her, that he loved her more than any other person on the face of the earth, everything a lovestruck teenager wanted to hear.

But she wasn't a teenager anymore. She sat down opposite him, crossing her legs and arms, a silent barrier.

"Connor, in my mind, your wedding is mixed up with the worst thing that ever happened to me—losing my parents and my aunt, that was the kind of pain which never heals. Losing you… I don't want to hurt you, but I don't even think about that anymore."

"Which is as it should be. I was never worth the worry or the pain, I know that. What you went through, I can't even imagine. All I am asking now is, can we be friends? And don't think I'm asking this to sabotage your new friendship with Harper. Both of you are wonderful women who deserve better than me, and I'm being selfish asking for your friendship, I know, but I would like it. I'm going to be in town quite a lot, and you'll see me around. I'd like for it not to be awkward."

Connor was right. Now that his arrogance had disappeared and she was seeing him clearly, she could see a man who was worn down by a bad marriage—of his own making, mind you—but who just wanted a quiet life. And it would be better not to make any enemies for herself, especially with old friends.

"Look, Connor, I'll think about it. That's all I can give you right now."

Connor nodded somberly. "And that's all I can ask. Thank you." He got up and handed her his empty coffee mug. "Like I said, I'll be around." He reached into his pocket and drew out a business card and handed it to her. "My number. You need anything, you give me a call, okay?"

Romy took it and nodded. "Okay."

She walked him to the door and was glad he didn't try to kiss her goodbye. Instead, he touched a fingertip briefly to her cheek and smiled. "Good job on growing up, beautiful. See you around."

She closed the door after him and went back into the living room. She flopped down onto the couch and took a shuddering breath in. *What the fuck was that? What the hell just happened?*

Ten years of pain and emotion flooded to the surface then, and she put her head in her hands and started to cry.

Milo flicked his phone onto speaker and set it down on the table gently. Harper had called him back, sounding sheepish, and telling him the truth about her little "dinner party."

Milo couldn't decide whether he was amused or furious. "Tell me, Harper, did I or did we not have a conversation about this already?"

"I'm fully prepared to be utterly passive-aggressive about this whole thing. It's not a *date* I'm setting you up on, it's a professional courtesy to two friends. All I'm doing is getting you two in the same room together so you can meet, that's all."

Milo sighed. "Fine."

There was a shocked silence on the other end of the phone line. "I'm sorry, what?"

Milo pressed his lips together, trying not to laugh. "So, I'll go along with your cunning plan, but I'm not going to be pressurized into exhibiting. So, none of that from you, deal?"

He heard Harper's relieved sigh. "Deal."

"Also, I get to call you *The Hooded Claw.*"

"The what-the-what now?"

Milo sighed. "Damn millennial. *The Hooded Claw. Penelope Pitstop.*"

"Oh, one of those old-time cartoons?" But Harper giggled wickedly, and he realized he'd been had.

"Do you require my presence at this dinner or not, you brat?" He asked tartly, then laughed. He'd woken up in a better mood than he had for months, maybe even years. The decision to sell the house had lifted a weight.

After he'd said goodbye to Harper, he pottered about the house for a while, and then he went up to the attic, where he kept his paintings. He lifted the dust sheets and pulled each canvas out carefully. He wasn't going to waver about exhibiting—no *way*—but he spent an hour figuring out which works he would send to the new little gallery in town, if he was.

Just for fun, he told himself, but he had to admit he was enjoying himself. Last of all, he pulled out the largest canvas.

Antigone. He ran his eyes over his most celebrated painting. He had known as soon as he finished it, it would be his masterpiece. His model, his muse, was Sarah, of course, but he had imagined her standing at the window of this house—a house she'd never even been inside.

But the vision had been so clear in his head. Sarah was meant to live here, and they had been destined to raise a family in this house.

A wave of grief hit him, but Milo refused to give into it. He placed the painting back in its rack and draped the dust sheets over it. His old agent, Dan, despaired at how he stored his life's work, urging Milo to put them into specialized storage somewhere, but the truth was simply that he needed them with him, even if he no longer painted or exhibited.

Jesus, Keys, you really need to get a life. There was a bar out in Salinas that he used to go to now and again with some old college friends. All of those friends were out East now, but it was the kind of bar a guy could go, watch a game on the flat screen, and chill out.

Decision made, Milo grabbed his keys and headed out.

Romy hadn't mentioned seeing Connor to Jae when he called to check up on her. She knew she would have to tell him eventually, but in the hours since she had seen her first love, she had vacillated between anger, sorrow, and nausea.

Now she lay in bed, determinedly *not* sleeping. She jiggled her legs impatiently and sat up, pushing the covers aside. Why had he had such an effect on her? She knew she might see him, but somehow, cognitive dissonance had kicked in, and she hadn't dealt with the reality of actually seeing him.

Also… that kiss. If Connor had been hoping the desire in her would be ignited by it, he would be sorely disappointed. *He was lucky I didn't kick his ass,* she thought grimly, padding quietly into the kitchen.

Romy grabbed a glass of water, drained it, and then decided to just make some coffee. Screw sleep, she could get on the internet and pin some more images to moodboards—that was Romy's kind of procrastination.

When the coffee was made, she went to the balcony and opened the sliding doors a crack. The cold night air hit her skin, but she still stood there, cradling her coffee and enjoying the quiet. The street below was empty of traffic, and there had been a small rain shower because the asphalt was slick with water.

Romy stared at the shimmering reflection of the streetlights and thought about Harper's invitation. If Milo Keys did indeed turn up at the dinner... *holy hell*. She would finally meet her idol. A thrill ran through her. She had already decided that she would not press the subject of him exhibiting at her gallery—in fact she wouldn't mention it at all.

Instead, she would concentrate on getting to know *him*, even if for just that one evening. Harper had told her that Milo didn't have many friends because he was such a hermit, but Romy wondered if it was because people were too careful around him when it came to mentioning his wife. She knew what that was like. The sympathy that turned to discomfort. The avoidance of eye contact, and then of any sort of contact.

After the accident, after the month-long coma, and after she'd finally learned how to walk again, there had been a wash of people she barely knew come to her grandmother's house to pay their respects. It lasted maybe a week. Romy hadn't cared at the time—she just wanted to go to sleep and never wake up. It was only the fact that she knew, eventually, her already elderly grandmother wouldn't be able to care for Jae—that's what kept Romy going. Her cousin was still too young to comprehend the horror of the accident, but he too would have to grow up fast.

Which is probably why he "big brother's" me, Romy thought with a smile. She closed the sliding door and dumped the rest of the coffee in the sink. On her way back to her bedroom, something caught her eye near the front door. An envelope.

It had been shoved under the door, and there was no writing on the front of the envelope. Romy picked it up and opened it. She pulled out a cutting from a newspaper, by the looks of it an old newspaper, or at least one that wasn't very recent. She unfolded it, and a pang of sharp pain went through her. It was an obituary... for her mother and father, and her aunt, too.

There was no letter with the cutting. Romy frowned. Why on earth would someone think to shut this into an envelope and put it under her door? What was the point? To cause her pain? Why?

Romy shook her head, set the envelope on the kitchen counter, and went back to bed. It was odd, sure, but it was just a newspaper cutting.

It was only when she woke suddenly a few hours later that she wondered if it had been intended as a threat.

SIX

"THAT IS WEIRD." HARPER said, frowning as she led Romy into her house. Well, 'house' was a bit misleading. *Try mansion or castle,* Romy thought with a grin. Harper caught her looking around with wide eyes and grinned sheepishly.

"Yeah, yeah, I know, it's ridiculously big, especially for just me, but it's been in the family for years."

"Hey, no judgement here, it's gorgeous." And it was. It was an eclectic mix of the classical and the minimalist, and it worked perfectly. Romy wondered if this is where Harper had lived with Connor, and Harper seemed to read her mind.

"Yup, this was indeed the marital home. Connor wasn't happy that he had to leave, that was clear, but luckily my prenup was airtight. I got this and a hunting lodge out in the woods."

Romy felt her face burn but just nodded. She hadn't yet told Harper that she'd seen Connor, but she had decided she was going to, and was even ready to ask her advice about what he had said. Romy might have known Connor longer, but Harper knew him better, she was sure.

But right now, Connor was the last thing on her mind. In a few moments, she would be meeting her idol, her inspiration.

Milo Keys was running late, apparently, but he had promised faithfully to be there soon, Harper told her with a grin.

"If he knows what's good for him, he wouldn't dare back out now."

Romy followed Harper into the kitchen and was surprised to see that there was no staff there, even though the kitchen counters were covered with cooking ingredients and half-finished dishes. Harper picked up a knife.

"My favorite hobby, cooking. If I hadn't been so busy with the family's foundation, I would have loved to have trained as a chef."

Romy offered to help, but Harper waved her into a seat. "No, I got this, you're a guest."

For the next twenty minutes, the two women chatted while Harper worked and Romy began to relax. Despite all the grandeur surrounding her, Harper really was very down to earth, and Romy began to warm up even more to the other woman.

As Harper slid the dish she was making into the oven, Romy found her courage. "Harper, I think you should know. I saw Connor yesterday."

She waited for Harper's reaction. Harper closed the oven and stood up, turning to face Romy. "And how was it?"

Before Romy could answer, the doorbell rang, and they both started a little. Harper chuckled.

"Great timing as always. That will be Milo." She saw the nervousness creep into Romy's expression and patted her arm comfortingly. "Hang loose, lovely. He really is a sweetheart."

Harper disappeared out of the kitchen and Romy stood up, tidying some cups to have something to do with her hands. Her heart was thumping painfully against her ribs. She heard a deep, melodic male voice talking to Harper as they returned to the kitchen, and then, there he was. Milo Keys.

Romy had seen photographs of him, of course, but she wasn't prepared for just how handsome this man was. She was reminded of a line from a movie, something about a really gorgeous actor being "photoshopped" as he was just *too* good-looking to be real. That was Milo Keys. He towered above both Romy and Harper, and his smile was pleasant enough, but his eyes were wary.

"Hello."

"Hi… Mr. Keys, it's very nice to meet you." Romy almost got the entire sentence out without her voice shaking. She cursed herself silently and offered her hand to him. He took it, his huge hand dwarfing hers.

"It's Milo, and good to meet you, too. I knew your father a little."

Romy nodded but then there was an awkward silence. Finally, Harper broke it. "Jesus, you two. Milo, this is Romy, Romy, this is Milo. Who's hungry?" She rolled her eyes at them and Romy couldn't help but giggle, and she saw Milo crack a smile. "Let's take our drinks out onto the patio. The beef daube won't be ready for an hour or so."

Now that the ice was broken, Milo asked Romy about her gallery and she told him about her life in Manhattan's art scene. As she had promised herself, she didn't mention him exhibiting in her gallery once. She was also glad that Harper didn't mention it; she had asked her friend not to earlier. "I do not want to pressure him in any way that will make him uncomfortable," she had told Harper.

Milo seemed to relax a little when he realized she wasn't going to use this dinner to try and get him to show his work. There was something both serene and sad about the man, but Harper, at least, was great at bringing people out of themselves, and Romy was learning.

She got to study Milo more while they ate Harper's incredible stew. He and Harper obviously had some kind of brother/sister relationship going on, and he teased her mercilessly, making Harper scream-laugh so infectiously that Romy was a little jealous.

But it served to put Milo at ease, and after dinner, they lounged around Harper's living room, drinking wine and chatting.

"So," Milo said eventually, "I never did get to know how you two met."

Harper and Romy looked at each other and laughed. "Well, we knew each other vaguely years ago, but this time, well, I had a nutty in my car. That day you called me out, Milo. I was crying in my car, and Romy... found me. Offered me a drink. From her hip flask," Harper said, with a wicked grin, "she always has it on her. Pure moonshine."

Romy was giggling furiously. "You are such a liar, Harper Van Warren." The wine was making Romy feel a little loopy, so she leaned over to Milo and stage-whispered to him. "It was *Johnny Walker Blue*."

Milo grinned, and it was like the sun had come out. "A woman of taste."

Romy clinked her glass against his. "You know it."

"Pssh. Don't believe a word, Milo, she has a still in the back of that gallery. Peach moonshine, sweet and delicious, but don't eat the peach. It'll kill ya."

Harper was actually slurring her words now, and Romy and Milo busted up. "I honestly have no idea what you're saying. You drunk, girl." Milo steadied Harper as she stood up and wobbled.

"I think I'd better go make some coffee." She stumbled into the kitchen.

Romy grinned at Milo. "Should we go help her?"

"Nah, she'll be fine." He was half sitting, half lying back in his chair. He smiled lazily at her. "So..."

"So?"

"I'm surprised you haven't given me the full court press."

Romy shrugged. "I didn't want to come on too strong." For some reason, her own words made her blush, but before she could look away, his gaze fixed steadily on hers.

One beat.

Two.

Romy felt that look all over her body. Her nipples hardened, and a pulse began to beat between her legs. Her chest felt tight.

"Milo—"

"Hey, who takes sugar?"

Romy blinked and then chuckled as Milo rolled his eyes at Harper's drunken shout. "None for me, doofus,"

"Nor me, thanks."

"'Kay"

"Sheesh," Milo said, grinning as Romy laughed.

"You two have a great friendship."

Milo nodded. "We do. We've known each other forever, but it's only lately that we got close."

"It's nice. My cousin, he's like a brother to me, and we have a similar vibe—always busting each other's chops. He's at Berkeley."

"Harper said. And he helps you out at the gallery?"

"Just while I'm renovating. Or remodeling, really, there's hardly any actual renovating to be done. I was lucky."

Milo nodded. "That building was a good space. I never understood why it stood empty for so long."

Romy frowned. "You know the gallery?"

Was it her or did he look a little shifty? "Well, Harper told me where it was."

"And you came to check it out?"

Milo hesitated then laughed. "I'm busted. Yes, I did, I'm sorry. Like the biggest creep, I did."

"Not a creep at all," Romy told him, her face flushing again. "You are always welcome, anytime. Just to hang out, I mean."

There was another loaded silence, but his eyes were warm. "Thank you, Romy."

She swallowed hard. Why did this man make her feel such different emotions at the same time? He was gloriously sexy, and yet sweet-natured, too. Romy didn't know if it was a false sense of security or the wine, but she leaned forward and put her hand on his. "I'm so sorry about your wife, Milo."

It was like a switch being turned off. His smile dropped and he looked away. Romy was horrified. "I mean, look, I'm sorry, I shouldn't have…"

"It's okay." But the flat monotone of his voice said otherwise. Romy wanted to cry.

"Milo—"

He got up suddenly, moved away from her. "Actually, Harper, I should be going. I left Sailor on his own at the house."

Romy felt frozen as the next few minutes passed with Harper saying goodbye to Milo, her lovely face creased with concern at the strange atmosphere between Milo and Romy.

When Milo was gone, Harper came back into the room and looked at Romy. "What happened? What did I miss?"

Romy felt cold inside. "I'm an idiot, that's what's wrong. God, I'm—" The tears that had been threatening came now, but she dashed them away with her hand. "I had too much to drink. I told him I was sorry about Sarah… Jesus, I'm a moron."

"What's moronic about that?" Harper sat down next to her, frowning. "Milo talks about Sarah all the time, why would he take offense now?"

"Because he doesn't know me!" Romy's voice was rising now, and she dragged a deep breath into her lungs before she could spiral into a full-on panic attack. She had met her idol, her inspiration, and she had thought there was something there, and now... she had blown it.

God damn it...

She shook her head. "I have to go, Harper. Thank you for a lovely evening."

Harper tried to persuade her to stay, have some coffee, and calm down, but Romy insisted in calling a cab. Harper waved her off, and as she drove away, Romy looked back to see her friend still staring after the cab, looking worried.

So, she'd ruined Harper's evening, too. Romy closed her eyes and dropped her head into her hands. Clumsy, awkward, and a party pooper. She would call Harper in the morning and apologize.

Thankfully, her driver wasn't a talker, and the journey back into Monterey passed in silence. It was only when they had almost reached her street when he slowed to a halt. There was some kind of party that had spilled out onto the street, and it was blocking the road towards her place.

"I can back up, go around a different route?" The driver looked back at her uncertainly, but Romy shook her head.

"I can walk from here."

She tipped him generously and stepped out into the cold night air. She was glad for it—it helped sober her up. She tried to slip quietly past the revelers, but one of them asked her to dance with him, and he twirled her around once before letting her go. She grinned at him and, in relief, made her escape.

She could still hear the party as she walked up to her condo and let herself in. Immediately she knew something was wrong. A cold draft blew into the kitchen from the open sliding door of the balcony.

Romy's body tensed. Had she left it open? It had happened before, and she had been out there sipping some tea before she got ready earlier. Slowly, she padded towards it. It would be difficult, but not impossible, for someone to climb up to the balcony, but they would really have to want it.

She slid the door closed and stood, listening. Nothing. No noise from the apartment. She could hear her own heartbeat in the silence.

There's no one there. Romy breathed deeply and put her bag down. She moved carefully through the apartment, checking each room before she finally relaxed. Paranoia was the last thing she needed right now.

She shook it off and went to take a shower. The hot water spraying on her body helped calm her down and sober her up. Afterwards, she slipped into fresh sweats and grabbed her book from the nightstand. She knew she wouldn't be able to sleep; her mind was roiling from the events of the evening, and she hoped the book would distract her, at least a little. Romy walked back into the living room—and froze.

The sliding door was open. For less than a second, Romy's mind went blank with fear—and then there were hands on her back, shoving her and she was falling... falling...

She felt an explosion of pain, and then there was nothing.

SEVEN

MILO GOT HOME AND immediately took Sailor out for a walk. He needed the air, he needed to calm down. Why the hell had he reacted that way? It had been a sweet thing for Romy to say, hell, anyone who knew anything about him would have said the same.

So why did he have such a visceral reaction? Milo shook his head now, angry with himself. *You know damn well why. Because at that moment, you'd been thinking about how much you would like to kiss Romy Park. How you would have taken that sweet mouth of hers and covered it with your own. Fisted that glorious dark mane in your hand and...*

"For fuck's sake, stop." He growled to himself, now. But when Romy had mentioned Sarah, the whole fantasy had come crashing down. He resented her for that, and he knew it wasn't fair, but there it was, *damn it.*

Sailor bumped his hand—he'd had enough of his walk now, and Milo turned for home. Jesus, he'd really fucked it up, hadn't he? In the morning, he'd apologize to Harper then go to the gallery and do the same for Romy. Hell, he might even agree to her showing one of his...

Really?

Was he actually considering that?

Milo sighed. *First things first.* He had some apologies to make.

But when he drove to Monterey in the morning, the gallery was closed up and empty. He frowned. He could have sworn Romy told him she was always there before seven a.m. He peered in through the windows to see if she was out back, but he saw no sign of movement.

"Hey, buddy, can I help you?"

Milo turned to see a vaguely familiar man smiling at him. Nick? No, Nico. The other man seemed to recognize him too.

"Oh, hey, Milo."

"Nico. Look, I'm sorry, I was looking for Romy. Romy Park?" He didn't want to seem too familiar. Nico's smile faded.

"She's not here?"

Milo shook his head. "She wasn't expecting me or anything, but I was under the impression she was here every day this early."

"She usually is." Nico banged on the door. "Ro? Romy?"

They stood for a moment, then Nico took out his cell phone. "Give me a second."

"Sure."

Milo moved away to give the man some privacy and couldn't help wondering if Nico and Romy were more than colleagues. He checked himself—he was thinking like some lovesick schoolboy.

Nico shook his head. "Straight to voicemail." He looked back into the gallery and Milo could see uncertainty in his eyes. "I don't know, man. Something feels hinky."

Milo nodded. "Do you have her cousin's number?"

"Yeah, good idea." He placed another call, and Milo listened to him talk to Jae Park, watching the other man's expression change.

"And she won't mind? Okay, sure, no, I'll go there. I'll call you back soon." He ended the call. "Jae hasn't heard anything. Could be she just slept in, he says, but I could tell—"

"—he's concerned?"

"Yup. Anyway, he gave me her address, and I said I'd go and check up on her."

Milo nodded and hesitated before looking at Nico. "Mind if I tag along? I was with her last night and there was... let's just say I might have upset her, and I want to apologize."

Nico considered. "Well... yeah, I'm sure that would be okay. Let's go in my truck."

Milo looked up at the condo. The fact the balcony door seemed to be open was either a good thing or very, very bad news. Nico was right. Something felt hinky. Nico rang the buzzer for Romy's place, and they waited for an answer.

Nothing. Nico and Milo shared a look. Without saying anything more, Nico buzzed the super. A pleasant-faced, middle-aged woman named Jeanie came to greet them. She asked for their IDs and then said she'd take them up.

At Romy's door, she knocked twice, then opened the door.

"Romy? Romy, dear?" Milo followed Nick and Jeanie into the condo. "I'll see if she's overslept, dears," Jeanie said, giving them a meaningful look that told them to stay out of Romy's bedroom. Milo and Nico split up, Nico went to the kitchen, Milo to the living room.

At first, Milo didn't comprehend what he was seeing, that the unconscious, bloody pile on the floor was Romy. A glass coffee table was shattered around her, and she lay still, too still, amongst the debris. The shock was ice in his veins, constricting his chest before he reacted.

"Guys! She's here!" He dropped to his knees next to Romy. "Hey, hey, sweet girl... can you hear me?"

There was blood spattered all over her face and neck, and Milo was careful when he reached to check her pulse. To his relief, it was there and reasonably strong.

"Jesus!" Nico was there, followed by Jeanie, who gasped in distress.

"Nico, call 911."

Romy moaned a little as Jeanie put her hand on Milo's back. "I'll get a cool cloth."

Milo nodded, not taking his eyes from Romy's face. Her eyelids flickered, and she opened them, looking directly at him. Her brow creased.

"Milo?"

"I'm here, sweetheart. You're going to be okay… we're calling an ambulance."

Romy shook her head, winced and tried to sit up. "I'm okay."

"You're really, really not. Romy, just lay still."

But she ignored him, and, giving up, Milo helped her sit up. She didn't appear to be actively bleeding anymore, but there was a myriad of cuts on her face, neck, and chest. Jeanie brought over the damp cloth and began to dab at her face. Romy winced but smiled wearily. "I'm okay, really. I don't… I don't really know what happened…"

Her attention drifted and Milo, worried she was about to pass out, picked her up out of the glass and laid her gently on the couch. Nico came over then. "Paramedics on the way. The police, too."

Romy frowned. "The police?"

Nico nodded but didn't elaborate. Milo smoothed Romy's hair back from her forehead and her eyes met his. "Do you remember how you fell, Romy?"

"No. I remember coming home from…" Her eyes lid away from his then, and he realized with a pang, that she remembered the scene he had made at Harper's house.

"Romy, it's okay, really. I'm sorry about last night." He could feel the curious glances both Nico and Jeanie were giving him, but he ignored them. "I was an idiot. You were very sweet and I just… forgive me."

Romy gave him a weak but genuine smile. Underneath her olive skin, she looked very wan, and there were dark circles under her eyes. "Do I really need an ambulance? I don't want to waste their time."

But Milo insisted, and when the paramedics got there, they recommended they take Romy to be checked out in the emergency room. Milo rode in the ambulance with her, while Nico followed in his car. Nico volunteered to call Jae, and Milo waited in the relatives' room while the doctor examined Romy. Milo wondered if he should call Harper, but as he took his phone out, Nico was back.

"Jae's driving down from Berkeley. I told him Romy seemed okay, but he insisted."

"Maybe it's for the best. After all, we're hardly her family." Milo smiled at him. "Just friends. You?"

"Just friends, too. She's a cool kid, though."

"I agree."

Nico sat down next to him. "I haven't seen you in town for, god, months. Maybe even years. I heard about your wife. I'm sorry, man, that must have been rough."

Milo's throat closed, but he forced himself to nod. "It was. Thanks. How long have you been working with Romy?"

"Since she called me about the gallery. To be honest, and I keep telling her this, there's not that much I can do for her, but she insists on keeping me around. I think it gives her a confidence boost. It's a big step she's taking for someone so young."

"Yep, sure is."

"And I appreciate all the help."

They both started and stood as Romy limped in. Both Milo and Nico rushed to help her, but she waved them away. "I told you, I'm fine."

The doctor appeared behind her, rolling her eyes. "As she keeps saying, but Romy, you've had a pretty bad concussion, and you're going to be real sore for a few days." She looked at the two men. "Do either of these belong to you, Romy?"

"Nope." Romy seemed a little disgruntled, and Milo didn't know why, but he found her sulking adorable.

The doctor sighed. "Whatever. You two are now in charge of making sure she gets home okay—unless I can make one last plea for you to admit yourself overnight?"

"I refer you to my previous 'nope.'"

Milo hid a smile, and Nico grinned. Romy glared at them both. "I don't need babysitting."

"Okay, then." The doctor scribbled on her notepad. "Well, I won't be the one who signs your death certificate when you throw up in your sleep and choke on it, so what do I care?"

Even Romy's lips twitched at the doctor's snark. "Fine."

"Your cousin is on his way," Nico told her, and Romy relaxed a little.

"See?" She shot a smug look at the doctor, who shrugged.

"You experience any headache or dizziness, you take it easy, and if it doesn't resolve with sleep and painkillers, come back in."

Romy's face softened. "I will. And in all seriousness, thanks, doc."

Milo insisted on Romy riding shotgun in Nico's truck, and he sat in the back, listening to them talk sporadically. Despite her earlier sass, Romy looked all done in. There were a few butterfly stitches on her face, but she told them none of the cuts were that deep.

"Some of these bruises are going to be grim. I might have to layer on some pan stick to hide them." She sighed. "I keep thinking maybe I was drunker than I thought last night." She turned to Milo in the back. "I wasn't blackout drunk, though, right?"

"Not even close. We were joking around, but none of us were." His voice trailed off. Didn't he excuse his awful behavior by blaming the drink? He looked up and met Romy's eyes. There was no accusation in them. She smiled, a soft smile of friendship. Milo couldn't help but smile back.

"So, I don't know, I..." She gave a sigh of frustration and closed her eyes. "I just don't know."

Back at her apartment, she studied the debris of her coffee table. "Well, that sucks."

Something was beginning to tug at her memory, but her head was beginning to pound, and she didn't want to face it.

"I'll clear this up," Nico said, heading to the kitchen "you got a dustpan?"

"Under the sink."

Alone with Milo, Romy felt shy. "Thanks for coming to look for me."

He smiled at her. "You're welcome."

"You came to see me at the gallery?"

He nodded. "I wanted to apologize for how I acted at Harper's place. It was... I was just taken by surprise."

"I'm sorry I upset you."

"You didn't."

Milo reached out and touched her cheek and she felt a flush pass over her entire body. She leaned into his touch for a moment, then drew away. She felt a wave of fatigue, probably the concussion her doctor warned her about. "I think I better get some sleep."

"Good idea. Listen, I'll stay until your cousin gets here. You shouldn't be alone."

Romy felt her face burn. "I don't want to inconvenience you."

"You're not."

She thanked him, and then Nico, who had finally found her dustpan and was clearing up the glass. Romy walked to her bedroom and got into bed.

She closed her eyes, but her head swam, making her feel nauseous. She opened them and stared at the ceiling. What the hell had happened last night? She remembered being upset, leaving Harper's place. Dancing? She remembered dancing...

...she remembered the door to the balcony being open. Her stomach lurched and she stumbled out of bed to her bathroom, only just reaching the toilet before throwing up.

"Hey, you okay?"

Milo was at the door now, and she shook her head. He came into the bathroom and smoothed her hair back as she retched until there was nothing else to bring up. Milo's handsome face was creased with worry. "I think maybe you should go back to the hospital."

Romy shook her head. "No, it's not that... I just remembered what happened."

"What is it?"

Her throat constricted as she stared at him with fear flooding her veins. "It wasn't an accident. Somebody pushed me."

EIGHT

THE DOCTOR HAD BEEN right. Romy ached everywhere, and it was difficult to get up the following morning to go to the gallery. Jae had arrived soon after she and Milo had talked about the assault, and she had made Milo promise not to say anything. "I want to be absolutely sure before I say anything. Jae... he gets anxious if he thinks I might be in trouble. I don't want to do that to him."

Milo had wanted to call the police, but Romy had told him no. "I promise, when I feel better, I'll go make a statement, but it's not like they can do anything now." She saw the uncertainty in his eyes. "Promise me, Milo. Leave it to me."

Milo had promised her, and she thanked him. He'd left with Nico when Jae arrived, and the younger man had been so grateful to the older men for helping Romy, that it made Romy smile.

When Milo had gone, Jae made a face at her. "That was Milo Keys?"

"It was. Why are you surprised?"

"I don't know." Jae sat on the edge of her bed. "I imagined someone older. I've heard you talk about him for years like this unattainable hermit, and yet here he is..."

"...holding my hair back while I throw up. Yep. I know how to make a good impression." She grinned as Jae laughed, before her cousin's eyes turned serious.

"You scared the crap out of me."

"It was just an accident." She shifted uncomfortably in the bed. "I just need a solid twelve hours sleep, a crap ton of coffee, and I'll be okay. I'm sorry to drag you all the way down here."

"Don't be. It got me out of a test." Jae grinned at her. "Moon wanted to come, too, to check up on his 'woman.'"

Romy laughed. "That boy is an incorrigible flirt."

Jae's smile faded a little. "Actually, he's going through a hard time, at the moment. He won't want me to tell you, but I'm really worried about him. He's not eating."

Romy sighed. "I did think he looked too thin last time he was here."

"You know Moon, he normally loves his food. It's just lately—" Jae shook his head. "I shouldn't be bothering you with this, especially now."

"Moon is our family," Romy told him. "We stick together, we fight together, like we always have. Next time you bring him down, I'll cook." She grinned at Jae's grimace. "Okay, I'll order in a feast and make him eat his body weight."

Jae smiled at her gratefully. "Look, I'm here now. Get some sleep, and we'll figure everything out in the morning."

When she was alone, Romy stared up at the ceiling. Her mind was too hectic to sleep, and she shifted, moaning softly as her aching body protested.

Someone had pushed her. The more she thought about, the more she was convinced she was recalling the truth. She could feel the way two hands had been shoved, flat, against her back.

She had a memory of falling, then of a quick, agonizing pain when she had fallen through the glass coffee table.

Someone broke in, was about to burgle me, and I came home. They just wanted to steal from me, is all. I just got unlucky.

But the doubt that lurked in her mind was far more insidious than she was reasoning to herself. Romy couldn't help but wonder if the break-in and assault wasn't tied to the obituary that had been shoved through her door. Something was hinky about all of this.

But she was determined not to let it distract her from opening the gallery. So, the next morning, she was at the gallery before seven a.m. Now that all the trash had been removed and the walls had their first coat of paint, she was beginning to see where she would place the artwork—that was, if she could get off her ass and begin to call in works from local artists.

Romy gathered up the pile of mail from the doorway and began to sort through it. Another plain envelope fell out of the pile, and her insides twisted a little as she opened it. The relief when a flyer for a local restaurant fell out was palpable.

It was a couple of hours later when she heard a knock at the door. When she walked out to answer it, she was surprised to see Connor smiling through the glass door at her.

She opened the door. "Hey."

Connor stepped into the gallery; his eyebrows knotted as he frowned at her. "I just heard what happened. I stopped by your place, but there was no one there. Should you be here?"

He brushed his fingertips over some of her stitches. Romy drew away, smiling to lessen the slight. "I'm good, it's just a few cuts and scrapes. No biggie."

She walked back into the gallery and offered him a cup of coffee. Connor nodded.

"Thanks. I'm serious, Ro, I heard you were hurt real bad."

Romy indicated herself. "Obviously not too bad. I'm good Connor, but thanks for asking."

She wasn't sure why she was irritated by his presence. Maybe it was because when she heard someone knocking, her heart had leaped in anticipation that it might be Milo. The disappointment at seeing Connor instead was making her grouchy.

"I don't like it that you're here alone," Connor was saying, shaking his head. "It's not right. Maybe I should—"

"Let me stop you there, Connor. There is *no* scenario where you should be doing anything for me. We do not know each other anymore, we're not friends." Romy put her hand up as he started to protest. "I appreciate your concern, I really do, but this is none of your concern, thank you."

He stared at her for a long minute, and she couldn't read the expression in his eyes. "Is it so wrong that I want to protect you?"

Romy met his gaze steadily. "It's inappropriate. I know you mean well, but I'm not yours to protect." She sighed, hating that she was having to say any of this. "Connor, really, we don't know each other at all. It's been ten years since we even spoke to each other at any length."

"Ah. I get it. You're punishing me, for marrying Harper. For that I don't blame you, it was the biggest mistake of my life. After letting you go, of course."

Romy turned away so he couldn't see her rolling her eyes. The arrogance of this man was staggering. "No, Connor, I'm not punishing you for anything. We were kids who fooled around with each other, that was all."

"I remember I was your first."

Ugh. Romy opened her mouth to ask him to leave but then heard another voice in front of the gallery, and this time it *was* the voice she wanted to hear. She couldn't help the delighted smile that spread across her face.

"We are in here, Milo. Come through, please."

Then he was there in her doorway, his green eyes twinkling at her. "Hey, you."

"Hey yourself." Her eyes dropped to the tray of coffee in his hand. "Milo Keys, is that a vanilla latte?"

"I remembered you love it, so yes, and I remembered that you prefer it with half a shot, even though technically that's not coffee." He grinned at her.

"Is, too."

"Is not. I..." His voice trailed off as he caught sight of Connor, who was leaning against the wall watching their interaction with a sly smirk on his face. Milo's smile faded almost immediately. "Connor."

Connor nodded. "Milo."

The atmosphere was icy cold then, and Romy sighed. She took the coffee from the tray. She smiled at Milo, hoping to ease some of the tension in the room. "You are a lifesaver, Mr. Keys."

For a moment, Milo kept staring at Connor, but then his gaze shifted to Romy, and his eyes softened. "Anytime."

"Well now that you've delivered the lady's beverage, we were in the middle of a discussion, so—" Connor made a shifting motion with his hands. Milo studied him with dislike, and Romy shook her head, disbelieving Connor's rudeness.

"Actually, Connor, Milo and I have business to discuss, so if you wouldn't mind."

Connor's eyebrows shot up in surprise, and he looked annoyed, but to Romy's relief, he didn't argue.

"I guess I'll see you later. You owe me a dinner sometime, Romy. We need to talk." He shot a smirk at Milo. "About *us*."

Romy gritted her teeth. "I'll see you around, Connor."

She waited until Connor had gone before she let out a frustrated hiss. "Asshole. Deluded, arrogant *asshole*." She risked a look at Milo, who looked mollified by her cussing.

"I take it he wasn't the most welcome guest."

"Damn right. What did I ever see in him? Ugh, ugh, *ugh*." Romy shook her head. "But anyway." She smiled and Milo. "I would much rather have coffee with you." She blushed to her roots at how that sounded, but then decided it was the truth, so what did it matter?

Milo gaze down at her and the breath caught in her throat at the softness in his eyes. "And how do you feel this morning?" He touched a fingertip to her cheek. Unlike when Connor did it, Romy didn't pull away this time, instead she put her hand over his, holding it to her cheek.

"It feels a lot better now."

For a moment, she thought he might kiss her, but Milo just smiled and looked around. "Hey, this place is really coming along."

Romy chuckled, releasing his hand. "Thanks for saying so, but it's still a mess."

"Ah, now, come on." He flicked a switch, and the lights came on. "Okay, so you need some more white paint, but the lighting is great, plus in the big room, you have the natural light from the big picture window."

They walked around together, and Milo pointed out the good points of what she had done and advised on what could be improved. Romy listened to all of it, drinking it all in, starstruck.

They stood in front of the main wall. "Obviously, this will be the main display, the focal point of any exhibit."

"Are you calling in yet?"

Romy took a deep breath in. "I haven't started. I know, I

know, I should start to schedule the artists, but in a strange way, I'm terrified. Scared they'll say no. Worried they'll laugh in my face. My old boss, Sebastien Yverneau, he told me to just go for it, and that he would help, but—"

"You want to do it on your own."

Romy nodded. "Is that naïve?"

"It's brave."

She flushed bright red. "I don't know about that."

Milo smiled at her, then nodded at the blank space. "You know what would look good there?"

"What?"

"*Antigone*."

For a moment, Romy thought she must have heard wrong. Then she shook her head. "Don't joke about that, Milo, please. It means too much to me."

His gaze was steady. "I'm not joking."

A beat of silence, two... three... then, to her mortification, Romy burst into tears. Milo chuckled and wrapped his arms around her as she sobbed. "I didn't realize it meant that much to you."

"*Omsgoshfragglemush...*" Romy's face was buried in his sweater, her voice muffled by the wool and her tears.

Milo laughed. "Well said." He released her and offered her a napkin from the coffee tray. Romy wiped her eyes and blew her nose loudly.

"I can't believe it. I can't... what changed your mind? I know you were dead set against showing again—"

"Because you didn't ask." His voice was so soft, she wanted to cry again. "Because you didn't once try and manipulate me into doing this." He offered her his hand, and she took it. He drew her close. "And because you deserve some good luck. Romy, we don't know each other well... *yet*, but we seem to keep being thrown together, and I find myself... I haven't been out in public much for the last couple of years. But I woke up this morning excited because I was going to come here." He touched her cheek again. "That's really something, Romy Park."

Romy's body was crying out for him to kiss her, to touch her, but something held her back from throwing herself into his arms. He was offering friendship and the biggest coup in the art world for years. To *her*... But that was all. Sarah's specter loomed large over his life, Romy knew, and so there was a limit to what he was offering.

But what he was offering was beyond what she had ever even dreamed.

"Milo, are you sure?"

"Yes." He didn't hesitate in answering, and then as she grinned widely, he laughed. "I enjoy shocking you, Romy Park."

"To my core, Milo." She shook her head. "I can't believe it."

He touched her arm. "Believe it. I'm not going to paint anything new, but you're welcome to go through my attic and pick out whatever you need."

Romy's eyes bugged, and she sat down on a pasting table with a thump. "This is actually happening?"

Milo grinned. "It is. But I have to tell you... I'm not selling. So, you may just want my work to be the thing that draws people in. Man, that sounded arrogant."

"It's not arrogant at all. You know your worth, and so does the art world, Milo." She got up and went to him. "Are you ready for the scrutiny that this will bring? The invasion of privacy?"

Milo nodded, his smile fading a little. "I know. But maybe that's what I need. I've been..." He cast around for the right word. "Stagnating."

Romy giggled. "The last adjective I'd use to describe you, Milo, is *stagnant*."

She ran her hands through her hair, blowing out her cheeks. "I can't believe this."

Milo laughed. "Well, believe it. Listen, why don't you come out to my place tonight? Harper's bringing pizza—homemade, I believe—so there'll be a chaperone, if that worries you."

She met his eyes. "It doesn't." The way he held her gaze made a pulse beat furiously between her legs. "But it will be nice to see Harper, and I'm dying to meet your dog."

Milo beamed. "Then it's settled." He looked around. "So, you want some help?"

In the end, Milo stayed to help Romy paint the walls again, and at lunchtime, Jae joined them. He'd spent the morning studying, taking a class long distance over the internet so he wouldn't have to play catch up. He looked a little stressed when he arrived, Milo thought, but when Romy told him about Milo's offer, his mood lifted, and he grinned at the older man.

"Dude, you don't know how many years I've had to listen to Ro waxing lyrical about your work. This is incredible. Sincerely, thank you, man." He hugged Romy, and Milo watched the two younger people, his heart lifting. He hadn't known he was going to make the offer to Romy until the words came out of his mouth, but he knew as soon as he said them, he'd made the right decision. It felt right in his soul.

And what was more, the joy in Romy Park's eyes—he was actually making this kid's dreams come true, and that was an incredible feeling.

Except…

Romy Park was no kid. She was a beautiful, vital, intelligent woman, and he hated to admit it, but she'd gotten under his skin.

Milo made the excuse that he was going out to grab some lunch and ducked out of the gallery for a while. He realized he hadn't felt this content in years, just being around Romy and her younger cousin. His mind went to Connor Small, and his smile faded. It wasn't that he thought Connor was any sort of competition for Romy's heart; the wary expression in her eyes when he'd seen them together convinced him of that.

But Connor Small was a conman. Now that Milo thought about it, he disliked the man even before Sarah had worked with him, or since Milo had gotten to know Harper better. Harper always had been too good for Connor, that had been obvious from the first meeting of the couple together.

Milo wondered at the history between Romy and Connor. He didn't think it was his place to ask or to warn Romy about his womanizing ways. Romy was a smart enough girl on her own. He pushed the thought of Connor aside and went down to a local sandwich bar he liked to grab some lunch for Romy and Jae.

At the sandwich place he studied the order board, realizing he didn't know whether Jae was vegan or vegetarian or had any other dietary restrictions. Romy seemed to like whatever was put in front of her, he thought with a grin, remembering the beef Daube that Harper had cooked for them. He was so lost in his memory that he didn't realize the queue had disappeared in front of him, and someone prodded him in the back impatiently.

Milo turned around to apologize and stopped. A familiar face was behind him. Farron Lee, a dissolute Englishman who had lived in Monterey for many years and wore a neckerchief under his loose artist's smock, looked equally surprised to see him.

"Well, Milo Keys… This is a bit of a shocker. How are you?"

Farron had been supportive of Milo's early career, when he'd just been starting out. Farron's gallery was one of the oldest in Monterey, its owner having the gift of schmoozing and networking and not caring who he stepped on, on the way *up*. It had made Farron many enemies, but many fans, too, and he'd seen his competitors' galleries close one by one as the recession hit.

Milo couldn't say, in all honesty, that he liked the man, but he respected him and was grateful for the early help. In fact, the only misstep Farron had ever made was not appreciating the worth of *Antigone*, before it debuted. To his own credit, he knew he'd fucked up but never held it against Milo when he went with a different gallery in San Francisco.

Milo nodded to him now. "It's good to see you, Farron, you are looking well."

"You're a good liar, Milo Keys." Farron gave him a cynical smile. And the truth was, Farron looked twenty years older than his fifty-five. Milo guessed it was something to do with the smoking—Farron had resolutely refused to give up his habit of sixty cigarettes and a half bottle of bourbon a day, even on his doctor's advice. Milo had heard that Farron had been given only a few months to live a couple of years back, and now he was losing the red hair that had once been his pride and joy, and however voluminous his artist's smock was, it couldn't hide the scrawny man underneath.

"I saw you this morning, going into the Park girl's gallery. I take it she is a friend?"

Milo nodded. "She's just starting out," he began warily. He didn't want Farron to take against Romy just because she was a competitor. "She's been honing her craft in Manhattan the last few years and decided to come home."

"Ah, so it is Jin's kid?"

"Yes." He'd forgotten that Farron and Jin had been friendly before the accident. "If you like, you can come meet her."

Farron waved his hand dismissively. "Maybe another time. Order your sandwich, there's a

good chap. I need some calories."

Jae had been teasing Romy ever since Milo left to go to get lunch.

"Someone has got an admirer."

Romy tried to dismiss it, but she couldn't help the huge grin on her face. "Jae, this is a professional relationship."

"*Sure,* it is." Jae rolled his eyes. He hoisted himself up onto one of the tables and studied his cousin. "When was the last time you had a boyfriend, cuz? Or shouldn't I ask?"

"You should not ask. Besides, there really is nothing to tell, either then or now. I'm just concentrating on my business," Romy said rather sniffily, but then chuckled when Jae gaped at her in disbelief.

"Ro, the man is gorgeous, and he gets all heart-eyes when he looks at you."

"What the hell are heart-eyes?" Romy giggled when Jae opened his eyes wide and pretended to moon lovingly at her. "Oh, stop. He's a grown-up, and I'm just, well, me."

"We'll see."

It was Romy's turn to roll her eyes, but she changed the subject. "Well, he's certainly going to kickstart our launch. Which reminds me, I need to seriously start looking around for a caterer and get some invitations printed."

There was a panic rising inside her then as she thought about the magnitude of what she was about to do, but she tamped it down. This was what she had dreamed of, after all.

Milo returned with an armful of sandwiches and sodas, and they picnicked on the gallery floor. Romy listened to the two men chat easily and was glad they got along. She used the time to study Milo. Never in a million years did she ever think he would agree to show with her, let alone show *Antigone.*

But maybe Jae was right. Every time she was near Milo, her body would react in a way that she wasn't used to, and it unsettled... and *thrilled* her. After avoiding any kind of relationship after the accident, and then throughout her time in New York, the thought of suddenly being attracted to someone in such a primal way was unnerving.

After lunch, Milo made his apologies and left to go see Sailor. He gave Romy his address in Big Sur. "Are you sure you don't want me to pick you up?"

"No, no, of course not. I'll find my way there."

He smiled down at her. "Then I'll see you tonight."

Romy felt her face burn as she smiled back at him. "Tonight. See you then."

NINE

HARPER LOOKED UP AS her housekeeper knocked on her bedroom door.

"Hey, Mary, what's up?"

Mary shifted from foot to foot uncomfortably. "Miss Harper, Mr. Small is here. He… he insisted on coming in. I couldn't stop him."

Harper sighed but smiled kindly at the middle-aged woman. "It's okay, Mary. I know how Connor is. I'll go down and see him."

Connor was already sitting in the living room when Harper found him.

"Hello, Connor."

"Hey, babe."

Harper swallowed her irritation. *You don't get to call me babe anymore, jackass.* "While it's always good to see you," she said mildly, "I do have plans this evening."

"With the artist again?"

Harper sighed. "I'm having dinner with Milo, yes."

Connor smirked to himself. "You realize he's been sniffing around Romy Park, right? He was there today when I caught up with her."

66

Ah. So that's what he wanted. Information. "Milo doesn't have to sniff around anyone. He and Romy are friends. I introduced them, actually."

Something flashed in Connor's eyes. Jealousy? Rage? He smoothed his pants slowly.

"Matchmaking, Harper?"

She didn't answer him. "What is it you needed, Con?" She went to the bureau and opened it. "I trust your monthly allowance has been paid?"

She took out her checkbook anyway, knowing he would probably moan about something that was now 'out of his means.' Connor got up and came to her, putting his hand on her arm.

"No, Harper. I don't want your money."

She caught a whiff of alcohol on his breath. "Connor, did you drive here?"

"Don't change the subject."

"From what?"

"Romy... and the artist."

"Milo. His name is Milo, as you well know. We went to enough functions with him and Sarah over the years, Connor. You know his name."

"I don't give a fuck what his name is." His hand closed around her wrist and began to squeeze, painfully.

Adrenalin shot through Harper. She knew where this was going. In their ten-year marriage it had happened twice before.

Connor knew where to hit her to hide the bruises. Not this time. Harper twisted her arm away from him. Was he really so bent out of shape abut Milo and Romy that it made him violent? For some reason, the thought was terrifying.

She kept her voice calm. "Mary? Would you call a cab for Connor, please? We're going to have a cocktail before he goes."

Mary appeared at the door, shooting Connor a wary look and

giving Harper a nod. Harper knew Mary had smelled the booze, too. "Of course, Miss Harper."

"*Miss Harper,*" mocked Connor when Mary had gone. "Don't you feel awkward with her calling you that?"

"It took me long enough to train her not to call me 'Madam' or 'Miss Van Warren,' Connor. I'll take it." Harper kept her tone mild as she made a martini, no olive for Connor.

As she handed it to him, he smiled at her, but there was no warmth in his expression. "Nice of you to cover for me with the help." He sipped his drink and sighed. "Damn. No one makes that like you, Harp."

She sat down opposite him, praying that Mary would tell the cab driver to hurry. There was no way she was leaving the house before Connor.

He was clearly in no rush to leave. "So, you're having dinner with Keys?"

"And Romy." Harper wasn't so noble that she didn't enjoy goading him. That would teach him for the wrist twist. "Like I said, we're all friends."

Connor mumbled something.

"I'm sorry, what was that?"

He smirked. "I said, never took you for an Eskimo sister."

Harper frowned. "I have absolutely no idea what you're talking about."

Connor laughed, but just then, thankfully, Mary came to tell them the cab was here. Harper stood up and was grateful when Connor did the same.

As she saw him to the door, he suddenly stopped. "We have a meeting soon, right?"

"At your lawyer's office. Monday, Connor. Two p.m."

He suddenly looked a little desolate. "How did we come to this, Harper?"

Not this again... the never-ending cycle. Anger, antagonism... regret. Every time. "Let's look to the future, now, Connor. We can at least be friends."

He nodded sadly, and Harper watched him walk to the cab and get in. She closed the door quietly, then leaned against it, sighing. Mary watched her carefully.

"My niece taught me a new word to describe a man like that, Miss Harper."

"And what was that?"

Mary grinned. "I believe it was 'douchebag,' Miss Harper."

Harper laughed, her tension easing. If *Mary* was calling Connor a douchebag... "I think that's a perfect description, Mary. *Perfect.*" She patted her housekeeper on the arm. "I'm going to finish up getting ready, Mary, then I'll be out of here. You will get yourself home safely, right?"

"Of course, Miss Harper. Have a good night."

"You, too, Mary."

Harper ran lightly upstairs and finished her makeup. She wrapped a light shawl around her shoulders and took a few deep breaths. Connor always did this to her, unsettled, disturbed her and even now, months after they split, he could still... touch her heart.

She glared at herself in the mirror. *You're an intelligent, reasonable, grown woman. What the hell? Forget him.*

But as she got into her car and started the ignition, she had to steady the tears that threatened again, because, despite everything, she knew the horrible truth was that she still loved her ex-husband.

Romy pulled up to the gate of Milo's place, her eyes wide. The place really did look like a Gothic mansion. There was an unexpected drama to it that she hadn't expected from the stoic

Milo. The gates slid open without her having to buzz, and then, as she pulled her car up to the house, she saw Milo waiting for her, a smile on his gloriously handsome face.

Romy's stomach disappeared and as he opened her door for her and offered her his hand, she took it, feeling breathless. "Hi, Milo."

"Welcome to Dracula's castle," Milo said with a grin, and she laughed. He bent to kiss her cheek. "Harper's five minutes behind you. Come on in."

Romy walked into the main foyer of the house, a little overwhelmed. Inside, it wasn't at all what she expected—no decaying staircases covered with cobwebs—instead it was bright and modern and spacious.

Milo led her into the huge kitchen, and his dog lumbered over to say hello to Romy. She crouched down and ruffled the St. Bernard's ears. "Oh, you are so handsome," she said to him and planted a kiss on his silky head. Sailor nuzzled close to her, and she hugged him.

"He likes you."

"He's beautiful. Huge." She giggled as Sailor, excited over his new friend, knocked into her and made her wobble. Milo caught her as she toppled backwards.

"Sailor, calm. Sorry about that." He steadied her, and she smiled at him gratefully.

"It's okay. If I wasn't a guest, I'd be rolling around on the floor with him." She flushed red when she realized how that sounded, and Milo raised an eyebrow, a grin on his face.

"Really? I'll keep that in mind."

He offered Romy a drink, but she shook her head. "I never do, not even one, when I'm driving."

"Good sense. I have some non-alcoholic beer or some soda." In the end, he made her a virgin cocktail of fruit juice and grenadine, grimacing when Romy, her sweet tooth satisfied, declared it the best drink ever. "It's pure sugar."

"And you say that like it's a bad thing?" Romy twinkled at him, and he touched her cheek briefly.

"Don't blame me if you end up in a diabetic coma."

Realizing too late, he winced, but Romy just smiled. "I promise I won't."

There was a delicious tension between them, and Romy, for once, just reveled in it. "Going to show me your etchings, Mr. Keys?"

Milo led the way upstairs. Like the first floor, he had gutted the place, giving the whole house an airy, open feel that Romy liked. It reminded her of him, much more so than the haunting exterior.

In the attic, she suddenly got nervous. She was about to see his work in the flesh, and suddenly she didn't know if she was ready. Milo seemed to notice the shift in her mood. "You okay?"

Romy nodded. "It's just... a big moment."

"They're just paint and canvas, Ro."

She smiled at his easy use of her nickname—it strangely put her at ease. "Don't keep me waiting, Keys."

He laughed and began pulling canvases from under the dust sheets. Romy felt a thrill go through her as he set each one out for her to see. They were incredible, masterworks of color and content, dimension and diorama. He had captured the coastline around Big Sur and Monterey perfectly, and the portraits were even better. There was so much history and emotion in the eyes of his subjects, and then, finally, he brought *Antigone* out to show her.

Romy let out a long breath. "Oh, Milo."

He didn't say anything, simply stepping aside and studying the painting with her. Sarah Keys' portrait was even more remarkable than Romy had dreamed. Up close, she could see every emotion in the subject's eyes, and it was a myriad of things—sadness, love, beauty. Romy opened her mouth to say something profound, but words would not come. The only word she could think of for it was heartbreak.

Unblinkingly, she slipped her hand into Milo's and squeezed. His long fingers twisted with hers and they stood there for a few moments in silence, just taking in the painting. Finally, Romy found her voice.

"If you want to change your mind, I wouldn't blame you in the slightest. She's... She's so lovely, I don't blame you for wanting to keep it for yourself."

For a moment, Milo didn't say anything, but then he turned to her. He drew her close and put his arms around her, burying his face in her hair. Romy held him tightly, wanting to take away all of his sadness. She sensed this had been more traumatic for him than his jokey manner had given away, and she was incredibly moved that he trusted her enough to be here with him. She meant what she said; if he changed his mind about showing *Antigone*, she was absolutely fine with that. It was more than a painting—it was a memory.

After a moment, she looked up. "Are you okay?"

Milo nodded slowly; his green eyes serious. "For the first time in a long time, I think I am." He stroked the back of his fingers over her cheek. "And you have a lot to do with that, Romy Park. I know you understand loss, but what I'm feeling now isn't loss. It's... hope."

Romy stared up at him, nodding, understanding. They gazed at each other for a beat, and Milo bent his head and brushed his lips lightly against hers. It was a brief, sweet kiss, but it sent shivers down her body. "Milo, I—"

From down the stairs, they both heard the doorbell ring. For a beat they froze, then, breaking apart, both of them chuckled softly. "I guess Harper is here." Milo offered Romy his hand, and she took it. They went downstairs and let Harper in. Romy saw her friend's eyes drop to their clasped hands, and a small smile played over her lips, but she didn't say anything to them.

It wasn't until after dinner when Milo was making coffee that Harper said anything to Romy. She leaned over in her seat and nudged her friend. "Come on, don't keep me in suspense. You and Milo, hey? I don't want to take credit, but I could see it coming from a mile off. I'm delighted for you both."

Romy flushed, but smiled at her friend. "There's nothing to tell really, yes, there does seem to be something between us. I like him very much."

She kept her voice low, feeling shy. Harper grinned at her. "You know, I can always make myself scarce if you two want to—"

"We are definitely not at *that* stage yet," Romy laughed, her face burning, "but thanks for the backup."

Milo returned with the coffee then, and Romy shot Harper a warning glance. Harper took the hint and changed the subject. "So, it's official? You'll be Romy's first exhibitor?"

"I would be honored." Milo smiled at Romy. "Truly."

Romy felt her throat close up with emotion. "It would be all *my* honor." She cleared her throat, embarrassed. "I just have to figure out the rest of it. When I told Sebastien Yverneau, my old boss, he said he could come out for a few days to help me set up, make sure I've ticked every box."

"That was generous of him."

Romy nodded, smiling. "That's Sebastien. He taught me everything I know about the art world." She looked at Milo. "And he's another huge fan of yours, so get used to being fan-boyed and fan-girled over. You'll be sick at the sight of us by the time the exhibition is over."

"Would never happen." Milo's eyes were soft on hers.

"You have caterers and wait staff yet?" Harper interjected, and Romy shook her head.

"Actually, I was hoping to pick your brains about that. I have a budget, but not a huge one, so I wanted to know the best people to hire to fit it."

Harper nodded. "I know someone who could do the catering for you for practically nothing."

"Who?"

Harper beamed at her. "Me. Do you know how many parties I have catered in my life? And ask Milo, I always do all the cooking and all the prep myself. I would be happy to do it for you, free of charge, too, including the food."

Romy gaped at her. "I couldn't possibly let you do that; it's too much."

"No, it's not. You deserve all the luck, Romy, and I'm in a position to help. Why wouldn't I?"

"Let her help, Ro," Milo encouraged her with a smile. "You know as well as I do that art is a cut-throat business, especially in such a small town as this. Your competition won't be kind, regardless of how successful you are. A lot of them will try to shut you down. So, take all the help you can get."

Romy hesitated. What Harper—and Milo—had offered was incredible and beyond what she could have hoped for. But something inside her told her it was too much. However fond she was of them both, and they of her, it was still true that they hardly knew each other.

Harper seemed to read her mind. "Sometimes there's no ulterior motive, sweetie."

Romy laughed self-consciously. "I know. It's just—wow, this is really happening, isn't it?"

Milo, sitting next to her on the couch, smoothed a comforting hand down her back. Her skin tingled at his touch. "It is. And we have your back, Romy Park."

TEN

IT WAS THE EARLY hours before they finally stopped talking about the gallery opening, and Romy was nervous. Was Milo expecting her to stay? She wanted to—desperately—but she also knew that she wasn't ready to take things to the next level with him.

If there *was* a next level to go to. *You're presuming an awful lot, Park.* Thankfully, Milo came to her rescue.

"Now, are you sure you're not too tired to drive? Because I can drive you back myself or call a cab?"

"No, I'm fine."

Milo hesitated at her car, tipping her face up to his. "I'm loathe to let you go off into the night. Isn't that ridiculous?"

She shook her head. "No. But…"

"But…" He smiled down at her and then kissed her again, softly, just a brush of his lips against hers. "Send me a text message. Let me know you got home okay. I'll worry."

"I promise."

He opened her door for her, and she got into her car. Her body was screaming at her to stay with him, to throw away all of her inhibitions—and her clothes—and make love to this wonderful man.

But her head won. It was too much, too soon. Still, she watched him in the rearview mirror as she drove away until she rounded the bend and drove along the coastal road back up to Monterey.

Her bubble of happiness lasted until the morning. She allowed herself to sleep in a little the next morning, and when she got up, yawning as she padded into the kitchen, she didn't expect Jae to be sitting at the breakfast bar, his eyes glued to his laptop screen, his expression furious.

Romy rocked back a little. "What's up, bro?"

Jae looked up, then turned the laptop around. "Read this."

Romy grabbed the coffee pot before she sat down at the counter and began to read. The coffee went cold. She read through the article on a local Monterey website twice before she met Jae's gaze. "What the actual fuck?"

"Is word-for-word what I said. Who would write this?"

Romy shook her head, lost. The article was a character assassination of her, for chrissakes. According to the writer, she was an upstart who barely qualified as an art curator, having been *coddled* by her former employer, Sebastien Yverneau, who was known for his 'liking' of young Asian American women. The evidence for this, apparently, was that his previous assistant was from Hong Kong. It didn't matter, apparently, that Ling Mai was very happily married to an Ivy League professor—a *woman*.

Miss Park, said a source, traded on her good looks and made a big deal of her past tragedy, an accident in Monterey, California, which took the lives of her parents, her aunt, and several other Monterey residents. 'Of course, she never mentioned who was to blame for the accident,' the source went on, 'and she never showed any remorse for the other victims.'

"What the actual fucking fuck is this fuckery?" Romy was incensed, and Jae nodded grimly.

"Right? I've never seen anything as petty and spiteful. This is all bullshit." He pulled the laptop towards him. "I did some digging. This article comes verbatim from a forum page, probably uploaded by the same writer. They don't moderate the articles—apparently, they enjoy being sued."

Romy shook her head, calming down. "We're not suing anybody. We're not even going to acknowledge this thing exists."

"Ro, this thing is slander."

"Libel, actually, it's written down, but yes, it's all lies." She blew out her cheeks, calming herself. "If we respond to this crap, it'll never go away."

"You can't bury your head in the sand about this stuff, not when—" Jae broke off and just shook his head, and Romy frowned.

"When what?"

Jae sighed. "When someone broke in here and attacked you."

Romy sat down heavily. "Who told you?"

"Nico. Don't blame him, he thought I knew. He said you remembered someone attacked you, pushed you into the coffee table. Then this?"

Romy was quiet. "There's something else, too." She got up and went to her desk, pulling out the obituary. "This was put through my door a few nights ago."

She handed it to Jae, wondering if she was doing the right thing. Jae never liked to talk about the accident that took his mother's life. He'd only been eight when it had happened, but the scars ran deep. Their grandmother had told Romy when she woke from her coma that Jae had come every day after school to sit with his cousin. Sometimes, Nari said, Jae would creep onto the hospital bed and hug himself to Romy's side.

My little koala, Romy thought to herself now, as she watched Jae read through the obituary. He sighed and put it down. "Well, it's not explicit, but it's kind of threatening."

"But why would anyone threaten me? No one here knew I was coming back, and it's not like I'm going out of my way to annoy anyone."

"Apart from the obvious. Your competition." Jae met her gaze. "And Connor."

"Why would Connor attack me? He's made it perfectly clear he wants... he assumed I wanted him back. Yeah," she added with a grin, as Jae snorted. "Why did no one tell me back then that he was such a douchebag?"

"Because we all fall in love with the wrong person when we're teenagers."

"Says the teenager."

"Only for another three weeks." Jae said with a grin. "And I've always been older inside."

"True." She smiled at him fondly. "So, who are you in love with?"

"Ha, we're not talking about me. Connor sounds like just the type to put you in danger, then do the whole rescue-the-maiden act. If you weren't going to go back to him out of long-lost love—"

"I can't see it, honestly." Romy sighed. "Look, let's just get on with our lives. If anything else happens, we'll work out how to act then."

"All right." Jae met her gaze. "But next time, don't hide anything from me, Ro. Please."

"I promise."

Jae drove back to Berkeley later that morning, and Romy went to the gallery. Nico was already there, having let himself in with the keys Romy had loaned him so she didn't have to be there all the time while he and his crew were working.

Nico grinned at her as she opened the door. "Hey, kiddo."

"Hi. Wow, Nico, is this the same place as yesterday?" Romy could hardly believe what she was seeing. The free-standing walls that divided up the large showroom were built with the lighting fixed into them. With a few layers of paint, they could be up and running by the end of the week, Romy realized.

"You like?"

"I do, very much. You guys have been working like demons."

Nico smiled. "Also… a surprise. Come with me."

He led her through the backrooms and to the small room she had designated as her office. He pushed the door open and stood aside to let her in.

Romy stepped into the small room and gasped. "Nico!"

The room had been cleared of all debris and trash and painted in the same bright white as the rest of the gallery. The window had been refitted, and shelves crafted from driftwood adorned the largest wall. They were decked out with some of Romy's books she had brought from home and a couple of potted plants. There was a table in lieu of the desk that Romy had on order and a brightly colored cushion on the small wooden chair.

"My friend made the cushion for you. We just wanted to do something nice for you after the accident."

Romy shook her head. "Nico, this is so sweet of you. Really, I'm overwhelmed."

"It's not much, but I hope—"

"It's amazing." Romy felt close to tears. "Nico…"

"Hey now, don't do the weepy thing. I'm a guy and completely useless with a woman's tears. Really, every stereotype in the book." Nico grinned, and Romy laughed, grateful for his joke.

"Okay, I promise. But I owe you one."

"Nope. Comes with the job. I look after my clients."

He smiled again, then made himself scarce. Romy looked around her office again, chuckling softly to herself. The upset of this morning had been erased by this simple act of kindness, and she snapped a few photos and sent them to Jae. *The good ones outweigh the bad, every time.*

Jae sent back a 'thumbs up' emoji and a smiley face.

"Romy?"

Her heart leaped when she heard Milo's voice, and she went to the door. "In here."

And there he was, walking down the small hallway. "Hey. Nico let me in, I hope you don't mind."

"Of course not." Why did he make her feel so nervous and yet excited at the same time? He smiled down at her, and Romy couldn't resist standing on her tiptoes and kissing him. His lips met hers and his arms went around her, and the kiss went on… and on… and on…

Finally, they broke apart and Romy flushed bright red. "I… um…"

Milo chuckled. "That was unexpected… and very, very pleasant."

Romy wished her face would stop burning, but she couldn't keep the smile off of her face.

"Come in and see the office Nico made for me."

She took his hand and Milo stepped into the office—Romy noticed he had to duck his head to get through the door. "Wow, this is great."

"Right? Such a sweet gesture." Romy felt like she was rambling, her hands were shaking, and she felt breathless. Milo drew her close, kicking the office door closed behind him.

"Take a breath, Ro. It's okay. It's just me."

"Yes, but it's *you.*"

Milo threw his head back and laughed. "I'm really not that impressive."

"I beg to differ."

He bent his head and nuzzled his nose against hers. "Then perhaps," he said in a low voice, heavy with emotion, "you'd better kiss me again."

His mouth covered hers, and Romy sank into the kiss. His tongue caressed hers as the kiss deepened, and his hands slid into her hair, his fingers twisting in the thick strands. Romy slid her arms around his waist. He was so tall, so big, that she felt tiny in his arms.

She could feel the hot length of his erection through his jeans against her belly, and her body felt flushed and hot with arousal. A pulse beat hard and steady between her legs. Milo's lips, gentle at first, crushed hard against hers as their desire built, and eventually, Romy had to break away for oxygen.

"I hate to say this, but we need to stop. There's a fleet of contractors just two doors away and if we, um, go at it, they'll hear everything."

Milo grinned. "Regretfully, I think you're right." He cradled her cheek in his palm. "We have plenty of time, Romy. We don't need to rush into anything." He kissed her again. "As much as I'd like to."

"Anticipation."

"Yes, indeed."

Romy sighed and leaned into his arms, which Milo wrapped tightly around her. "I have to confess... this is a strange feeling for me. I never thought, after Sarah..."

Romy looked up at him, nodding. "It must be, and I understand if you want to pull back. As much as I would hate it, I really do understand. I've spent the best part of a decade avoiding any romantic ties." She grinned at the surprise in his eyes. "That shocks you?"

"Well, yes." He chuckled, shaking his head. "Have you seen yourself?"

She flushed with pleasure at his compliment. "I'm nothing special."

"I beg to differ," he said softly, repeating what she had said to him earlier. His thumb traced over her cheek. "You're a beautiful woman, Romy, but it's not your looks that I'm falling for. Okay, well, part of it is, I'm only human," he added when she rolled her eyes at him, embarrassed. "But no, it's your passion for life, for art, for your family. The fact that although you had every opportunity, you respected me and my former attitude to exhibiting."

They both laughed, and Romy kissed his cheek. "And yet, here you are, stuck with me and my gallery. Ha, my upstart gallery." She remembered the article on the website and shook her head.

Milo frowned. "Huh?"

"Oh, just some malicious crap on a website this morning. Take a look." She cued it up on her phone and handed it to him, watching his expression change as he read it.

"What the hell?"

"Yup. Someone's got it in for me."

Milo met her gaze. "Romy…"

"Jae already beat you to that suspicion. He knows about the attack, by the way, and the obit that was shoved through my door. But, Milo, doesn't this seem more bitchy than threatening?"

Milo considered. "It could be. I don't like the pattern that's emerging, though."

"You think they're all linked?"

"I honestly don't know. But it makes me uneasy."

Romy sighed. "I just don't know who would have anything against me."

Milo reread the article again. "Well, the good thing is it's just on a message board."

"A Monterey-specific board. Who knows how many people read that thing." She took her phone back from Milo. "But there's no way I'm going to let it distract from your opening."

"It's *your* opening, Ro, but I agree."

There was a knock at the door. "Come in."

Nico smiled at them both as he came. "Hey, sorry to interrupt. Romy, I need your opinion on something out front."

"No problem."

The rest of the morning was spent on discussions of the opening, and at lunchtime, Harper turned up with some draft menus and some finger food samples. "I'm thinking the usual, canapes and champagne. We don't want to overfeed them, but a few sumptuous bites would satisfy them. Elegant and classy."

"Two words that absolutely don't describe me," Romy had the hiccups after scarfing down some of the canapes Harper had brought with her. Milo grinned at her.

"Doofus."

Harper couldn't help the smug look on her face as she looked between them, and Romy arched an eyebrow at her friend. "Got something to say, Harper?"

"No, no. Just taking credit, is all."

They shared friendly teasing and jokes as they discussed the opening, then when Harper had left, Milo looked at Romy regretfully. "I have to get back to Sailor."

"You can always bring him here, you know. Anytime, or if you need a dog sitter."

"Thank you." Milo got up and opened his arms, and Romy went into them. He kissed her. "I hate to leave you here alone."

"Nah, I got Nico and his crew, I'm fine."

"Can I call you later?"

Romy smiled at him, nodding. "You can call me anytime, Mr. Keys."

He kissed her again—really, he thought, he could kiss Romy Park all day, every day and never get tired of it—then said goodbye.

Milo went out to his car, but he didn't immediately drive back to Big Sur. Instead, he went a couple of blocks and got out again. He opened the door of a gallery and stepped inside. Farron Lee looked up in surprise, then his expression changed when he registered the annoyance on Milo's face.

"Hello, Milo... what's going on?"

"You tell me, Farron." Milo pulled out his phone, flicking to the article Romy had shown him. "First of all, why did you write this piece of filth about a woman who has done you absolutely no harm?"

He shoved the phone at Farron, who glanced at it, feigning disinterest. "Nothing to do with me."

"Oh, please, don't embarrass yourself any more than you already have. This has your spite all over it. What I want to know is, why? And another thing."

"What?"

Milo's anger was threatening to brim over now as he stared at the other man. "What I want you to tell me, Farron, is this. Did you have anything to do with Romy's assault, and if so, why the hell would you want to hurt her?"

ELEVEN

HARPER TRIED TO KEEP her mood as light as she had felt with her friends as she drove to her lawyer's office, but it was difficult. When she saw Connor's car in the parking lot, she rolled her eyes. Connor had at least three cars, but he'd driven the oldest, most banged up one to the lawyer's office.

Of course, he had. Still, Harper thought as she got out, the Audi was still in better shape than most people's vehicles, and anyway, they weren't here to discuss money. All that had been settled. *At least, I hope it has.* She had been very generous in the divorce settlement. Even though she had known Connor wanted a monthly stipend, her lawyers had negotiated a huge one-off payment, mostly to protect the rest of the Van Warrens' fortune.

And Harper, ever kind-hearted, had given Connor a monthly sum out of her own pocket, even if it was a lot less than he had wanted from the Van Warren Foundation. It was worth it to her to keep him from sniping at her. And it had worked…

…for a while. Harper sighed and made her way into the lawyer's office. Today should be a formality. It was just to remove Connor's name from her will, but no doubt he'd try and stall her on some technicality.

But instead, he surprised her. He sat quietly next to his lawyer, nodding and agreeing to everything Harper had requested. "No problem."

God help her, but Harper was suspicious. After they'd all shaken hands and Harper and Connor were walking out together, she asked him if everything was okay.

"Yes, sure. Why?" The small smile playing around his lips told her he knew exactly why she was asking.

"Cut the act, Connor. I was expecting some pushback."

"Why? Because I'm a soulless, bloodsucking, money-hungry asshole?" His smile didn't reach his eyes.

Yes, actually. "No, because, well, going by previous meetings."

"We're not married anymore, Harp. It's quite usual for divorced people not to be in their former spouse's will."

Patronizing idiot. "Well, I'm grateful for the quick meeting."

"You busy?"

Harper nodded. "I'm helping Romy with her opening. Catering for her."

"Really? That's cool. She got any artists willing to show with her?"

Harper felt more than a little smug. "She has the biggest coup in the art world, Connor. Milo Keys."

She hated herself for the way she enjoyed seeing Connor's face drop. "Keys? She got Keys?"

In more than one sense. "Yes. He made the offer to her over the weekend."

Connor stopped walking. "Huh."

"Why are you surprised?"

"I'm not, not really. Romy was always going to do well. I'm happy for her."

Right. "Well, I have to go. Good seeing you, Connor." Ugh, she sounded as fake as the sentiment.

Connor just nodded and got into his car, seemingly distracted. Harper waited until he had pulled his Audi out of the parking lot to drive off herself. That went way too well, she thought as she pulled the car into traffic. *Way* too well... what's Connor up to?

She had a horrible feeling that whatever it was, neither she, nor Romy, would like it.

"Yo, Romy, we're heading out for the night."

Romy looked up from her laptop and smiled at Nico. "Okay, see you tomorrow. And thank you again for this." She waved her pen around in the air, indicating the office. "It's so sweet of you."

"You're welcome. Listen, it's getting dark out. You'll be okay on your own?"

Romy smiled at him. "I'm a big girl, Nico. I can kick ass."

"I bet you can. Good night."

"Night."

For the next couple of hours, Romy was too absorbed in her work to notice how late it was getting. She felt pleased at her progress, however, managing to outsource the flyers for the event and calling in some favors. It was only when her cell phone rang at ten p.m. that she looked up.

She was surprised when the caller ID told her that Sebastien was calling from New York.

"Hey, boss. Isn't it like three a.m. there?"

There was a short silence. Romy frowned. "Seb?"

"Romy... did you just call me?"

"No, of course not. Why?"

"Hanna answered the phone. She said someone who sounded like you began to cuss her out."

Romy felt an icy cold shock. Hanna was Seb's long-term

girlfriend and a good friend to Romy. "I would never do that. What on earth? Is Hanna okay?"

"She's fine, it's just we're a little confused, is all. I knew it couldn't be you, but Hanna said—"

"Can I speak to her?"

There was a rustling, and then Hanna came onto the end of the line. "Hey, Ro."

"Hey, buddy. Listen, I didn't call you. I swear. This is so strange. What did the person say?"

"Just a lot of cussing, really, then they put the phone down. It's just... it did sound a little like you."

"Han, when have I ever cussed you out? Or anybody, for that matter?" Something was niggling at the back of Romy's mind, but she couldn't get a grip on it.

Hanna laughed, sounding relieved. "I couldn't believe it either. I know you wouldn't do it. What was even weirder was... it sounded like it was cut off at either end, you know? Like whoever was speaking had started before the line connected and was still in mid-flow when it cut off."

Romy frowned. "Can you remember exactly what you heard?"

Hanna sighed. "There was a lot of the 'f' word. Something like '*fucking fuck is this fuckery.*' It would have been funny if..."

"Hanna, I have to go," Romy interrupted her friend. "I'm so sorry this happened, but I will get to the bottom of it, I promise."

She said goodbye, feeling cold. She remembered all too clearly what she had said to Jae that morning when he showed her the malicious article. *What the fucking fuck is this fuckery...*

Hanna *had* heard Romy's voice. The question now was, how?

The answer made Romy want to throw up. Someone had bugged her home.

Her fingers hovered over Milo's number then she set her phone down. Nope. She wasn't going to be *that* woman. Whatever was happening between Milo and herself was embryonic. Fragile. And she didn't run to the nearest guy when she was in trouble, she'd never done that, and she wouldn't now.

Romy grabbed her keys and locked up the gallery. Now, she was mad. *Quite possibly literally*, she thought as she started her car and drove the few blocks to her condo. On her way up to her home, she made sure she said hello to any of her neighbors she passed. *I might need you in a crisis if some crazy is targeting me...*

Fuck it. She went into her apartment and listened to the silence. Nothing was disturbed, and there was no sense that anyone else was there. Still, she snagged a knife from the butcher's block and checked every room, every closet, every corner. Now that she knew no one was there, she felt like a ninja as she padded quietly through her home.

She flicked on a playlist from her phone and connected it to the Bluetooth speaker. She turned it as loud as she felt comfortable with—and that wouldn't upset her neighbors—and went to all the places she thought a bug might be hidden.

The entire time she was searching, she was more and more aware of how ridiculous this all was. At the same time, there was an unease in her soul, a nagging thought that this was just the beginning. Was someone really trying to run her out of town... or worse?

She found one weird-looking thing under the couch, a small piece of plastic with a sensor. But that was it. She put it into an empty mason jar and screwed the lid on tightly.

Of course, I could have just found a piece of trash, and I'm a crazy lady. Romy shook her head. *No.* Someone had recorded her voice and played it to her former boss as a nuisance call.

Romy scowled at the mason jar as if it were the perp. "Douchebag. Okay, now I'm just talking to a damn jar."

She gave it a childish shove, then had to catch it before it slid off the countertop. "Go. To. Bed. Woman."

When she got into bed, she checked her phone. A smile finally crept across her face, and the tension in her body eased. An image of Sailor, his big goofy face filling the screen, had the words "Sailor (and his dad) would like to take you for lunch tomorrow—how about it?"

Romy laughed. She typed in a quick reply. *Wuff, wuff, bork, wuff, bork, bork. (* translation: I would love to have lunch with you and your Dad xx)*

Back came two emojis—a paw print and a heart.

Despite everything, Romy went to sleep that night with a smile on her face.

TWELVE

ROMY SIDE-EYED THE MASON jar with the 'bug' in it as she ate her breakfast the next morning. She'd slept fitfully and felt grouchy and irritated. Only the fact she would be seeing Milo later was keeping her from going back to bed.

She showered and dressed casually but added a little makeup and blow-dried her long hair into soft waves. Her jeans were her favorite brand, a slight kick flare, and she paired them with a pretty, floral top and a navy blue blazer. Her well-worn Chucks finished the outfit.

She dabbed a little perfume on her pulse points and added a delicate gold chain. Romy checked her reflection out and nodded. Smart, functional but with feminine twist—perfect for a lunch date. She tried to cover up her dark circles with some concealer, but they refused to be covered.

On the ride down to the gallery, her spirits lifted. The day was bright, clear, and warmer than it had been for the last few days. At the gallery, Nico and his team were already at work, and Romy could tell that before the week was out, her gallery would be ready for some artwork to be hung, if only to check out that everything worked aesthetically.

"Nico, the work you've done here, wow."

"Just doing my job. It was a good building to work with."

The door behind her opened, and Romy turned to see Nan, her old friend, smiling at her.

"Hello, stranger."

"I'm sorry I haven't been around much, honey. Mom's been sick, and I've been out in Carmel with her. Hey, this place is really coming along." Nan looked around the gallery appreciatively and smiled at Romy. "You were right. This was the right decision, this place."

Romy nodded. "Come back to the office. Nico has worked his magic there, too."

She made them both coffee, and they sat in the bright office, the window open, enjoying the view down to the ocean. "Catch me up, Park. I really wanted to get together with you, but you know how it is."

"How is your Mom?"

"Oh, fine. She's just getting old, is all. Forgetful. But what about you? I hear rumors…" Nan grinned, wiggling her eyebrows at her.

Romy was a little shocked. There were already rumors about her and Milo? "Not much to tell."

"Not according to the man himself. He says you had a very… what was his word, again? Intimate reunion."

Romy blinked. "Huh?" She frowned and then groaned. "God, Nan, please tell me you're not talking about Connor Small?"

"Who else? I remember you and him in high school. God, you were so crazy over him. I always thought he was a little too… you know, pretty boy, but—"

"Nan, there is no way on this earth that Connor Small and I would or will ever be intimate." Romy shuddered, and Nan gave a shocked laugh.

"Ro, I have to tell you. That was the opposite reaction I was expecting, given how... effusive Connor was about you." Nan shook her head, her face flushing a little. "I'm sorry, I... I don't quite understand."

Romy took pity on her friend. "Nan, I was a kid back then. I didn't realize what a self-absorbed idiot he was." She sighed. "As a matter of fact, I've become quite close to his ex since I've been back."

The expression on Nan's face changed, became guarded. "Well, sorry for bringing him up."

"What's up?"

"No. Nothing. Just... I always thought the Van Warrens were... a little, haughty, is all. Not our type."

Romy half-smiled. "I admit, I used to think so, too. But then again, I didn't really know them. Connor, by all accounts, was the one who made his mind up to marry into money. From what Harper tells me, she fell in love."

Nan's face softened. "Well, Connor always had that easy charm." She looked away from Romy's gaze, and then two spots of pink bloomed high on her cheeks.

"Nan Sommers... Connor? Really?"

Nan chuckled softly. "He was always yours, Ro, so I never said anything. Then I met Huck, and there was that."

"But now Huck has gone, and Connor is single." Romy got up and went to her friend and hugged her. "Darling, if Connor is who you want, go for it. But just know, if he hurts you, I'll break his legs."

Nan laughed but shook her head. "I don't think that's going to happen, Ro. He seems pretty keen on starting things back up with you."

"Speaking of things that will never happen." Romy said darkly, then half-smiled. "Actually, although I meant it when I said there's not much to tell… I have… I mean, there's someone I have feelings for."

"Oh, is it the handsome contractor?" Nan at least had the decency to lower her voice, nodding in the direction of the main gallery where Nico was working. Romy colored.

"No." She hesitated, feeling that if she put a name to her burgeoning relationship with Milo, it would be bad luck. "Let's just say… he's unexpected."

Nan groaned. "Always so secretive. You haven't changed."

Romy felt the sting of her words. "What does that mean?"

"You always played your cards close to your chest, Ro. Even when we were kids, I never thought I really knew you." She smiled at her. "There's nothing wrong with that, of course. You were like your dad—quiet, reflective. Nothing like your mom."

"She had that Italian spirit, all right. Huh. I never realized I was a closed book."

"Not closed. Just… bookmarked."

Romy had to laugh then. "I like that. *Bookmarked.* Well, alright, how's this for opening up? I am seeing Milo Keys."

She watched Nan's expression change from smiling to shock to wariness. "Really?"

"It's very early, very, *very* early." She checked her watch. "I'm actually having lunch with him in an hour."

Nan nodded, but Romy couldn't help noticing that her friend seemed non-plussed. "What is it?"

"Just… he's a little strange, isn't he? He lives in that huge place in Big Sur, on his own, and he rarely comes out in public. He's a good-looking man, but you're not telling me he hasn't got bodies buried in his basement. Losing your wife like that has got to mess with your head."

Romy swallowed hard and looked away from her friend. "You don't know him."

"And being back here for a month means you don't really know him, either. God, here I go again, putting my foot in it. Sorry, Ro, I didn't mean to be a downer. Just be cautious, is all I'm saying."

Romy nodded, but she was unsettled by Nan's words, and when her friend said goodbye a few minutes later, she sat in her office, staring blankly at her computer screen.

She argued with herself for a moment, then typed 'Sarah Keys, Monterey' into the search engine. She recognized the dark-haired woman in the images that came up, of course. Milo had captured his wife in exquisite detail in *Antigone*, and it was a little surreal to see her as she was in real life. Sarah Keys had long dark hair, flowing in waves around her shoulders and a wide, warm smile. There were photographs from her job—she had been an architect, and there were several professional-looking shots of her. Romy liked the mischievous look in her eyes even in those images. *We would have been friends.* The thought came unbidden, and Romy laughed at her own presumption.

She saw the death notices and, feeling guilty, clicked on some of them. Sarah Keys had been found by her husband, an eight-inch knife buried in her abdomen, a suicide note nearby. Milo had insisted they investigate Sarah's death as a murder, but the evidence all pointed to it being a horrible, tragic suicide.

Romy felt a little sick to her stomach. In the photos taken at Sarah's funeral, Milo's utter desolation and heartbreak were harrowing to look at. More than that, the man looked broken and confused, as if his world had shifted on its axis out of nowhere,

I guess it did. I know how that feels. Her heart ached for Milo. Sarah's death had come out of the blue. Romy read the articles that followed the funeral, which soon shifted from sympathetic to painting Milo as a crazy man who wouldn't accept his wife's death.

I don't blame you at all, she thought fiercely, *you fight for the truth, Milo. I believe you.* None of it made sense. By all accounts, Sarah was successful in her career and was still as head-over-heels in love with her husband as the day they married. They were planning children and a future.

Romy shut her laptop, suddenly feeling intrusive. How was this any better than someone bugging her place? She shook it off and got up, just as she heard a muffled bark. She smiled and went to the door. "Sailor? Is that you?"

A large shape lumbered down the dimly lit hallway and launched itself at her. Romy laughed, rocking back onto her ass as the dog covered her in kisses. "Hey, boy… how are you doing?"

"Sailor, don't pre-empt your dad." Milo followed his dog, and he offered his hand to Romy, who took it. He pulled her to her feet, using the opportunity to draw her close and press his lips to hers. "Hello."

Romy kissed him back. "Hello to you, too."

Milo smiled down at her, and she cupped his face in her hand. He leaned into her touch. Sailor wuffed, annoyed at being so rapidly forgotten and nudged Romy's hand. Romy laughed as Milo rolled his eyes. "He doesn't like to share."

"Bad luck for you, dog," she said to the animal, who gave her a huge wolfy smile and nudged her hand again.

"Well, actually, lucky for all of us that it's a great day out there. I thought we could have a picnic."

"Sounds good to me."

"Um, Romy?"

They both looked around to see Nico at the end of the hallway. "Sorry to interrupt. Can I have a word?"

"Of course." Romy shot Milo a quick smile and went to see Nico.

Nico seemed a little off, she thought, but all he wanted her for was to sign off on some paperwork. She scribbled her name on the sheets and handed his pen back to him.

"You okay, Nico?"

"Sure." He looked at Milo. "You two have a good date."

"Thanks, we will." Milo's smile was pleasant, but when he and Romy walked outside with Sailor, he made a face. "Uh oh. I think someone's nose is a little out of joint."

"Who, Nico? Why would it be?" But then she remembered that Nico had asked her out a few weeks ago. "Oh, heck." She told Milo as they got into his car, and he shrugged.

"You don't owe him an explanation. It was one time."

"I guess, I just don't need an atmosphere at work." She smiled at him then. "But, really, it's nothing to worry about. It's just good to be here with you."

"Likewise." He leaned over and kissed her again. "I was dreaming of those lips all night."

"Sweet talker."

"Wuff."

Romy and Milo laughed as Sailor stuck his head between them. "Honestly, Sailor, am I going to have to fight every other man in this town for Romy?"

Romy flushed, feeling a little awkward, but then she met his gaze. "No," she said softly, "you're not."

His answering smile erased any doubts she had that this man wasn't interested in her. It was a smile of delight, shy and happy. Later, Romy would wonder if that was the moment that she knew she had fallen hard for Milo Keys, maybe even the moment she fell in love with him.

THIRTEEN

MILO DROVE DOWN TO Monterey State Beach where dogs were welcome, and although there was a '*dogs must be on leash*' rule, most of the other dogs were running free. So Milo risked letting Sailor loose. The dog immediately headed for the water.

"Just to warn you, the car will be blessed with the special aroma of soggy St. Bernard on the way back."

"I can live with that."

"It's a treat."

Milo took Romy's hand, and they walked a little, watching Sailor play with some other dogs. Milo indicated a bench halfway up the beach, and they set out their lunch there.

"I bought a few subs. I didn't know what you liked. Apart from, you know, all food."

Romy laughed. "You know me too well already."

Milo hid a grin as she sank her teeth into a meatball sub and immediately squirted her top with marinara sauce. "Ah, dang it."

Milo swiped the blob of sauce up with one quick movement, and then, making Romy laugh, he smeared it on his own cheek. "Who's messy now?"

She leaned over and kissed his cheek clean, before brushing her lips against his. "Thank you for the food... and the help."

He cradled her face in his hands. "Hurry up and eat. I need to be kissing you more."

Romy chuckled, and they finished their lunch, watching Sailor play in the water. Milo got up to dump their trash in the refuse bin. Then, as he walked back, he came around to Romy's side of the bench and sat behind her, slipping his arms around her waist. Romy leaned back against him.

He buried his face in her hair and breathed in. She smelled of soap and fresh air, and she turned her head to smile at him.

"God, you're beautiful."

Romy flushed. "You need glasses, but thank you."

"Hey, I'm an artist. I should know."

"Doofus."

"Hey, that's my line."

Romy kissed him. "Hush your mouth."

"Whatever you say, as long as you keep doing that." Milo smiled down at her, and as her lips met his, he sank into it, wanting to feel every soft moment of the kiss.

He hadn't felt this way about anyone since Sarah, and he had assumed he never would. He couldn't even define why he was so drawn to this young woman, except... they fit. And they had ever since the day they had met—which was what had freaked him out so much at that first dinner at Harper's.

He felt like he'd known Romy Park forever, and that was an oddly unsettling feeling at first. Now, though, he leaned into it. He'd forgotten the heady phase of new love, but this woman had gotten him sleepless and looking forward to the moment he would be with her again.

"Milo?"

Milo snapped out of his reverie. "Yes, sweetheart?"

Romy turned around in his arms, her face serious for once. "Do you think you'll ever paint again?"

He had been waiting for this question for a while. "I can't answer that. Which in itself is new for me, because before you came into my life, I would have said no, right away. Without even thinking. Now…"

"Now?"

He kissed her. "Now, you have me looking at art supplies."

He loved the excitement in her eyes. "I'm not promising anything, Romy. But…"

"I won't pressure you, or anything, I promise. I was just curious. Your gift is remarkable, Milo Keys. And that's all I'll say."

She slid her fingers into his short hair, her warm eyes on his. "I'm crazy about you. I know I should play it cool, but I can't."

Milo crushed his lips to Romy's and kissed her so fiercely that his head swam. He didn't care that the other people on the beach were watching—all he could see was her. Romy.

Finally, they broke apart, panting for air. "Now that was a kiss." Romy looked as stunned as she was flushed with pleasure. They gazed at each other for the longest moment.

Milo traced the curve of her cheek with his finger. "Romy, have dinner with me. Tonight. At my place."

There was a flicker of nervousness in her eyes, but she nodded. "I would like that."

Milo took a deep breath in. "And stay. No pressure… there are plenty of guest rooms. But stay."

Slowly, she nodded, and a sweet smile spread across her face. "I would like that, too."

They walked back to the car, Sailor, having exhausted himself, trotting obediently beside them. Milo drove back to Monterey, and they spent a good few minutes kissing goodbye.

"I'll see you tonight."

"I won't be late."

She was still smiling when she went back to the gallery, and thankfully, Nico seemed to be in a better mood. He didn't mention Milo, just walked her through the progress.

"Honestly, Ro, a couple more days and we're done. I've hired someone in to come finesse the details, but you're good to go."

Romy took a shaky breath in. "Wow. We're doing this." She smiled at Nico. "Nico, you have made this process so much easier than I could have ever wished, thank you. You will stay in touch, promise me? And come to the opening?"

"To Milo Keys' first show in a decade? Hell, yes."

Romy was relieved Nico didn't seem to harbor any ill-will for her new beau. "You're not just a contractor, you know? You've become a real friend. I'll never forget what you did for me after the assault."

Nico's face clouded. "It still bugs me, Ro. Will you let me come check out your security? Put my mind at rest that you're okay up there on your own."

Romy considered, remembering the mason jar on her kitchen counter. "Actually, that might be a good idea. I want to pick your brain about something."

Nico turned the mason jar, peering in at the small square of black plastic.

"Well… I don't know, Ro. I'm not an expert, but it does seem weird." He looked at her. "And you say someone recorded your voice and played it to your old boss?"

"Yup. I had to deny it was me, of course, because… well…" She trailed off, shaking her head. "But what with the attack, the weird obituary being sent to me, and now this… someone wants me out of here. Oh, and there was a bitchy article about me online, but that doesn't seem to have gained any traction so…" She sighed and sat down heavily. "But the intrusion… *again*, Nico."

He nodded, his face grim and set. "Look, it's not my place, but I think you should move out. Whoever is targeting you knows you live here alone. He—or she—has heard everything you've said or done. Your most private moments."

He colored and looked away, and Romy grinned to herself. "Then he or she would have been very bored." Her smile faded. "But it does creep me out. And I just don't know what reason anyone would have to want to spy on me or try and drive me out."

"Or hurt you."

"That, too." She shook her head. "It pisses me off. I don't want to have to move out of here, but neither do I want my privacy invaded."

"Look, for now, I'm going to check around, see if I can find any other, anything else suspicious, let's say, and I'll ask around about this thing."

"Thanks, Nico, I appreciate it."

Romy made some coffee while Nico checked the entire condo. After a half-hour, he came back to the kitchen and dumped a pile of the small plastic pieces on the counter.

Romy's heart sank. "No."

"Afraid so. Every power outlet and in your air conditioning, too. I'm sorry, Romy."

"I should report it to the police."

Nico nodded. "I would. Between this and the attack, it's cause for concern. Look, I'm going to put extra locks on your balcony doors and the front door. I'll clear it with the super, but under the circumstances…"

"I really appreciate it, but not tonight. I have someplace to be in an hour so."

"Fair enough. I can do it tomorrow."

She walked him to the door. "I mean it, Nico. Thank you. You're a real friend."

He smiled down at her, and not for the first time, Romy thought how handsome he was. So, why did he do nothing for her? Maybe she could set him up with Nan.

"Ro, just take care of yourself. I would hate for you to come to any harm." He hesitated. "I had a friend once. She got hurt by someone who was obsessed with her. And she didn't make it. I still miss her, even now."

"I'm so sorry, Nico." Romy was appalled by the grief in his eyes.

"Thanks. So... please, take care. I won't lose another friend."

"You won't, I promise."

He smiled at her sadly and then turned away, before turning back. "Don't promise that, Romy. You know as well as I do that none of us know what's around the corner. None of us."

And then he was gone.

FOURTEEN

THINKING ABOUT WHAT NICO had told her for most of the drive
out to Big Sur had tamped down some of Romy's nerves, but as
Milo's place came into view, her heart began to beat hard against
her ribs.

She'd packed an overnight bag and then forgotten her
toothbrush, so she'd stopped at a drugstore to pick one up. As
she was paying, the end cap of condoms mocked her until she
grabbed a box and added it to her pile of items. Why, in the
twenty-first century, was she still so embarrassed about buying
condoms? Wasn't it the safe thing to do?

The cashier didn't even blink as Romy paid for her things
and then shoved them deep into her purse, skulking out of the
drugstore like she'd robbed the place. In the car, she allowed
herself a laugh at her own dumb behavior.

But...

The fact remained she'd only ever slept with one person, and
even then, it had only been a handful of times. She barely even
remembered it. Romy chuckled to herself. She wondered how
Connor would feel about that.

She'd thought herself in love with Connor, but now she knew

it had been nothing more than a teenage crush. The desire she felt for Milo Keys was overwhelming. She felt breathless when she imagined him touching her. Her whole body yearned to be skin-on-skin with him.

Now as the gates of the Keys mansion slid open, she saw him outlined against the doorway, and her breath caught in her throat. She was really going to do this, sleep with this gorgeous man in front of her.

Her hero. Her inspiration.

And now... her lover.

Milo opened her car door, and she slid out into his arms.

"Hi." Her voice shook, and Milo smiled.

"Hello again." He bent his head to kiss her, his lips firm against hers, but she could feel him trembling as much as she was. The kiss deepened, and something clicked in Romy's mind.

She wanted him, and there was no reason to wait... none at all.

Milo was clearly a mind reader as he picked her up and carried her into the house. Romy dropped her bag and kissed him again as Milo climbed the stairs with her in his arms.

In his bedroom, he lowered her gently onto the bed and covered her body with his. His kisses were long, sweet, and their tongues curved around each other's as if they wanted to consume each other.

"God, Milo..."

He smiled down at her, his green eyes soft but excited. "Are you sure, Romy? Because you say the word and we'll stop."

She shook her head. "No... don't stop..."

His hands were under her top, stroking a delicious rhythm on her belly with his fingertips. Her own hands fluttered nervously at his shirt buttons, fumbling with them in her excitement.

She pushed his shirt aside and ran her hands over the firm

planes of his chest. The man worked out, but he wasn't crazy-ripped, and she liked that. There was some softness to him, and although his hips were slim, they didn't jut out at the bone.

She kissed him again and tentatively slid her hand down to his groin, stroking his stiffening cock through his pants. Milo moaned, burying his face in her neck, kissing her throat before trailing his lips along her jawline.

"I want you, Romy Park, so, so badly..."

Romy hooked her legs around him, tangling her fingers in his hair. "I want you, too, inside me, Milo..."

Their clothes didn't stay on too long after that. And, god, he was magnificent, but Romy was elated by the blatant lust in his eyes. Milo kissed her lips, her throat, then all the way down her body, taking each nipple into his mouth in turn, lashing his tongue around them and making Romy's body catch fire.

"God, Milo..."

He looked up and smiled at her. "Your body is sensational, Romy."

"Flatterer." But she blushed with delight at his obvious admiration. His lips were on her belly now, and then, as she gasped with pleasure, his tongue found her clit.

The man has skills, she thought as every cell in her body ignited. Milo's fingers dug hard into the soft flesh of her inner thighs, pushing them apart as his mouth covered her sex and he brought her to near abandon.

"Wait..." She could barely catch her breath. "I want to come with you inside me."

She felt his deep, throaty chuckle against her sex, and then he was kissing her again. She could feel his rock-hard cock against her thigh. "Want to help me with the condom, darling?"

She helped him roll it down his hot length, and then he was hitching her legs around his waist. Romy gazed up at him as he slowly entered her, shivering with blissful release as he filled her and began to move. They found their rhythm slowly, locking eyes, Milo's fingers entwined with hers, his strong legs supporting him as he thrust into her.

"Romy, Romy, Romy…" His sweet whisper made tears come to her eyes, and she gave up every last thing that was holding her back and gave herself to him completely.

Milo's pace quickened, and Romy tightened her thighs, clenching herself around him, wanting to give him as much pleasure as he was giving her. She was too breathless to speak so she just crushed her lips against his as they both neared their climax.

His hips slammed against hers and she tilted her hips so he could go deeper as she moaned and gasped and writhed beneath him. "Romy… I'm close…"

Her orgasm exploded through her and she cried out as stars danced in her vision. Her back arched, her belly pressing hard against his as she felt him come, too, his body shuddering with the force of his climax.

They collapsed back onto the bed, and Milo kissed her, both of them drenched in sweat.

"God… Romy…"

She wrapped her arms and legs around him, never wanting to let him go. The feel of him inside her was like nothing she had ever dreamed of, and although she knew he would have to withdraw, just for the moment, she relished this moment of connection with him.

They caught their breath, and then, with a regretful smile, Milo slid from the bed and went to the bathroom to deal with the condom. He returned to her side, kissing her softly. "Damn condoms, a necessity but always a mood killer."

Romy laughed, curving into his arms, her head on his chest.

"I don't think anything could kill this mood, Milo Keys." She looked up at him. "That was incredible."

"Right back at you, beautiful." His arms tightened around her, and he pressed his lips against her forehead. "Damn, Romy... I thought I could hold out until after supper, at least, but you got out of that car and—"

He was teasing her now and she joined in. "What can I tell you? I'm a floozy."

"A *floozy*?" Milo started to laugh as she nodded.

"A slattern, a strumpet."

He laughed but shook his head. "You are none of those things."

"Well, okay, but you know what I am, especially in this moment?"

He stroked her cheek with his thumb. "And what's that?"

Romy looked up at him, her eyes loving but serious. "Yours," she whispered.

For a moment, she wondered if she had said too much, but then Milo gave a groan of desire and rolled her onto her back, kissing her until she had to beg for oxygen. "And I am yours, Romy Park. Always, always yours."

They began to make love again, and soon any thought of food was forgotten. Milo was a generous lover, and Romy followed his lead, hoping her lack of experience didn't mean she was lacking. He was intoxicating, knowing exactly how to touch and caress her.

It was almost dawn before they finally collapsed back on the bed, exhausted and sated. Milo gathered her into his arms.

"Sleep, my darling. We have all the time in the world to talk."

She kissed him softly. "Milo... tonight has been incredible."

She felt his deep chuckle rumble through his hard chest. "More than I can say, little one."

They feel asleep quickly, wrapped around each other.

The sound of her cell phone broke through her sleep, and Romy opened her eyes. Slipping out from Milo's arms—and god, he looked cute when he was asleep—she padded downstairs to where she had dropped her bag the previous night. Sailor came lumbering to greet her, and she fussed him and let him out to pee before she snagged her phone.

As she rummaged deep into her purse, she was aware that her body ached in the most pleasant way. Her thighs felt sore from being pushed apart by Milo and her sex felt swollen and tender from the pounding of his cock. Romy had never felt more beautiful or feminine.

She grinned to herself. *Stop mooning, check your phone, and then you can go back upstairs to that glorious man and start over again.* Romy chuckled to herself as she pulled her phone out of the depths of her purse.

Milo had woken to an empty bed and was just sitting up when he heard the scream from downstairs. Naked, he darted down the stairs as Sailor began to bark furiously. He saw Romy bent double, sobbing uncontrollably, holding onto her phone.

Milo gathered her up in his arms, trying to calm her. He took the phone from her and said hello. A young man's voice, shaken, answered him. "Who is this?"

"I'm Milo Keys, a friend of Romy's... is this Jae?"

"No." The young man gave a sob. "It's Moon. Moon Kim. I'm a friend of Romy's, too... and Jae's..."

"Moon," Milo remembered Romy telling him that she considered Moon family. He spoke gently now as he held Romy tightly. "Moon, what's wrong?"

"It's Jae," Moon said in a faint voice. "He's been stabbed."

FIFTEEN

THE DRIVE UP TO Berkeley seemed endless, and Romy felt edgy and tearful the entire journey. Milo had insisted on driving her himself, and she couldn't stop apologizing for causing him inconvenience.

After the fifth time, Milo put his hand on hers. "Ro, stop saying you're sorry. This is what couples do, they support each other. I'm just so sorry this has happened."

Romy entwined her fingers between his. It made her feel safe, somehow. The way he had reacted when she was a sobbing mess, she would never forget. He talked to Moon, reassured the young man and got the details of what had happened.

Jae and Moon had been out at dinner with friends and were returning to their dorm when it happened. As Moon walked into the building, he heard someone call Jae's name. Turning, he saw a figure in dark clothing, hooded, appear to push Jae. Jae staggered back and whirled around, and Moon saw blood blooming across his friend's chest.

His reaction was to yell, go after the assailant, but the attacker swiped at Moon with the knife, catching his bicep. Then Jae collapsed and all Moon could think of was getting help for his friend. The assailant disappeared into the night, and Moon held Jae in his arms as they waited for the ambulance.

"He didn't lose consciousness," Moon told Milo, his voice dull from exhaustion and shock, "so that's one good thing. They're operating on him now. Can you bring Romy?"

Milo had reassured him, and then after saying goodbye, he had lifted Romy into his arms and held her.

"Sweetheart, Jae's being cared for. Moon says the doctors are very optimistic he'll be just fine. Right now, we're going to go upstairs and shower, eat some breakfast. Then we'll drop Sailor off with Harper—she won't mind—and I'm going to drive you to Berkeley.

Romy closed her eyes now. The view outside was incredible, and usually, she felt joy when travelling up the coast, but today, all she could think of was getting to Jae. The thought that somebody would target Jae made her feel sick at heart—and what was worse, why? Moon had told Milo that there didn't seem to be any financial motive—Jae wasn't mugged. There had been no attempt to rob him, so...why?

She felt Milo looking over at her, and she opened her eyes. "I'm sorry."

"Ro."

"Sorry." She chuckled softly. "I can't help myself. It's just... Jae is my brother, you know? He and Moon are my family." Romy blew out her cheeks. "If I could get in a room with the person who attacked them, I tell you, Milo... they'd regret it."

Grief and anger made tears well in her eyes, and she looked away from Milo, not wanting to burst into tears again. In the span of just a few hours, she had gone from a dream to a nightmare.

Milo drove on a few miles, then pulled into a gas station. "We need coffee, I think, even if it is gas station coffee."

"I'll come in with you."

While Milo put gas in the car, Romy wandered around the store, randomly picking up bags of potato chips and packs of jerky. She grabbed a six-pack of soda and took them to the register.

"And whatever gas number four is using. Oh, and two coffees, please."

"Sure thing." The clerk rang up her purchases as Milo walked in. Romy smiled at him. "I got this."

Milo started to protest, but she waved away his offer to reimburse her. He carried the coffee back to the car as Romy dumped her snacks in the footwell of the passenger side. She looked at him apologetically. "When I get stressed, I eat."

Milo smiled. "You snack away, sweetheart."

Romy ate her way through an entire bag of spicy snacks as they drove, Milo casting amused looks at her. "You weren't kidding."

"Nope. I'm a stress eater." She put the bag down. "Milo, tell me again how Moon sounded. Was he trying to put a good spin on things?"

"Honey, honestly, I don't think the poor kid was anything but in shock. I don't think he had it in him to smooth the edges."

Romy nodded. "I hope so."

Alta Bates Campus Emergency Department was as busy as they expected it to be, and Romy felt like they walked miles before she saw Moon, his slight figure curled into a plastic chair. He saw Romy and got up, almost running to her. His arm was heavily bandaged, and Romy was shocked about how thin and frail her friend looked. She wrapped her arms around him and held him. He felt like he might break, and he was trembling badly.

She stroked his silky hair. "It's okay, darling, I'm here now."

She felt him nod. "He's in recovery, Ro. They said... they

said they couldn't tell me much but that the surgery went well. They were waiting for you." He drew away from her and looked at Milo. "Hi."

Romy introduced them, and Milo shook Moon's good hand. The height difference between the two men might have been amusing in other circumstances. But Romy could find no humor in anything right now. Moon's skin was pale white, and there were dark shadows under his eyes.

"The police want to talk to you, too," Moon said, his voice wracked with exhaustion. "They were grilling me practically the whole time Jae was being operated on." He sighed and wobbled a little. Romy put her arms around him to steady him.

"Sweetie, you need some rest."

"I'm not leaving him."

Romy stroked Moon's hair back from his face. "I wouldn't ask you to. Is there a relatives' room where we should wait?"

They had the room to themselves, and Romy made Moon lie down on one of the couches. She covered him with her jacket. "Try to sleep, darling. I promise I'll wake you when there's some news."

She sat at his side while he fell asleep. Milo rubbed her shoulders. "Sweet kid."

Romy watched as sleep erased most of the stress from Moon's lovely face. "He really is. He got shoved out by his family a lot—nothing abusive—just there were a lot of kids, and Moon got forgotten in the mix. So, he grew up with Jae and me." She stroked Moon's cheek. "He's too thin."

There was a knock at the door, and a middle-aged woman came in. "Hi… Miss Park? I'm Detective Ames from crime unit."

Romy stood and shook her hand. "My cousin is in recovery at the moment."

"I know." Det. Ames looked down at Moon's sleeping form. "How's he doing?"

"Exhausted." Romy's tone hardened a little. "He says you grilled him?"

"We had to, a little. We had to make sure that this wasn't a hate crime."

Romy blinked. "What?"

"That they weren't targeted by some homophobic assholes."

Romy glanced at Milo, who looked as confused as she did. "As far as I know..." she trailed off. *Of course. Of course...* it had been staring her in the face this whole time. Jae and Moon. *Of course.* Something about that made her heart lift a little. "Do you think it might be?"

"We still don't know. We know the assailant knew your cousin; he called him by name after all."

"Definitely a 'he'?"

Det. Ames nodded. "According to Mr. Kim, yes. Look, I don't want to pressure you, but I could do with a little background information. Do you have some time now?"

Romy looked at Milo, and he nodded. "I'll stay with Moon."

"Well, okay, but, Detective," Romy looked back at the other woman, "the moment the doctors say I can see Jae..."

"Of course. I won't take too much of your time."

Milo stayed with Moon while Romy went with the detective to another room.

"Would you like some coffee?"

Romy shook her head. "No, thanks."

There was another detective, a young man, waiting for them, and Romy wondered if he had helped question Moon. Whether he'd been mean to him. He nodded politely at her but didn't smile. Romy started to feel uneasy.

"Is there something you're not telling me?"

Det. Ames exchanged a look with the other detective. "Romy, this Jim Halsey from the Monterey Police Department. I called him this morning, and he very kindly came here to meet with us. I understand you were assaulted in your apartment a few weeks ago?"

Romy rocked back. "How did you know that?"

"A Mr. Kays filed a report with us," Det. Halsey spoke at last. "He said that you didn't want to make a statement, but he didn't think it should go by without being reported, at least."

"He never told me that." Romy couldn't find it in her to be mad at Milo. He was just looking out for her. "But, yes, that's what it seemed to be. But what does that have to do with the attack on Jae and Moon?"

Det. Ames pushed her iPad over to Romy. On the screen, a photograph of a note. Romy squinted but couldn't make out the writing. "This was pushed under Jae and Moon's door. It reads: '*This was just a warning. Tell her next time it'll be her, and it'll be permanent.*' We think the 'her' the notes refers to is you."

Romy swallowed hard, dread making her chest tight. "I don't understand any of this."

"I'm going to ask you the most obvious question, Romy. Do you know of anyone who would want to hurt you?"

"I really don't. I've asked myself the same question since the attack and there's no one."

Det. Halsey looked skeptical. "No bad break-ups? Either here or in New York?"

"No." Him mentioning New York jogged a memory. "But, my apartment was bugged."

Both detectives gaped at her. "What?"

"I should have mentioned it." Romy rubbed her head. "Someone—and I assume it was whoever broke in—bugged my apartment. They recorded me and called my old boss, played some, um… they recorded me cussing and used it to call my old boss." She shook her head, almost smiling. "Fuck, this sounds ridiculous now that I'm saying it out loud. My contractor went through my place, found them all. Well, we think they're bugs; neither of us are experts."

Det. Ames sighed. "So, fingerprinting would be pointless at this stage."

"The place is a rental. I'd expect there to be all sorts of fingerprints." Romy rolled her shoulders, the tension back.

"So… no mad exes?" Det. Halsey was studying her carefully, and Romy began to feel uncomfortable.

"Really. No."

He shifted in his seat. "And you're with Mr. Keys?"

"Yes." Romy was starting to get irritated. "Why?"

"I hear things in town. In Monterey. There was talk you were getting back together with Connor Small after his divorce, that him splitting with his wife was the reason you came back to Monterey."

"And where, or rather, who did you hear that from? Connor? He's deluded." Romy couldn't help the bitterness in her voice. She'd had about enough of Connor Small. "But he's not violent. Nor does he have any reason to threaten me. I came back to Monterey to open an art gallery and to be closer to my family. Jae and Moon. That's the only reason."

"We understand you're friendly with Mr. Small's ex-wife."

"Yes. We've become friendly since I've been back in Monterey."

"And you don't think that would upset Mr. Small?"

Romy snorted. "I really don't give a crap if it does."

"I hear you." Det. Ames smiled at Romy, and Romy relaxed a little. Det. Ames got it. Det. Halsey, on the other hand, was annoying her.

"Det. Halsey, I'm just guessing here… are you friendly with Connor?"

"Not at all, I can assure you."

"It's just you seem to want to fight his case. Like I owe him something?"

Halsey's face softened. "I'm sorry you feel that way. It couldn't be further from the truth." He glanced at Ames, who gave him a slight nod. "What I'm about to tell you… I'm breaking all the rules, but it might give you some clarity. We have evidence that Mr. Small was physically abusive to his former wife."

Romy blinked, the shock of the police officer's words sinking in. "What?"

"He *is* violent, Romy. That's what we're telling you." Ames sighed. "When you came back, did Connor approach you? Make any advances?"

Romy nodded. "Yes. In fact, he kissed me—and it definitely wasn't welcome, but he seemed so sure I would be glad to see him again. Now that I think about it, it was a little strange—even for someone as arrogant as Connor."

"You used to date, right?"

"For a few weeks back when I was eighteen. Then he married Harper."

"Gotcha. So he made an advance, and you turned him down?"

"Yes. I made it very clear I wasn't interested."

Det. Ames gave her a smile, an 'I get you' smile. "Anyone else?"

Before Romy could answer, there was a knock at the door. Milo opened the door. "Excuse me, detectives. Romy, the doctors say you can see Jae now."

Romy was up and halfway out of the door before Det. Ames could even say anything. "We'll continue this later, Romy."

"Sure, sure." But Romy's attention was anywhere but there now, as she hurried to the room where they'd taken Jae.

SIXTEEN

HER COUSIN WAS PALE, dopey from the anesthetic, but his smile when he saw her made Romy's heart soar. She went to him and carefully put her arms around him. To her relief, he felt a lot more sturdily built than Moon was, and his answering hug was firm.

After a moment, Romy eased out of the embrace and studied him. "How are you feeling, darling?"

Jae grinned. "Fine. Sore, but fine. I think I was lucky. The docs say the knife missed anything vital so there's that. I just have to heal." He nodded at the blood bag hanging above him. "Got me some extra hemoglobin."

"God, Jae." Romy's legs suddenly wobbled, and she had to sit down quickly. She leaned over and took his hand. "I'm so sorry, honey."

"Not your fault." Jae slid his eyes over to Milo, who was hovering near the door. "You must be Milo."

"Hey, Jae. Good to meet you, buddy."

"Likewise." Jae smiled at him, then Romy. "Ro… I'm okay. It was just some jerk who wanted my wallet."

Romy glanced at Milo before speaking. "Jae, they think it

was something to do with me. They found a note at your place. It was a warning... to me."

Jae's smile faded. "What?"

"Yep. Apparently '*next time*,' it'll be me—and permanent."

Milo made a noise, and she turned to look at him. He looked distressed. "Milo, I'm sorry. I don't know why any of this is happening."

"Jesus."

Jae squeezed Romy's hand. "You know we won't let anything happen to you, right?"

"I do know that, but I hate the fact that you got hurt because of me."

"It wasn't because of you. It was some psycho." Jae leaned back on his pillows. "Do the police have any leads?"

Romy hesitated. "Connor."

"That makes sense."

"Yep." Milo's face was grim. "Son of a bitch."

Romy gave an involuntary shiver. "I just don't know."

Moon came into the room then, balancing four cups of coffee in his hands. He smiled at them, and then Romy watched his eyes softened as he looked at Jae. "I have contraband."

He set the coffee down and went to Jae's side. They hugged for a long moment, gingerly, but Romy could sense the emotion in the embrace. How had she not seen this? The love between them was obvious.

Later, Milo took Romy to the hotel room he had booked for them.

"Harper said she'd look after Sailor for as long as we needed to be away."

"I feel bad for dragging you away from your life."

"This *is* my life, Ro. With you."

120

She flushed and went to him, wanting to be wrapped in his arms. They stood there for a long time, holding each other. Romy buried her face in his sweater and breathed him in. It was strange; it felt weird to have somebody, to be a couple, when she had survived on her own for so long, and yet, the sheer excitement of new love was still there. She looked up at him.

"Thank you for everything, Milo. I don't know how I would have gotten through the last twenty-four hours without you."

"You would have. Well, maybe not the sex part." He grinned, and she laughed, feeling some of her tension ease. "But you're stronger than you think. You held your own with those detectives."

"They want to talk to me again." She sighed. "I don't want to believe Connor could do this." She was silent for a moment then gasped slightly. "Hell, I forgot to mention the online article."

"That, I can help with. I meant to tell you that was nothing to worry about. It was Farron Lee."

Romy blinked. "The gallery owner?" She thought about it. "Okay, so, that makes sense, kind of, except he's established in Monterey, almost a legend. Why would he have to badmouth me?"

"Because you're young, you have history in the town, and people adored your mother and father. Plus—and this sounds so conceited, but—you have me. You have *Antigone*. That's a big coup. Jealously is a powerful motivator."

"So it seems. How did you find out?"

Milo sat on the edge of the bed. "I confronted him. The tone of the post was him all over—bitchy, mean-spirited."

"Wasn't he friends with my father?"

"As much as Farron Lee can be friends with someone. There's something else to this, though." Milo met her gaze steadily. "He was in love with your mother. You remind him of her." He told her the rest of the conversation with Farron, that the other man had been unrepentant at first, but when Milo asked him if he wanted to hurt Romy, he had broken down and admitted he was just in pain because of Romy's resemblance to her late mother.

"Oh." Instantly, Romy's anger dissipated. "Oh, that poor man."

Milo looked askance, but Romy shook her head. "No, honestly. Unrequited love is a bitch."

"And so is Farron. I doubt your mother looked at him twice."

Romy half-smiled. "Probably not. I know what kind of relationship my parents had." She touched his face. "They adored each other, they were best friends. You can't fake that."

"No, you can't." Milo slid his hands around Romy's waist and drew her close. "I adore you, Romy Park."

"And I, you."

Milo buried his face in her belly, and Romy stroked his short dark curls. "It just feels so right being in your arms."

She felt him nod. He gently laid her back on the bed and cradled her in his arms. "We'll go back to the hospital later, but I think you should eat something and rest."

"I could do with a shower."

He smiled at her and kissed her. "I'll order room service, then I'll join you."

Romy stepped under the hot stream of water and sighed as the warmth eased the tension in her body. The water streamed through her long dark hair, and she closed her eyes. A few moments later, she felt Milo join her and, smiling, opened her eyes. "Well, hello."

He drew her close, and she reached down to stroke his cock against her belly. God, she loved every inch of this man's body. He put a finger under her chin and tilted her face up so he could kiss her.

Romy felt her body respond, her sex flood with warmth, and she pressed her body against his as the kiss deepened. After they broke apart to breath, she grinned at him. "Mr. Keys, I do hope you brought a condom into the shower with you, because if you don't make love to me right now, I might explode."

Milo laughed, then reached over to the soap dish, plucking a condom packet from it. "Always prepared, my love."

She helped him roll the condom down his hot length, then he picked her up, both of them laughing as the slippery shower floor made them wobble, but then he was sliding inside her, and Romy shivered with pleasure.

They made love slowly, enjoying every sensation as the water pumped over them, before Milo gave up and lifted her onto the bathroom floor and hitched her legs around his waist. Romy smiled then as he slammed himself into her again, her back arched up and her head rolled back, completely under his spell.

Afterward, they ate dinner, wrapped in their robes. Romy hadn't realized how hungry she was as she tucked into the fat, juicy burgers and shoestring fries. "God, so good. Do you think Harper would judge us for just eating burgers and fries?"

"Ha, no way. Harper can grill like the rest of us."

They chatted idly while they ate their meal, then showered again and dressed. Romy checked her watch. "We have an hour before we have to be back at the hospital."

"Then let's talk. Let's try and figure out who's behind all of this. Or rather... Connor. I can absolutely believe he did this."

Romy frowned. "Obviously you've seen him over the last decade more than I have. He worked with Sarah?"

"And she couldn't stand him. She said he was a pretty boy who traded on his looks, that there was very little else to recommend him as a person. She could never understand what Harper had seen in him."

"His charm. Believe it or not, he can turn it on. I remember, back when I was a teenager, I fell for it. He had this ability to make you feel like the only girl in the world who could possibly capture him. It's not an uncommon trait."

"He's a conman."

Romy nodded. "Yes, that's it exactly." She sighed. "He hurt Harper. Not just emotionally. The detectives told me that she didn't want to press charges, but he beat her, Milo. I want to kill him just because of that."

Her jaw set grimly. "Did he ever come onto Sarah?"

Milo nodded. "It got to a point where she was miserable going into work if she knew he was in the office." He was silent for a moment. "I just didn't know how sad she was. Sarah would hide things from me sometimes. I hate that. I hate she didn't feel like she could trust me to be on her side. I failed her."

"No."

"Yes. I failed in some respect to our partnership, our marriage." He looked at Romy, bottomless grief in his eyes. "And I don't know how, or what I was supposed to do, to help her. Romy, promise me. You will tell me everything. Everything. You will let me in because if something happens and I could have helped…" He slid his hand into her hair. "Promise me."

Romy nodded, holding his gaze steadily. "I promise you, Milo. I'll tell you everything."

SEVENTEEN

HE HAD FOLLOWED THEM back to their hotel. He knew she had talked to the police at the hospital, but he was certain she wouldn't have even mentioned his name. Why would she?

Romy had no idea he was watching, waiting. The previous evening, after following her to Milo Keys' home, his rage had known no bounds when, from the road, he had watched them kiss. There had been no doubt in his mind that they were about to have sex, the way they held each other, kissed each other.

So, the decision to hurt her cousin had been an easy one. Ruin her first night with Milo with the worst news. He had nothing against Jae Park or his pretty boyfriend, but he had to admit, there was something satisfying about sinking his knife into another human's flesh.

He'd missed it. That sensation of the blade plunging into the soft skin. It had been a couple of years since he'd felt it.

Sarah Keys. He still relived every moment of her murder. Her 'suicide.' He could barely believe that the police had ruled it as Sarah taking her own life. He'd stabbed her once, surprising them both, as she tried to get him to leave. She hadn't believed what he'd come to tell her. She was angry, and he lashed out. Once.

She had stumbled backwards, the hilt of the knife protruding from her belly, blood blooming across her white shirt. The look in her eyes… pain, shock, confusion.

He watched her drop, gasping for air. Just one stab wound, but he'd severed her abdominal artery. She bled out in front of him, and with her last breath, she'd asked him why.

She didn't live long enough for his answer. Her lovely eyes glazed over, and he watched the pulse in her neck flicker and stop. He'd had enough sense to clean every one of his fingerprints from the place, from the knife's handle. He could still smell the salt-and-rust tang of her blood in his nostrils.

And he'd felt… exhilarated. But the killing hadn't started some kind of bloodlust in him. He hadn't killed again, but he'd enjoyed Milo Keys' grief.

And when Romy had come back to Monterey, he had known. She would be his next kill, and this time, there would be no doubt that she had been murdered. He intended to make her suffer beforehand, though, break her emotionally, psychologically before he killed her.

He dreamed of her bleeding out in his arms. Of wanting to know why.

This time, there would be a good reason, the best reason for his revenge. He would make her pay for the sins others had committed to him.

And this time, his victim would know *exactly* why.

EIGHTEEN

JAE WAS DISCHARGED FROM the hospital after four days, and Milo had insisted on renting Jae and Moon an apartment near the college, one with added security. Romy had agreed, but she told Milo she would be paying for it.

Jae and Moon had thanked them, but Jae told them they would be paying their own way. "But don't think I'm not grateful to both of you. We both are. And thanks for finding this place, Milo. It's certainly more comfortable than the dorm."

Romy had gone to see the Dean to arrange the new living arrangements, and the Dean had been accommodating. "It was such a shock to us all," he had said.

Romy and Milo had hired movers to bring the boys' things to the new apartment, and they helped them move in. Nether Jae or Moon could carry anything, but they made coffee and ordered pizza and did as much as they could.

"Would the two of you just rest, for the love of God?" Romy complained but then laughed as they both looked like guilty puppies. She loved these two so much, and the relief that they would be okay was overwhelming.

The apartment had two bedrooms, but when Jae saw Romy

putting both his and Moon's clothes in the same closet, he grinned at her. "You guessed?"

"Only recently. How could I have been so blind?"

"We… well, we've only been lovers for about a year. We both struggled with coming out to each other, so we were just being… cautious. Ro, we never had any doubt that you would be supportive. We just needed time. We didn't hide it from you purposefully."

Romy hugged him. "I'm over the moon, ha ha. Although you have stolen my spare," she grinned at him, and he laughed.

"I'm still not confident Moon wouldn't leave me for you."

"As it should be," Romy made her expression of outrage, and Jae laughed.

"I don't think you'll need a jump-off, Ro, not from the way Milo Keys looks at you. I take it you're together?"

"We are." Romy flushed with pleasure and gave her cousin a shy smile. "He's amazing."

"He seems like a good guy. I like him." Jae's face paled, and immediately Ro was on alert. "Ro, relax. I'm just tired."

"Then, for the love of God, go take a nap." She waved him towards the bed and left him alone.

Moon and Milo were in the kitchen. Moon was making ramen, and Milo was on his laptop. Ro stood at the door and watched them chat, her heart warming to the way they seemed to get on so readily.

Milo looked up and saw her, and she grinned. "Just admiring my harem."

Moon snorted while Milo laughed. He opened his arms, and Romy went into them. "Sorry, Moon buddy, not sharing."

"Fair enough." Moon set three bowls of ramen, stuffed with freshly cut vegetables and succulent chicken in front of them. "Jae asleep?"

Romy nodded. "No problem, I'll just heat his up later."

Romy frowned. "Moon, where's your food?"

Moon pointed at the third bowl. "Right there, doofus." He smiled at Romy, who relaxed a little. "Jae's is still in the pot. Ro, really, stop worrying about me. I'm not anorexic. I know I've lost weight, but that's because... well, I've been exercising more because I've been taking dance classes."

"You have?"

Moon nodded. "I know I should have told everyone, Jae especially, but I wanted to make sure it was the right decision. Ro... I'm changing my major to Dance. In my heart it's what I've always dreamed of doing, but I always thought that... well, I needed some kind of business degree to get on in the world. But I was so bored. I wasn't putting effort into any of my work. My tutor called me and told me that unless I... well. He was kind, and told me if I wasn't invested now, then I never would be and to find something I was passionate about."

Romy got up and went to hug Moon tightly. "Darling, I think it's wonderful."

Milo nodded, smiling at Moon. "Good move, buddy."

They ate their ramen—the kid knew how to make delicious food—and talked more about Moon's decision. "The only thing Jae was disappointed at was that we'd spend less time together in classes. But he is loving the business stuff."

"What a nerd."

Moon grinned. "Right?" He looked at Milo shyly. "I might need advice if I'm going to make it in the arts."

"You got it, Moon. Anytime."

Later, when Moon had joined Jae in their bedroom, Romy and Milo went back to their hotel. There was a peace inside her now, despite everything. Jae would be alright, Moon would be happier, and they would be safer in the apartment.

"I just want to wrap them in cotton wool forever," Romy said to Milo as they undressed, "but I know I can't. What I can do is find out who is targeting me and why."

Milo frowned. "Let the police do their job, Romy."

"Oh, I will, but at the same time, it's my life." She sighed, sitting on the bed in her underwear. "I still can't believe Connor is behind this, but when we get back to Monterey, I'm going to talk to him. Get a read on whether he really is dangerously delusional or just conceited." She smiled at Milo. "Is it okay if I refer to you as my boyfriend?"

"That's what I am, sweetheart."

A warm glow was starting in her chest as he came to her and drew her into his arms. He rested his forehead against hers. "I am yours, Romy Park. My heart is yours." His lips brushed hers, quickly at first, then they crushed hard against her mouth.

Romy sank into the kiss, letting every cell in her body feel the pleasure of it. Her fingers tangled in his hair, and as he picked her up, she wrapped her legs around him. Even through his underwear, she could feel his erect cock nudging against her panties.

"I want you inside me," she whispered to him, seeing fire ignite in his eyes.

What had happened to her? From years of self-imposed celibacy, a few nights with this man had made her feel, finally, like a sensual, almost wanton woman. Milo laid her down on the bed and kissed from her throat down to her belly, before hooking his fingers in the sides of her panties and drawing them down her legs.

Romy squirmed with pleasure as his mouth found her sex, and then she squealed in shock as his teeth nipped at her clit. "Milo!"

She felt, rather than heard, his deep, throaty chuckle, and her head fell back as his tongue lashed around her clit, teasing it until it was swollen and so sensitive that when he nipped it again, an orgasm crashed over her.

He didn't give her time to recover before he was plunging deep inside her, and Romy clung to him as they moved together. She loved how they fit together so perfectly and how he seemed to know what turned her on. Even with his much greater experience, he was never selfish, but Romy wanted him to feel as much pleasure as he was giving her.

As they found their rhythm, she traced the length of his spine with her fingertips, and Milo shivered. "That feels so good."

"Tell me what you like, Milo."

"You."

"Ha ha, funny boy, I mean it." Romy slid her hand down and caressed his sac while his cock slid in and out of her. "Do you like that?"

His soft groan answered her question. She massaged him until he quickened his pace and she lost all control. As she came, she tightened her muscles around him and Milo gasped and came, hard. Both of them were trembling with the force of their climaxes, and Milo chuckled, panting for air.

"It just keeps getting better with you."

He cradled her in his arms, kissing her lips, her eyelids. Romy sighed happily. "Everything is going to be okay from now on, right, baby?"

"You better believe it."

But, of course, they were wrong…

NINETEEN

IT WAS A WEEK later when Romy finally met with Connor. It had been a week of getting the gallery ready for the first show, from finalizing the renovations with Nico to choosing which of Milo's works they wanted to show first.

Milo had blown her mind by telling her he would lend *Antigone* to her for as long as she wanted. Romy had swallowed the lump in her throat.

"You don't know how much that means to me, Milo. Really." She touched the frame of the painting. "It's such a lovely way to honor you and Sarah."

Milo nodded. "For me, it's like… finally saying goodbye to my old life, and saying hello to the new."

Nico, who was still working on the last steps, agreed. "It's incredible."

"You knew Sarah?"

"A little. Her architectural firm used us many times, and she was always a pleasure to work with." He looked at Milo, a sympathetic smile on his face. "Man, I was so upset when she passed. I'm sorry, man."

"Thanks, Nico."

Nico shook his head. "Guess we never know what's going on in someone's head. She always seemed so happy."

Romy felt a little awkward, but Milo just nodded. "I think it's a lesson to all of us. Talk to each other. Pay attention."

"Right on, man."

When Nico had gone, Romy made a face at Milo. "Sorry."

"Don't be. One thing I've always liked about Nico is that he doesn't bullshit. He tells it like it is. And... it hurts less when people don't tiptoe around me. I've accepted it. Sarah killed herself." He drew in a long breath. "Man, I never thought I'd say that out loud."

Romy slid her arms around him. "I want to dedicate this show to Sarah's memory. What do you think about that? Is it inappropriate?"

Milo smiled down at her. "It's an incredible gesture."

"Then it's decided." She kissed him, then sighed, glancing at her watch. "God. I have to go meet with Connor."

"Sure you don't need back-up?"

Romy smiled at him. "Nah, I'm good, it's just Connor. We'll be at the coffeehouse, and believe me, I won't be lingering after what I have to say to him."

Milo rubbed the back of her neck and Romy groaned. "That's good."

"More of that later, I promise. Will you stay over tonight?"

"Of course. At this rate, the person bugging my place will get nothing."

"How inconsiderate of us." Milo grinned and kissed her again. "Perhaps we should stay at your place one night and show 'em how it's done."

"You bet your sweet ass." Romy laughed, then grabbed her bag. "Listen... I'll call you when I'm done with Connor, and we'll go grab some food."

Romy found herself slowing down as she approached the café. She could see Connor waiting at the table in the window, and she felt herself dreading seeing him. *Don't be a coward. Get in there, say what you have to say, and after that, you need never speak to him again.*

She had realized over the last few days that her enmity toward Connor hadn't begun recently—it had begun the day he married Harper. The cruelty of inviting her to the wedding—why had she gone?

She had remembered one moment in particular. As Harper had begun to recite her vows, Connor had shot a look over to his mother. *Victory. Triumph.* Wendy Small had returned the look. Her boy had married money. That was all she cared about.

Romy was scowling at that memory as she went into the coffeehouse and Connor's eyebrows shot up. "Who got your goat, baby?"

Don't call me baby. She smoothed her expression out and nodded at the bar. "I'll just get a drink. Are you good?"

"I'm good."

Romy took her time at the bar, getting herself into the right headspace to deal with her childhood sweetheart. *Ugh.* He was barely that. Her teenage mistake. That was more like it.

Connor stood up as she came back to his table and pulled her chair out for her.

"Thanks," Romy said as she sat down and pulled off her gloves and coat. It was the day before Halloween, and the temperature outside had dropped to just above freezing.

It seemed apt for her mood. Connor smiled at her. "So, how have you been?"

"Fine, except for worrying about Jae. He was stabbed last week."

"I heard. Is he okay?"

Romy's eyes narrowed. "How did you hear?"

"People in this town talk. Is he okay?"

Romy wondered if Connor really cared. "He's fine. Apparently, some asshole stabbed him as a warning to me. I'm next apparently. And this is on top of being attacked in my own home and having the place bugged. All of that was just a warning."

She watched his face carefully. Connor frowned. "Warning? To you? For what?"

"Beats me. Do you have any idea, Connor?" *Enough with this crap. Let's get to business.* "Is it you? Because I have got to be honest here, you're the only person I know that has any motive at all."

Connor rocked back. "What the fuck? Why the hell would I want to hurt you, of all people, Romy? *Jesus.*"

Too late to back out now. "Because I turned you down. Because you thought I would come running back to you and I didn't. Because I'm in love with Milo Keys."

Hell. She hadn't known she was going to say that, and she regretted it the moment it came out of her mouth. Because Milo should have heard it from her lips before anyone else, especially Connor, did. *Too late now.* Connor's expression froze.

"Well. Congratulations. I take it he feels the same way?"

Romy said nothing for a moment, then: "Was it you, Connor? Did you stab my Jae? Are you so mad you want to kill me?"

"Fuck, no." He spat out the words, and for a second, Romy wondered if he would storm out. "How can you…" His voice broke, and he looked away from her. He took a few deep breaths. Romy saw other café patrons watching them curiously, but she didn't care. All she could see in her mind was Jae lying in that hospital bed. Moon with his arm slashed open.

Sarah Keys with a knife in her gut.

Romy blinked. What the hell was that? Where did that come from? She felt sick. Connor was staring at her, all pretense dropped now.

"How could you even begin to think I could hurt you, Romy? Haven't I made myself clear? All I want is... Jesus, to be your friend, at the very least. If there's really no chance of anything romantic—I'm not a monster." To Romy's shock, there were tears in his eyes. Connor breathed deeply, taking a few moments to gather himself before speaking again, his voice lowered. "I know what you must think of me. I dumped you for Harper, for her money. I'm an arrogant man, a greedy man. I know all of this. But I would never, ever hurt you, Romy." He sighed. "I'm not a violent man."

God damn it, he'd almost convinced her until that last line. "Funny, that's not what I heard."

Connor's head snapped up. "Did Harper say something?"

"Not Harper. People in this town talk." She shot his line back to him, and he sat back in his chair. There was active dislike on his face now.

"Well, well, well, aren't we the little detective?"

"I have no time for men who beat their wives, Connor. I have no time for assholes who think women somehow owe them something, or 'belong' to them. Yes, we once dated for about five minutes back in the day and, god help me, I thought I loved you. I didn't even know you, Connor. And you certainly didn't know me."

Connor snorted. "You keep telling yourself that, Romy. I expect you told yourself the accident wasn't your fault, too."

Romy rocked back. "What?"

"Come on, the whole town knows. You were driving the day of the accident. Your father, mother, your aunt... the people in the other cars."

136

"What the hell are you talking about? I wasn't driving!"

Connor smirked. "Hurts, doesn't it? Being accused of hurting people you love."

God, this asshole... "The difference is, Connor, that *I've* actually never hurt anyone."

Before she could react, Connor's hand shot forward and grabbed her wrist, his fingers biting into the underside of her arm. He pulled her close. "Listen to me, you jumped up little bitch, and listen good. I didn't stab your little cousin. I wouldn't touch that little fa—"

Romy tugged her hand free, and before she could stop herself, she slapped Connor hard across the face. "Don't you ever, ever call anyone that, least of all Jae. He's worth a billion of you, you slimeball."

Connor lunged across the table at her, but before he could grab her, someone hooked his arms under Connor's shoulders and hauled him back.

Jim Halsey. The detective investigating Jae's stabbing. He nodded at her, unsmiling. Connor struggled against his grip.

"That's about enough of this. Miss. Park, I suggest you leave now. I'll deal with Mr. Small."

Romy was trembling badly, but relieved. She grabbed her bag and darted for the door. She shot a look at Connor as she left. His eyes fixed on hers, filled with a murderous rage.

Romy looked away and made her escape. Tears blurred her vision, and her breath came in short, sharp gasps. What the hell had she done? Had she made things a million times worse?

She stepped into the street, jumping back as a car tooted its horn furiously at her. The bumper caught her calf, and Romy gasped at the quick pain. She sucked in some air as she stepped back onto the sidewalk.

Take a minute. Calm down. Breathe.

Dark spots bounded at the edge of her vision—*aww, hell...* she wasn't about to pass out, was she?

She felt hands on her shoulders then and started. "Romy, are you okay?"

Nico. She turned, opened her mouth to reassure him she was fine, but then no words would come out. The black spots in her eyes grew larger until she couldn't see, and she passed out.

TWENTY

ROMY OPENED HER EYES and stared up at the ceiling. White, plastic ceiling tiles. The smell of antiseptic and sickness filled her nostrils. She tried to sit up.

"Hey, hey, hey... easy now." Milo was there, and she stared at him.

"What happened?"

"You fainted in the street, sweetheart. Luckily, Nico was there."

Romy struggled into a seated position. She was in a medical cubicle, the curtains drawn around her. "I don't know why I fainted. I was just..." She sighed, shaking her head. "I was upset. The meeting with Connor did not go well. And I stupidly almost got myself mown down."

She became aware her calf was aching and pulled up her pant leg. "Ugh." There was a massive bruise forming, blood vessels burst under the skin, forming a maroon and purple mark.

"Maybe the docs ought to check that out." Milo frowned, touching the bruise lightly. His cool fingers felt good against her skin.

"I'm sure it's just a bruise."

But Milo insisted, and while she was being examined, he stepped out of the room. Romy watched the doctor's face while she examined her. "Doc? There's no chance I'm pregnant, is there?"

"Are you having sex regularly?"

"Yes."

"Then there's always a chance. Want me to run a test?"

"Would you? And keep it between you and me for now."

The doctor smiled. "Of course. Do you want to stick around here for the result or shall I call you?"

"I can go?"

"You can. Just take it easy for the rest of the day. We can't find any reason for your fainting except that maybe you just forgot to breathe. Try to remember to do that."

Romy grinned at the doctor, appreciating her dry humor. "I promise."

The doctor took her cell phone number. "I'll text yay or nay on your test result, okay?"

"Perfect, thank you."

She didn't want to stay in Monterey any longer that day so they went to the gallery, closed it up, and then Milo drove her back to his place in Big Sur.

He drew her a bath, and Romy soaked in it gratefully while Milo was in the kitchen, feeding a slavering Sailor and cooking a big pot of mac-and-cheese for them. Romy felt better as she dried herself, rubbing some arnica on the bruise and dressing in comfortable sweats. As she was drying her hair, her cell phone bleeped. A message from the doctor.

Nay. Hope that was the news you wanted.

Romy sighed in relief. As much as she would one day like to have kids with Milo—and, jeez, she was really thinking that far ahead?—now was definitely not the time. It was too soon in their fledgling relationship, and her life was in turmoil.

Plus, she kept thinking back to the look in Connor's eyes. He had professed his love, but there was nothing but hate in his eyes. Yes, she had humiliated him, in public nonetheless, but it had been nothing he hadn't deserved.

She felt a wash of anger again at his jibe at Jae. She picked up her phone again to text her cousin.

Hey you, are you okay? Love you and Moon so much xx

A few seconds later the reply came back.

Mushy, mushy. We're good, don't worry about us. We love you, too xx

Romy smiled to herself. If the people she loved were safe, then she could cope with anything else. She looked up as Milo appeared at the bedroom door. "Hey, beautiful."

"Hey, yourself." Romy got up and went to him. "Thank you for taking care of me." She slid her arms around his waist, and Milo bent his head to kiss her.

"Of course. I'll always take care of you as long as you want me to."

Romy smiled at him, then sniffed the air. "Food?"

Milo laughed. "It's almost ready. Come downstairs, and I'll feed you, woman."

Milo grinned as both Romy and Sailor salivated while he served up the creamy, extra-cheesy mac-and-cheese. Romy swept a forkful into her mouth, then waved her hand in front of it.

"Yeah, it's hot, doofus."

She took a swig of her water and grinned at him. "Burned my tongue, but totally worth it. This is delicious."

They ate their meal, holding hands across the table, but not talking. It seemed an evening for just being together and after supper, they vegged out on the couch and watched some dumb television shows.

Romy curled herself into Milo's body, and he buried his face in her hair. She smelled of fresh air and soap. A few moments later, he realized she had fallen asleep on him.

Milo smiled. He never thought he would have this again. This closeness. And what was even better was that he knew Sarah would be cheering him and Romy on. He didn't ever want to compare them, but there was something about Romy that reminded him of his late wife.

Soft. Sensitive. And a heart so big it could envelop the world. He pressed his lips against her forehead, and Romy opened her eyes. Her smile made his blood quicken. Her warm brown eyes gazed into his. "Milo..."

"I love you, Romy Park," he interrupted her, unable to keep the words in. "I know it's crazy fast, but I want you to know that. I'm in love with you."

"I feel the same way." She chuckled softly. "You beat me to it, but I was going to tell you this evening. I love you, too, Milo."

His lips covered her, and they kissed, a soft, caressing embrace. Milo drew away and smiled at her. "If we keep doing that, then things will happen, and I think maybe you should rest tonight."

Romy stuck out her bottom lip but then nodded, "You might be right. I do feel kind of washed out tonight. Lord knows why..."

She trailed off, and Milo frowned. "What is it?"

"Well, nothing really. Except I have noticed since we got back to Monterey, I've felt a little out of it. Nothing major, just lightheaded."

Milo nodded. "Maybe you should get checked out again. Romy..." He paused, not wanting to ask the obvious question, not wanting the answer, either way.

Romy looked up at him with wide eyes. "I'm not pregnant. The doctor did a test for me, and I wasn't going to say anything, but yes. The thought had occurred to me, too."

"But... you're not?"

"No."

"Right."

They sat in silence for a few moments, lost in their own thoughts before Romy gave a soft laugh. "That got heavy, quick."

Milo chuckled, kissing her temple. "Didn't it? Maybe we should have that conversation."

They gazed at each other and then busted up. "Nah, it's way too soon for that."

"Agreed." He smoothed her hair back from her face. "We need to enjoy this part more, without all the stress. I want to romance you."

"Fancy."

He grinned. "Woo you."

"Silver-tongued devil."

He tickled her, and she screeched with laughter, all the stress of the day melting away. He wrestled with her playfully until they were both breathless from laughing and Sailor was barking at them both.

Milo tapped the end of her nose with his finger. "You bring out my silly side, Miss Park."

"Good. I'm glad." She grinned at him, then groaned as his intercom buzzed. "No, no interruptions."

Milo got up, grinning. "Maybe it's a mystery pizza delivery." He laughed as her eyes lit up. "You can't possibly be hungry again."

"Want to bet?"

He chuckled, but his smile faded when he saw who was at the front gate. "It's Detective Halsey."

Romy sighed. "I was expecting him to call. Connor may press charges for me slapping him."

Milo buzzed the detective in and checked his watch. "It's already after eleven p.m. He could have come sooner."

His irritation only increased when he saw the look on Det. Halsey's face. His heart began to thump against his ribs unpleasantly. "Det. Halsey, if you're here to arrest Romy for slapping Connor Small—"

"I'm not. But I do need to speak with her."

"It's okay, Milo," Romy said from behind him. "Hi, Detective. I'm happy to give you a statement or whatever."

Milo stepped aside for the other man to enter. "Let's go in the kitchen."

He offered the detective a coffee, but Halsey shook his head. "No, I'm afraid I'm here with bad news."

He looked at Romy, who blanched. "Not Jae? Not Moon?"

"No, they're both fine, Romy. I'm sorry to tell you that earlier this evening, we pulled a body out of Monterey Bay."

"Oh god…"

Halsey nodded. "We just confirmed the identity. It's Connor Small, Romy. Connor Small is dead."

TWENTY-ONE

HARPER LOOKED HOLLOW-EYED AND exhausted as Romy rushed towards her. Once they had known Harper had identified the body and was at the precinct answering questions about her ex-husband, Romy had insisted on going to her friend's aid.

Halsey had agreed, and Milo had driven them into Monterey. On the journey over, Romy stared out at the dark night, trying to process what Halsey had told them.

Connor was dead. They hadn't been able to identify him immediately because he had been beaten to a pulp before being dumped in the water.

"Initial thinking is that he was unconscious when he went into the water and drowned. As far as suspects are concerned, we just don't know."

"We were here all night," Romy said, and Milo nodded.

"There's security camera footage to prove it."

Halsey had given them a slight smile. "That's useful, but we would like statements."

"Of course."

When Romy saw the desolation in Harper's expression, she went to her and wrapped her arms around her. "I'm so sorry, Harper."

Harper's body felt stiff at first, but then she leaned into the embrace. "I just don't believe it, Ro. How can he be gone?"

There were tears dropping down her face. "I know he was an asshole, I know that. But I just can't believe he's dead."

Romy didn't know what to say. Connor had been a waste of good oxygen, but she couldn't help but feel sad, too. There was no chance for his redemption now—maybe he'd finally gone too far with someone.

Milo hugged Harper, too, as Halsey came to find Romy. "Do you mind making a statement first?"

"Not at all." Romy squeezed Harper's hand and gave Milo a reassuring smile. "I'll be right back."

In the interview room, Halsey offered Romy a coffee.

"I'm all coffee-ed out today," she said with a sad smile.

Halsey nodded. "Obviously, with what happened earlier today, I wanted to talk to you. We all witnessed the argument. Could you tell me what it was about?"

Romy sighed. "I've been having some issues lately. Well, that's an understatement. You know that my cousin was stabbed, and I was attacked in my apartment. There is… *was*… only one person in Monterey with any kind of motive. So, I met with Connor and asked him directly if he was behind it. He got angry, which I expected, and then he got abusive. He accused me of being behind the wheel of the car when my family was killed ten years ago."

"Were you?"

Romy drew in a shaky breath. "I was *not*. I hadn't yet gotten my license at that time, which I'm sure you can check on." She drew in a deep breath. "My aunt was driving. She wasn't at fault either—a drunk driver crossed the median and ploughed into us. We, in turn, careened into another four cars. There were many fatalities." Her voice broke at the end of her sentence. "It was a damn drunk driver, and he died, too, and never faced the consequences of what he had done."

"It's okay, Romy. I'm sorry I had to ask."

She nodded, not trusting herself to go on. Halsey's expression was kinder than she'd ever seen it. "I know this is distressing, but I do need to know. What was your relationship with Connor back then?"

Romy sighed. "You have to remember, we were kids. He was charming back then. When Connor Small smiled at you, it was like a spotlight was on you. I was always very shy, very reserved, so when the most popular boy in town paid attention to you, it was a huge thing."

She rubbed her temple, aware there was a headache starting. "I spent a summer thinking we were forever. I lost my virginity to him on my eighteenth birthday. Three days later, he told me he was going to marry Harper, that he was sorry, but his father was making him do it."

She laughed without humor. "Of course, that was a lie, too. It was Connor and his mother who had arranged the whole thing. He had been dating Harper for months."

"Romy, I'm going to ask you a distressing question now, and I want you to know, it goes no further than these walls unless it significantly impacts our investigation. Do you think Harper Van Warren could have paid someone to do this?"

Romy fixed him with a steady gaze. "No. On my life, *no*, Harper would not have done this. Despite the divorce, she still loved him. I think she hoped that one day he would grow up and be the man he fooled her into thinking he was." She shook her head. "Believe me when I say there is no way Harper had anything to do with this. You saw her... she's destroyed."

"I did." Halsey sighed. "I know Connor slept around, but we're having trouble nailing down where he was after I left him at the coffeehouse this afternoon."

"He was angry."

"He was. I calmed him down, told him I saw him grab your arm, that you slapped him in self-defense, and that if he didn't calm down, he'd be spending the night in jail." He shook his head. "Maybe I should have thrown his ass in jail. He'd be alive now."

Romy felt cold to her core. "Det. Halsey… do you think he was behind what happened to Jae? To me?"

"I can't say for sure, Romy. We'll have to see. There'll be an investigation, obviously, because we need to find a solid motive for his murder."

Romy chewed her lip. "What if he just got into a fist fight, then fell into the water on his own?"

"That'll be investigated, too." Halsey stood and offered Romy his hand. She stood and shook it. "I'm sorry about all of this, Romy. In a way, I hope it was Connor who was guilty." He smiled at her. "I hate to think of anyone hurting you."

Milo was sitting by himself when Romy returned to the hallway. He got up when he saw her and hugged her tightly. "You okay?"

She nodded, relaxing against his big, warm body. "Where's Harper?"

"She didn't want to stay any longer. I asked her if she wanted us to go be with her tonight, but she said no."

Romy looked up at him. "You don't think she'll do anything silly, do you?"

Milo shook her head and kissed her softly. "No, sweetheart. Harper's strong, she just needs to grieve. I kept telling her, the man she married never existed, not really. Connor had already gone."

"I guess." She rubbed her face, feeling exhausted. "Let's go home, baby."

Milo stroked her cheek with the back of his fingers. "Good plan."

In the car on the way back to Big Sur, Milo reached over and took her hand. Romy, who had been staring unseeingly out of the window, turned and smiled at him.

"I love you."

"I love you, too. Romy, I've been thinking about what you said at the police station."

Romy frowned. "About Harper?"

"No." He squeezed her hand. "About going 'home.' Because, if you want it to be, it can be your home, too. Nothing would make me happier."

Romy was silent for a few moments, and Milo felt uneasy. "No?"

"I want to live with you, Milo. Nothing would make me happier."

His tension released, and he laughed. "God, you had me going then, Ro. I'm so glad, so happy."

She chuckled, but her eyes were serious. "It's just… in that house?"

"You don't like it?"

"I love it. It's stunning, and the views are out of this world. It's very you. But… in your mind, will it always be Sarah's home?"

Milo finally got why she was so worried. "Romy, Sarah never lived in that house. Yes, it was her dream house, but I bought it after she died."

"Oh."

"Yep. And, honestly, since we've been together, I've felt more at home there. But, just say the word and we'll find someplace new, someplace that we chose together. I'm sure Nan Sommers will be delighted she won't lose the commission."

Romy laughed then, her expression relaxing. "I expect she would." She leaned over and kissed him. "I love your house. It's so you, and Sailor loves it, too. I'd be honored to move in with you. But... I pay my way, Milo Keys. You've given me so much already."

"Not as much as you've given me, Romy. You gave me back the ability to love."

To his shock, Romy burst into tears, but she was smiling. He chuckled, reaching over to wipe her tears with his thumb. "Silly girl. Don't cry. I promise, from now on, only happy times."

TWENTY-TWO

OCTOBER SEGUED INTO NOVEMBER and then December, and by the week before Christmas, the gallery was ready to open. Romy, Milo, and Harper had decided on the eighteenth of December for the grand opening, and the few weeks after that terrible night in October had flown by.

Romy didn't go to Connor's funeral. She talked it out with Harper, who understood her reticence to attend. "I don't blame you, Ro," Harper had said. "He never gave you anything but sorrow, even if he had nothing to do with what happened to you and Jae. Let me bury him, and that's the end of it."

Romy had to admire Harper's strength, and she decided she would be more like her friend. Nothing more had happened since Connor's death; Jae recovered well, and he and Moon were coming down to stay with her and Milo for Christmas.

Romy smiled to herself. Her two 'brothers' had really bonded with her lover, and half the time they called, they called to speak to Milo. Romy loved the fact their little family was growing.

She had officially moved into the house in Big Sur in the middle of November. As she stood in her empty condo, she looked around. She had enjoyed living here, she realized now, but it had never been a home. The house in Big Sur—she and Milo referred to it as the Drac Castle—was home to her now, and she adored it. Sailor was also over the moon about the new living arrangements, and Milo complained, with a grin, that Sailor was always hogging 'Romy time' when they were just hanging out.

Now, as she checked her lists of things to do for the opening, Romy was excited. This was no time for nerves, this was it. She had done everything she could, the press releases were out, the invitations sent, Harper was ready to go with the food for the opening.

Milo was out of town for the day. He had decided to go visit Sarah's parents in person and tell them about his new relationship. "I'd rather they heard it from me than the papers when the exhibit opens."

Romy had hugged him. "They are welcome to come, please tell them that. This is for Sarah, too."

He had kissed her with feeling then. "You are a remarkable woman, Romy Park."

The day was cold but not overly so for December. Still, Romy shivered when the door of the gallery opened behind her and brought in a flurry of leaves and cool air. She turned—and stopped. A middle-aged man stood behind her, his tweed jacket shoved over an artist's smock, his watery blue eyes hidden behind thick spectacles. He shifted uncomfortably from foot to foot and seemed to be having a hard time meeting Romy's eyes.

Farron Lee.

"Hello." Romy kept her tone even. Milo had told her that Farron was the one writing bitchy articles about her and the gallery on social media, but Romy couldn't find it in her to be mad right now. Farron Lee had a bottomless sadness about him. "Mr. Lee?"

He nodded and cleared his throat. "I wanted... I wanted to come and apologize for my behavior."

Romy nodded, and when he didn't say anything else, she half-smiled. "Farron, would you like to have some coffee with me? I was just about to take a break."

She watched his eyes open with surprise, and a ghost of a smile flickered across his face. "That's very kind."

"Come back to the staffroom." She locked the gallery door and beckoned Farron with her.

While she made the coffee, she could feel him watching her. After she handed him the steaming mug, and he thanked her, she sat down opposite him. "You knew my mother and father."

"I did. They were wonderful people." He studied her face. "You look just like them... like her. Are you fiery, like your mother was?"

"I can be, but, no, I'm more like my father. Mama was a force of nature."

"You remember her well?"

Romy nodded. "Of course. I was eighteen when they died. They'd started to treat me not as a child but as a young woman. We were becoming... friends."

Her voice wavered as she recalled her parents laughing together in their bookstore—this very building. She could see them now, stacking books, her father teasing her mother by switching the titles around, categorizing them by color rather than alphabetically just to drive her crazy.

Romy remembered the little book nooks her father had made for her at home out of boxes and blankets. Yes, other people might call them forts, but in her family, they were places to go hide and bury yourself in a book.

"I remember everything about them. They're always with

me... I didn't get to say goodbye because of the coma I was in, but in a way, I'm glad. They're still here with me."

She looked at Farron who smiled at her. "You're a very sweet young woman. You remind me of her."

Romy just nodded. Farron sighed. "I suspect Milo told you why I was such an idiot with the article?"

"You didn't want to be reminded of my mother. And I look like her."

"It was selfish, and I'm sorry. She knew I was in love with her, but she neither encouraged it, nor did she shut me out. Giovanna knew how to make everyone feel wanted, without ever once giving you the impression she would cheat on Jin. I appreciate that, heck, I appreciated just being her friend. And your father... what a wonderful man."

Romy felt tears prick her eye then. "Thank you. Thank you for saying that."

"It wasn't your fault, you know? I sense you feel some survivor's guilt, but please. Don't. I know Jin and Giovanna would give their lives again and again so you could live, Romy. And they would be proud. So, so very proud."

Romy couldn't help the tears falling then, and she dropped her head into her hands and sobbed. She felt Farron's arm go tentatively around her shoulder. "It's alright, dear."

A decade's worth of grief seemed to fall out of her then. After a while, she became aware there was another voice there, and she looked up and wiped her eyes. Milo was talking quietly with Farron, who smiled back at Romy.

"I better go. Thank you for the coffee, dear."

He turned to go, but Romy stood up. "Farron, wait." She went to him and took his hands. "Thank you. Thank you for coming here today. Would you like to come to the opening?"

"Well..."

"Please. I would be honored if you did."

Farron patted her arm, still a little awkwardly, but smiled. "Then, of course I'll come."

"I'm sorry for crying all over you."

Farron's eyes softened. "Don't be. I think you needed that."

"I did."

Romy let Farron out of the gallery's back door, then returned to Milo.

"How were Sarah's parents?"

"They were good. They were happy for me. They sent their regards, but I think it's still too raw for them. They were touched that you were dedicating the opening to Sarah, but they also sent their apologies. They wouldn't come."

Romy nodded. "Well, that's their prerogative. I'm glad they didn't react badly to us."

Milo cupped her cheek in his hand. "They said it was wonderful, that Sarah would approve. I agree." He bent his head to kiss her. "What say we go grab a slice of pizza?"

Just at that moment, Romy's stomach gave an ominous groan, and she laughed. "Good idea."

Monterey was busy. It was a Friday night, and the bars and restaurants were full. Romy and Milo walked down to Cannery Row and managed to find a table in one of the eateries there.

As they waited for their food, Milo took her hands in his. "You look tired, my love."

"Probably from the crying."

Milo shook his head. "No, don't hide it. I know you've been out of sorts for the past few weeks."

Romy gave him a rueful smile. "Honestly, I can't get anything past you, can I? I don't know what it is. I've just been exhausted.

Even taking into consideration everything that's happened, I've felt just... drained. When they told me I wasn't pregnant, I wondered what the hell it was."

"Depression?"

Romy shrugged. "No, I don't think so. This feels more physical, like someone switched me off. Does that make sense?"

Milo frowned, but he nodded. "Sweetheart, maybe you should see a doctor."

"I think you're right." She smiled at him then. "Although you are the best medicine a girl could get, Milo Keys."

"Wow."

Romy giggled at his appalled expression. "Am I coming up on 'too cheesy?'"

"Nope. Look behind you." Milo grinned widely then, making her bust out laughing. He leaned over the table and kissed her, not caring who was watching.

TWENTY-THREE

AFTER THEIR MEAL, THEY walked along Fisherman's Wharf. It was distinctly less crowded down here on a cold December night, and Romy hugged her coat around her. Milo looked at her apologetically.

"Be right back," he said, nodding at the public restroom, and Romy nodded back.

"I'll be right here."

She walked to the edge of the boardwalk and looked out over the darkened ocean. Her face burned with the freezing air, but it made her skin tingle in a way she found pleasant.

It took a moment before a sense of being watched swept over her. Romy scanned her eyes over the now empty boardwalk, both ways, then turned to face the town. Her eyes raked the darkness, and she could see no movement, but there it was—the feeling someone was lurking in the shadows.

What a damn drama queen you are, Park. Even when there's nothing to worry about. She sighed and rubbed her face. Milo appeared then, and she didn't want to say anything to him, but she was glad when they turned back towards town and the bright lights.

It wasn't until they were almost back at the gallery and their respective cars that she felt nervous again. *Get in your car and drive home. That's all that's happening.* Romy kissed Milo, and they both got into their cars. "See you at home, sweetheart."

She nodded, smiling, but the expression faded when she got into her car. Milo's car pulled away, and she started her own car.

As soon as she pulled out into traffic, she saw it. A darkly-colored sedan was following her. Romy drew in a long breath. *Just drive. Don't get distracted.*

It could be a mere coincidence, but as she drove out on the coastal road down to Big Sur, the sedan was still there. He or she didn't attempt to harass Romy's vehicle, but still, the sedan just sat there behind her. Romy's hands flexed on the steering wheel anxiously. She drove steadily, within the speed limit, and focused on just getting to the house.

Still, her body was tensed the entire time, and when they got out onto the coastal road, she paid extra attention, not wanting to be run off here and tumble down the cliffs or into one of the huge boulders at the side of the road.

As she neared home, she flicked the button on the control pad Milo had given her to open the gates of the mansion. The house came into view, and she saw the gates slide open. Then she heard the sedan revving hard and driving up close behind her. The lights were blinding in the rearview.

Her heart began to beat furiously. "Fuck, fuck, fuck..."

Only a few feet to go. She flicked on the car's indicator—and the sedan moved into the other lane and roared past her, disappearing into the night. Romy turned her own car into the driveway, then mashed the button to close the gate behind her.

She let out a huge breath. *What the fuck is wrong with me?* She felt stretched, brittle. *It's just the culmination of everything that's happened plus the gallery opening. It's okay to feel like this.*

Milo was standing at the open door as she got out of the car, and Sailor squeezed past his legs to run out and greet Romy. She fussed the dog's silky hair and kissed his furry head.

"Hello, baby."

Milo grinned at her. "We were waiting for you."

"I know, I'm sorry, I was dawdling." Romy decided not to tell Milo about her fraught journey—it had come to nothing, after all.

Romy lay on her stomach as Milo kissed the entire length of her spine.

"Mmm. That feels so good."

"You taste so good."

Milo took her buttocks in his hands and kneaded them. "Cute butt."

Romy giggled, then yelped as Milo bit down on the soft flesh. "Milo Keys, you are a kinky son of a...oh!"

Milo chuckled as he thrust into her from behind, and Romy felt her sex flood with warmth as he moved inside her. Really, there was nothing like Milo making love to her to relax her body. He made her come once, then she turned onto her back and they made love again, their eyes locked, being completely in the moment.

She fell asleep in his arms, relaxed and chilled out. Outside, there was a rainstorm which had blown in over the ocean, and the rhythmic spatter of water against glass soothed her into sleep.

The dream began so pleasantly. She was walking along the shoreline, the ocean water lapping at her bare feet. She was naked under a loose white dress, her hair streaming down her back. She was holding hands with Milo, who smiled down at her.

"I love you so much. We will always be together."

She smiled at him as he stopped and kissed her. "Sarah—"

Romy frowned. Was that her name in the dream? It didn't seem right somehow. But as long as Milo kept kissing her, what did it matter what he called her? The ocean breeze picked up and swirled around her.

She heard voices. Jae. Moon. They were running towards her, their beautiful faces contorted with fear. She could hear them calling but couldn't make out the words. From other directions... Nico. Harper. Nan. Farron. Even Detective Halsey. All of them, panicked and desperate to get to her, but none of them could reach her.

She frowned and looked up at Milo, who was still smiling at her, but now his bright green eyes were solid black, and in them, she saw bottomless rage. "I'm sorry, Sarah... I have to do it... I have to make sure you will never leave me..."

He had a knife in his hand.

Romy backed away, shaking her head. "No... No... this isn't right... you would never hurt me... I'm not Sarah... I'm not Sarah..."

But as much as she tried to get away from him, he advanced on her. One hand came up to cup the back of her neck, and Romy tried to scream, but no sound would come out as Milo plunged the knife into her stomach over and over...

Romy woke up shivering, her belly cramping with the imagined pain. Milo was asleep beside her, laying on his stomach, one arm thrown across her. She was sweating. She slid out from under his arm and went to the bathroom to splash cold water on her face. Jesus, what a dream to have.

Still, it had unsettled her more than she would have expected, and she found she didn't want to go back to bed until she had talked herself down.

Sailor followed her downstairs, and they sat together on the couch. She ruffled his shaggy head and hugged him to her. "What the hell is wrong with me, Sailor boy? I have nothing to be stressed out about."

Sailor whimpered a little, then licked her hand. Romy shook her head. It was just a nightmare.

So why did she feel so on edge?

Get the opening over and done with, then it's Christmas. Jae and Moon were coming to Monterey for the holidays, Milo having invited them to stay with them for as long as they wanted. Harper would be with her family, but she was joining them for New Year's.

Romy tried to distract herself from her nightmare. She wanted to try and fix Nico and Nan up on a date—Nan had expressed an interest in Romy's friend and contractor, hadn't she? They were both coming to the opening…

"Hey."

She turned to see Milo, just in his boxers, his hair sticking up, standing in the doorway. Usually, she would have smiled, but the memory of the nightmare flooded back.

Milo, all love stripped from him, stabbing her…

She swallowed hard and forced a smile on her face as he came to sit next to her. "Hey."

"Couldn't sleep?"

She shook her head and kissed him back when he pressed his lips to hers. "No. Don't know why."

There was no way she was going to tell him about the nightmare. She could only imagine he would be terribly hurt and, after all, it was ridiculous. Milo would never hurt her; he had nothing to do with Sarah's death.

Milo scratched Sailor's ears. "Worried about the opening?" His tone was light, but Romy could tell he knew something was up.

Forgive me, my love, for lying just this one time. "I'm just stressed out. The whole schmoozing thing always gets to me, even though I've been doing it for years in Seb's gallery. But the stakes seem so high this time." She half-smiled. "I know it's ridiculous because people are dying to see your work again, and I couldn't have wished for a better show." She rubbed her face. "Ugh, ignore me. I'm being a drama queen."

"It's a big moment, Ro. The culmination of all your hard work."

She nodded. Milo stroked his hand through her hair, and despite herself, she relaxed into his touch. Milo leaned over and buried his face in her neck, kissing her throat. "Come back to bed, baby. I'll get you all sleepy and relaxed."

Romy gave him a genuine smile then and let him lead her upstairs to bed. They made love again, and as she held him, Romy stroked his face, gazing into his eyes. Milo Keys was incapable of hurting anyone, especially those he loved. It had been an anxiety dream, that was all.

Connor was dead, and she was just being paranoid. The opening was in two days, and after that, she could relax and enjoy the fact that this wonderful man loved her.

That she had finally found her person.

TWENTY-FOUR

MILO WATCHED ROMY AS she moved around the gallery, doing last minute checks on everything. Harper and Nan were in the staffroom, making sure all the canapes were ready and that the champagne was chilled. Romy had made him put on a suit, and he watched her now, clad in a dark burgundy dress which clung to her curves. Her dark hair was softly waved and pulled over one shoulder.

He caught her hand as she passed by him and drew her to him. "Have I told you how staggering beautiful you are?"

Romy grinned, a faint blush on her cheeks. "As long as you think so, that's all I care about. You look so handsome in your suit." She stood on her tiptoes to kiss him. "It's your night, Milo."

"Your night."

She rolled her eyes, smiling. "*Our* night, then. Compromise?"

"I can live with that. Listen, give me something to do, I'm going crazy."

"Milo Keys, are you nervous?"

He grinned wryly. "A little, I have to be honest." His smile faded. "To be honest, I'm scared that all the questions will be about—"

"—Sarah. I know." Romy's eyes were serious. "I think it's inevitable, so be prepared. If it gets to be too much, signal me. I'll run interference."

Milo bent his head and kissed her. "I love you, Romy Park."

"Right back at you, big guy."

Milo grinned—Romy was distracted enough by her own nerves.

"Eww, do you have to do that in front of us?"

They both turned to see Jae and Moon grinning at them. Romy gave a cry of joy and threw her arms around them both. Milo was glad to see them both looking healthy. Jae was almost completely recovered, and Moon looked like he had gained a little weight. He greeted them with a smile. "Thanks for coming, guys. I know we both appreciate the support."

"I came for the food," Moon grinned, and Romy laughed, high-fiving him.

"That's my Moonbeam."

"Ugh, you really dragging that nickname out of the past?"

She kissed his smooth cheek. "Live with it, Moonbeam."

Milo watched the younger three people teasing each other. This was his family now, and he loved them with his whole heart.

His eyes slid to the star of his show tonight. Romy had given *Antigone* pride of place, had lit the portrait beautifully and so well it almost seemed as if Sarah had come to life. Milo half expected her to turn in the frame and smile at him, enjoying his new family, approving of them.

He wished her family had been so accepting. It was his biggest regret, that he had lied to Romy over the rection he had gotten from Sarah's parents.

"She's hardly been dead three years, and you're moving on?" Her mother had sounded so harsh as her father had shaken his head.

"And you promised us you would never, ever show *Antigone* again. And now you're loaning her—giving my daughter—to your new girlfriend?"

Milo had tried to reason with them, tell them that both he and Romy respected Sarah's memory, but that he couldn't live his life like a monk. "Sarah wouldn't have wanted it."

"And she wouldn't want to be cast aside..."

Milo had lost it. "She will never be cast aside. *I* was cast aside. She left me behind. She took her own life and didn't care how..."

Too far. Sarah's parents had looked shell-shocked, and Milo had gotten up and left. On the car ride back to Monterey, he had to talk himself down. How had he lost control like that? All his resentment, his hurt, his bitterness had come flooding out of him. All of his anger at Sarah for leaving him.

He knew he was in love with Romy, but seemingly, he still wasn't over Sarah's death. It had been so out of the blue, so shocking, that he'd immediately suspected she had been murdered. But the police had come up with nothing. He was told in no uncertain terms that, although they were sympathetic to his loss, he needed to drop it before he was arrested for harassing the local police department.

"I'm sorry, Mr. Keys, I know it's hard, but your wife really did take her own life."

It was only when he met Romy that Milo had started to come alive again, and now that they were in a serious relationship, maybe it was time to put all his ghosts to rest. Which was why he'd hired a private detective to look into Sarah's life, both at work and before they had met. So far, the detective had come up with nothing. Milo asked him to investigate any interaction Sarah might have had with Connor Small—he knew she had loathed the man, but still, he could have had reason to hurt her if she'd rejected him, like Romy had.

He'd kept this from Romy, too. She didn't need to know. Whatever the detective found out, he would accept, and that would be that. The end.

He just hoped his sanity would hold up for the answers to his many, many questions.

Romy was busy, but she could still see the tension on Milo's face. She wanted to hug him and take away all that stress, but she knew she couldn't. Tonight was a big deal for him, for her, for them. Just a few hours, and it'd all be over.

She squeezed Milo's hand as she passed him, and he smiled at her. "Almost time, baby."

Jae appeared. "Hey, Ro, there's been a delivery. Several cases of what looks like really good champagne."

He handed her a note, and she read it aloud. *"For your first night, sweet Romy. Your mother and father would have been so proud. I will see you later. All my best, Farron Lee.* Oh, how wonderful."

Her throat got thick, and she took a deep breath, not wanting to cry and ruin her makeup. "Oh, no mushy stuff until later, kids, okay?"

The others laughed, and Romy grinned. She glanced at her watch. "Okay, peeps. Ten minutes."

"There are people outside already."

"Should we let them in?"

"Hell, no."

Romy snorted with laughter as Jae looked outraged, but Romy shook her head at him. "Let them in, Jae. It's December."

Moon rolled his eyes. "He'd let them freeze until it's exactly eight p.m., you know."

"Let them in, Jae."

Milo, Moon, and Harper were grinning as Jae huffed and went to open the door. A waft of cold air followed the first guests. Harper, Nan, Moon, and Jae handed out drinks, food, and goody bags to the first guests. Romy and Milo circulated, talking to every guest and introducing the gallery to them. There were plenty of journalists among them, too, and Romy found herself shielding Milo from the worst questions about Sarah.

After an hour, Romy made her welcoming speech, her voice shaking a little as she addressed the room.

"Well… hey, hello everyone. Thank you so much for coming tonight, the fact you've taken time out of your schedule to support the show and the gallery is incredibly touching, and I really appreciate it. Tonight, I am honored to present the work of someone you all know and who was the reason I went into the art world to begin with."

She looked over at Milo, and suddenly the rest of the world melted away. *God, I love you.* She smiled at him. "I never dreamed that my fantasy of showing Milo Keys would come true. But because of the generosity and the bravery of this man, here we are. Milo, would you like to come up and say a few words?"

Milo made his way to her side and kissed her cheek. "I love you," he whispered in her ear, sending shivers of pleasure through her. She handed him the mic and stepped back, but not before squeezing his hand. She watched as Milo, her big man, became shy in front of the audience.

"Hi everyone… um, well, I'm not used to this anymore so I'll keep this short. I never had any intention of showing my work again, especially *Antigone*, after my late wife's death." He turned to look at Romy and smiled. "It's not often a man finds his muse… *twice.* Tonight marks not only the celebration of my past, as a tribute to Sarah, but the excitement of the future. *Our*

MIA O'SULLIVAN

future. Romy Park came back to Monterey to open her gallery
in the same building her beloved parents owned their bookshop,
but she did far more than that. She gave me back my life."

Romy couldn't help the tear that escaped and dropped down
her cheek. Milo drew her into her arms and chuckled softly.
"Sorry to get mushy, folks, but you should know how much you
being here tonight means to both of us. So, please enjoy the show.
It's the first of many."

TWENTY-FIVE

LATER, AS THE GUESTS milled around and sold stickers began to appear on the works that Milo had decided he would sell, Romy took a moment to escape to the office and breathe. Tonight had been a success and she could hardly believe how well it had all gone. The art critics had been raving about the show—it would remain to be seen in tomorrow's articles whether they were merely paying lip service or if they genuinely loved it.

Romy let the tension of the run-up to the show dissipate now. It was over, a success, and the horror of the malevolent campaign against her was over now that Connor was gone. All there was left was, as Milo had said, excitement for what was next. She had found her person, her soulmate, in Milo Keys. Her career as a gallery owner was looking bright.

"Knock, knock."

She looked up to see Nico at the doorway and grinned at him. "Hey, you. I'm sorry, I didn't see you before."

"I only just got here. I'm sorry, honey. I had a call out in Carmel."

"You're here now, that's all that matters." She went to him and hugged him. "None of this would have been possible without you, Nico."

His arms tightened around her. "You're welcome, sweetheart."

"Hey."

Romy saw Milo appear from the hallway. His eyes flicked to Nico's arms around her, and Romy released her friend. There was something in Milo's eyes that made her frown. There was no way he was jealous of Nico, was there?

No, she was imagining it. Nico grinned guilelessly at Milo and clapped him on the back. "Hey, man, the show is great."

Milo relaxed, and Romy let out her breath. *That was a weird moment*, she thought.

"Thanks, Nico. You did a great job on the place."

"That's what I was just thanking him for." Romy went to Milo and slipped her hand into his. He squeezed it back, and she knew she had been imagining his jealousy. Milo knew she loved him. "I was just catching my breath."

"Good move. Almost everyone has cleared out now." He checked his watch. "It's almost midnight."

"I can't believe it's over."

"You did it, sweetheart."

"*We* did it." She smiled back at Nico. "Nico. Come with us. Let's go celebrate with our team."

After the last of the guests had gone, Romy closed the shades on the big picture windows, and her friends and family picnicked on champagne and some of the leftover food Harper had brought. They lounged on the floor in front of *Antigone* and chatted and laughed.

Romy lay with her head in Milo's lap, gazing up at him. His fingers stroked the patch of skin under her ear.

"So, what's next for you guys?"

Romy turned her head to see Harper, laying on her side, propped up against Jae's legs. Moon had fallen asleep, his face beautiful even as he snored softly, and Nico and Nan were playing finger soccer with a mashed-up piece of tin foil. Romy's heart warmed. *My family.*

"Right now? Wallowing in our victory and then Christmas. It's going to be a good one."

Harper smiled at them. "Honestly, I wish I could be with you, but my family has its traditions."

"Spend New Year's with us."

"That I can do."

Romy watched a shadow fall over Harper's face. "What is it?"

Harper shook her head. "It's just… the first one without… him. I know, I know he was a bad person but—"

"You loved him," Milo remarked. "Sometimes we can't help loving someone, even if we know they're toxic." He continued to stroke Romy's skin, but his voice took on a bitter tone that Romy wondered at.

Harper nodded. "Is it wrong that I still miss him? Even though our interactions were basically him asking for money over the last few months or arguing, I…" She sighed. "He never loved me. I don't think he was capable of loving anyone, and that was down to his mother. Love was unimportant compared to money. She instilled that in him. Also, that he was like a prince, the special one. Connor grew up believing he was entitled to everything."

Romy nodded slowly. "That's exactly right."

"His mother is a first-class bitch," Nico suddenly looked up from his game with Nan, and Romy was surprised to see the anger in his eyes. "I wasn't going to say anything, but she's been bad-mouthing you and Harper around town, Romy. No one pays much attention, but I heard her when I went to do some work at the country club. She didn't see me at first, but then she got real embarrassed when I heard her talking trash about you two."

"What did she say?"

Nico looked uncomfortable. "Words I don't care to repeat." He looked at Milo, an apologetic look in his eyes. "She was talking about Sarah, too."

Romy felt Milo's fingers stop stroking her skin. "What? Why would she?"

Nico sighed. "Seems she thought something had been going on between them before Sarah died."

"That's not possible." Milo shifted, and Romy sat up as he scrambled to his feet. He was clearly pissed. "Sarah hated Connor."

But later, on the drive home, Milo was quiet. Romy slid her hand onto his thigh, but he didn't react.

"Baby, are you okay?"

He nodded but stayed silent. At home, Sailor greeted them joyfully, and Milo fed him. As Sailor threw back his food like he hadn't eaten in years, Milo grabbed the dog's leash and clipped it onto his collar. "Going to take him out for a walk."

"Want some company?"

"It's okay. I won't be long." He didn't meet her gaze.

Alone, the tension had returned to Romy's body. It had been an emotional night, she reasoned, and Nico talking about Connor and Sarah had hit home. *Let him be, let him wallow as long as he needs.*

Romy went upstairs and stripped down, stepping into a hot shower and letting the warm water pound her body, easing her tired muscles. Afterwards, she blow-dried her long hair and rubbed moisturizer into every inch of her body. There was a draft of cold air which made her shiver, and she went to the window to close it. Outside, the ocean was dark and still, and the moon was full.

Romy leaned out to see if she could see the light from Milo's torch as he walked Sailor along the small stretch of beach below, but there was nothing. She hoped he was on his way back.

She slipped into a fresh t-shirt and shorts. Downstairs, she heard Sailor's muffled woof and the front door close.

"I'm back, baby."

Romy sighed with relief. Milo sounded a little more relaxed now. "Up here, I can come down."

"No, stay there. I'm coming up. You better be naked."

Romy laughed. Yep. Milo was feeling better. When he came into the bedroom, he stuck out his lower lip. "You have clothes on."

Romy pulled his lips down to hers. "Only so that I can perform a striptease for you." She slid her hand down to his crotch and squeezed his cock through his pants. "You okay?"

He nodded. "I am, I'm sorry, baby. My head got a bit messed up, but the walk helped. Only happy from here on out, right?"

"You bet that sweet ass of yours."

He chuckled and tumbled her to the bed as she pulled his shirt open and kissed his chest. Milo rolled her onto her back.

"The striptease is going to have to wait for another night. I need you naked right now."

Romy grinned. "Then strip me, big boy."

They wrestled around as they stripped each other, laughing and enjoying the feel of skin-on-skin, making love late into the night. It was almost dawn before they feel sleep, wrapped around each other. As Romy drifted off, she heard her cell phone bleep but couldn't be bothered to answer it.

And so, when she woke up the next morning, she woke up to a nightmare.

TWENTY-SIX

ROMY LEANED OVER THE toilet in the restrooms of the police station and threw up until there was nothing left but painful dry retches. She flushed and went out to the basins to wash her mouth out and splash water on her face. A woman emerged from another stall, frowning. She put her hand on Romy's back.

"Are you okay, dear?"

Romy nodded weakly. "I'm fine. Just a little sick."

When she was alone, she gazed at herself in the mirror, but all she could see was the video that had been texted to her that morning.

Sarah. Sarah being murdered by whoever was filming her. Romy had clicked unthinkingly on the link, and as the audio began, Milo had spun around from where he was cooking eggs at the stove. "That's Sarah's voice."

They both watched as the killer filmed a stumbling Sarah, who had obviously been drugged, as she tried to get away from him. *Please, no… why are you doing this?*

Then the horror of the murder. Sarah on the ground, helpless, the knife being plunged into her. Her gasps of agony. The blood, so, so much blood.

Romy had wanted to throw the phone away in shock, but Milo, pale-faced and shaking, caught her hand. "No. We have to take this to the police."

On the drive to the police station, she heard him muttering, "I knew it, I fucking knew it..." under his breath the whole way.

At the station, they had taken Milo to an interview room to question him, telling Romy they would talk to her next. As she sat outside, all Romy could picture was Sarah's lovely face, contorted with terror, then as she bled out, the way life had seeped from her and helplessness set in. Resignation. There was no message with the video, but the threat was implicit. The fact he or she had sent it to Romy meant one thing. Romy was next.

So she had run to the bathroom and thrown up. Now, as she wiped her mouth and went back outside, she felt helpless, too. What the hell was going on?

She dropped her head into her hands.

"Romy?"

She looked up to see Jim Halsey approaching her. "Hi."

"What are you doing here?"

She told him, and he cursed under his breath. "Jesus. Are you okay?"

Romy shook her head. "No. I'm really not. But not for myself, for Milo. He watched the video with me. They're talking to him now."

Halsey sat down next to her and rubbed her back. "I'm sorry, Romy."

"I thought it was over, with Connor being dead. I really hoped all this horror was done with."

Halsey nodded, but he looked as angry as she felt. Milo came out from the interview room, nodded to Halsey, then looked at Romy. "They want to talk to you now."

The police officers asked her all the same questions. *Who, what, where, why?*

She wished she knew why. Why the hell would anyone want to kill Sarah Keys? And her? What had she ever done to anyone? The questions came over and over again, and she answered them all patiently.

Outside, Halsey was talking to Milo when Romy was finished with the detectives. Romy went to Milo's side. He wrapped his arms around her. Halsey smiled at her kindly.

"We were just talking about added security at your home, and at your gallery."

Romy nodded, and Milo kissed the top of her head. "We'll figure it out."

Milo sounded defeated as they walked to his car, and Romy held his hand. "Milo, I'm so sorry."

They got in the car, but Milo didn't start the engine immediately. He stared out the windshield. "Is it weird that I feel... relief? No, not relief, vindication. I knew it. I knew she would never leave me. I knew it." He looked at Romy apologetically. "Not that her being murdered is better, of course not. I want to rip whoever killed her apart with my bare hands. But now we know he's out there." He slipped his hand onto her cheek. "I won't let anything happen to you, you know that, right?"

"I do know that. But maybe it's time we started to look into Sarah's life a bit more deeply."

Milo nodded. "I've already started. I have a private detective trying to dig up anything he can. I was always reticent to do so, not wanting to know the truth of whether Sarah may have cheated on me... I don't believe she did, but there's always the possibility." He sighed heavily. "I just have deal with whatever the private detective finds. The question is, how is what happened to you tied in? Because I believe it is, don't you?"

"I do." She studied him for a moment. "But I don't know why. The first thing that happened, to me at least, was that I was sent the obituary."

"Had we met?"

Romy squinted as she tried to recall. "No, but Harper had arranged that first dinner." She smiled. "Where I massively screwed things up."

"You did no such thing, baby. I was just taken by surprise." He smiled softly at her. "And god, I'm so thankful Harper decided to matchmake."

Romy grinned. "Right back at you. So, back to the thing, I got the obit that day."

"Do you still have it?"

"Yup." She rummaged in her purse. "For some reason, I kept it in here. It's just an obit, though, no threat, nothing." She handed the scrap of newspaper to him, and he read it through.

"There were multiple fatalities apart from your family?"

"Yes, but that's all I know."

He handed her back the paper. "Maybe we should look into who else was affected by the accident. Maybe there's someone with a grudge?"

Romy frowned, although her heart sank. "The accident wasn't our fault, though."

"But you were the only survivor. Maybe there's someone out there who thinks their loved one should have been the one. Let's see what we can find out."

She nodded. "Okay. It's a place to start after all. But how are you tied into this? How was Sarah?"

Milo started the car at last. "I don't know, sweetheart, but we're going to find out."

He pulled the car out into traffic and followed them away from the police station. So, the secret was out. The secret he had held close to him all of these years. Sarah's murder.

She had been the first, but not the last. Tracing everyone connected to the accident had taken years—and nearly all of his savings. Making them pay had been his reward.

Sarah, yes, she had been the first. He hadn't been sure he would be able to go through with killing someone, least of all a woman, but it had been terrifyingly easy.

And pleasurable.

He'd stabbed Sarah once and watched her die, filming the whole thing. When he killed Romy Park, he would take his time, making sure she suffered. Hell, he'd already messed with her medication. The first time he had broken into her condo, he'd noticed the antidepressants in her bathroom cabinet. So, when he'd gotten into the condo the second time, the time he placed the recording devices in her outlets, he'd painstakingly emptied out all of her medication capsules and swapped the drugs with corn flour.

He knew from experience how messing with antidepressants can fuck a person up. That she hadn't flipped out entirely yet was strange, but maybe she had been weening herself off the pills.

No matter. She would be dead soon. He just wanted to make her suffer before she died.

He wondered if she'd gotten yet that she and Milo Keys were connected in ways they could never have dreamed of. He wondered if, when they made love, or when they lay in each other's arms making plans for the future, if she had any idea that the man she loved was a liar.

He would enjoy telling Romy as he sank his knife into her soft, vulnerable flesh.

TWENTY-SEVEN

ROMY KNEW IT WAS for the best, at least for now, but it still rankled with her that Milo had asked Nico to install better security at the gallery. She had argued that she needed a walk-in, open-door policy, and that a locked gallery door was not conducive to success, but both Milo and Nico were firm that she be extra cautious. "Just until they catch the asshole who did this," they reasoned.

The police were in agreement. Halsey came to see Romy—she was glad to see him because it meant she could have her gallery door open while the detective was there—and told her they were now reopening the investigation into Sarah's death.

"Obviously, now that we know Connor is unlikely to have sent that video from beyond the grave," Halsey smiled grimly, "we're looking at anyone who can connect you and Mr. Keys."

"I think you can call him Milo at this point... Jim."

Halsey chuckled, his face softening. "Good point." He looked around the gallery. "This place is looking good." He nodded at a middle-aged couple who were admiring *Antigone*. "Looks like you might have another sale."

"Oh, that one isn't up for sale. It's too important. To Milo, and to be honest, to me, too."

Halsey looked a little confused. "Forgive me for saying, but…"

"Why does a portrait of my lover's dead wife mean so much?" Romy laughed softly. "*Antigone* is the reason I went into art. Come, look."

The couple had moved on now, and Romy beckoned Halsey over to the portrait.

"Look at the expression in her eyes. What does it say to you?"

Halsey studied the painting for a long time before replying. "She's reflective… not unhappy, but somber. There's humor there, too, the slight crinkling at the corner of her eyes… love. Wow." He blinked. "You're right. There's so much there, much more than just a portrait of a beautiful woman."

"Exactly." Romy studied Sarah's face. "And to kind of answer your question, this is the painting that brought Milo and I together. Sarah brought us together. I never met her in real life, but I feel as if we would have been friends. Does that sound crazy?"

"Not at all." Halsey smiled kindly at her. He looked around some more. "So, how's it going to work with the extra security?"

"I'll be hanging around."

They both turned to see Nico grinning at them. "Before you start arguing, Ro, Milo agrees. You need someone here, and I know you won't hire an actual bodyguard."

"He has that right." Romy wasn't happy, but she sighed. At least Nico was a friend, and she enjoyed his company. "But don't you have other contracts?"

"I had a gap in my schedule."

Halsey said goodbye after a while, and Romy was glad. At least with Nico here, she could have a steady and uninhibited flow of customers. It was Christmas Eve, and tonight Jae and Moon would be here. Romy would close the gallery for three days, and she, her boys, and Milo would spend the holiday eating, drinking, and playing games.

She couldn't wait. She needed this normalcy, the fun of just being happy, at least temporarily. Her body felt taught, and she needed the release of being silly with her brother and her lover. Nico was out back, one ear listening for if she needed him.

At almost four, it was dark outside. She looked up as the door opened, and Farron Lee came through the entryway. She beamed at him.

"Hello you. I was hoping you would stop by again."

Farron looked surprised as she hugged him, but he kissed her cheek. "I promised I would. I came to bring you this."

He reached into his pocket and drew out an envelope. He handed it to Romy, and she opened it, expecting a Christmas card or something. Instead, she drew out a photograph.

Her hand flew to her mouth, and tears filled her eyes. "Oh, Farron…"

The photograph was almost twenty years old, but the images were sharp. Romy stared down at her mother and father, arms locked around each other, laughing. The way they looked at each other… Romy felt her heart pump faster. Farron was watching her with a smile on his face. He pointed out the small nine-year-old girl.

"And who is that little pickle?"

"It's me." A tear fell down her cheek. "And look… the baby… that's my Jae." She turned and hugged Farron again, tightly. "You don't know how much this means to me. I have hardly any photographs of us all together."

Farron hugged her back. "I'm sorry I didn't find it sooner, dear." He studied her as she drew away and frowned. "You look exhausted. Is there something wrong?"

Romy ended up telling Farron everything, locking the front door and taking him back to the staffroom. The older man listened, nodding along.

"Why would anyone want to hurt you?"

"Milo thinks maybe it's to do with the accident." She was quiet for a moment. "Farron... did you go to the funeral?"

He nodded. "I did. A lot of townsfolk did. Your mother and father were loved, really loved."

Romy swallowed over the lump in her throat. "The other people who died... did you know any of them?"

"One or two I had seen around town, but I wouldn't say I knew them. Seventeen people died in that accident."

"I know." She chewed her lip. "When I woke up, all those months later, my grandmother didn't want to talk about it, so we never did. Even Jae and I haven't talked about it in detail. Obviously, he was so young when it happened, when my aunt died. While I was in the coma, my grandmother was busy taking care of him, arranging the funerals, and sitting with me in the hospital, so she never wanted to talk about the accident."

Romy sighed and rubbed her head. "What she did for us... I think it wore her down in the end. I don't think she ever processed the loss of her children."

"Your grandmother was a remarkable woman."

"She was." Romy shook her head. "But I'm getting off the topic. We—Milo and I—are trying to find an old link between us, something we think is to do with the others who died in the accident, something that connects he and I. Finding out about the others in the accident seems like the way to go."

"You know, it was only ten years ago. At the inquest, there was mention of video evidence, at least that's what the papers said. I wonder if it's still available."

"Or maybe..." Romy took out her phone and flicked to a video streaming site. "Maybe someone's uploaded it. You never know." She typed in the details into the search engine, then frowned. "Nothing."

Nico came into the room and leaned over her. "Try less description. Try 'Monterey, car wreck, and date.'"

Romy did as he said and pressed enter. Three results came up, and suddenly she couldn't breathe. If these videos did indeed show the accident, she would see her parents and her aunt die. She would see their car being driven into the back of the other vehicles, the pileup, the hideousness of the carnage.

She felt Nico's hand on her shoulder. "We're with you, Ro."

Romy looked up at him, and then Farron, who nodded encouragingly. She saw grief in his eyes, too. With her free hand, she reached out and took his hand as she pressed play.

She let out a groan. "This video has been removed due to copyright."

The two men let out sighs, and she knew they felt like she did—frustrated. The next video was of another wreck. The final video started as just a dashcam, following the stream of traffic on a rainy, dull day.

Romy watched as the car ducked and weaved through the heavy traffic, and then, when she saw her family's blue station wagon, her heart began to pound.

I'm looking at my parents alive, right now. I'm watching the last moments of their lives. What were we doing? What were we thinking...?

"Honey, you can do better than Connor Small, you always could. The fact that he married that poor girl for her money. I never liked the Van Warrens, but that girl is a sweetheart. Poor Harper. Ugh." *Giovanna Park, sitting next to her eighteen-year-old daughter,*

squeezed her hand. "You deserve the best man... or woman, whatever your preference."

Jin Park grinned around at them from the passenger seat. "Hell, honey, your mama's desperate for you to realize you actually like girls."

Romy laughed, despite her misery. "After today, I might."

"That's my girl. At least you won't get knocked up."

"Vanna..." But there was humor in her father's admonition, and he and Giovanna smiled at each other.

"I'm okay, really. Unless I can find someone who looks at me the way you two look at each other, I'll happily stay single forever."

"Mushy." Giovanna made a face which made them all laugh.

"What's this idiot doing?" Her aunt spoke from the driver's seat, staring at the rearview.

Jin looked around, his handsome face creased with concern. He spoke rapid Korean to his sister, who replied in the same, and Romy knew he was trying not to panic his wife and daughter—Giovanni had trouble learning her husband's first language, but Romy understood more than her father knew. The conversation sent chills down her spine.

"He's trying to kill us."

"Is it him?"

"I think so. Try to get away from him."

"What do you think I'm doing—Jin!"

The other car slammed into them, knocking the wind out of them, and again before Romy could understand what was going on, she cried, "Mom! Dad!"

"It's okay, honey, hold on... hold on..."

It was the last time she ever heard her father's voice. One last crash, and then the car was flying, and she was screaming, her aunt was screaming, her mother...

Then a crunch and darkness. Silence. Romy slipped in and out *of consciousness, the smell of gasoline and wet asphalt in her nostrils along with a rust-and-salt tang she knew could only be one thing.*

Blood.

With all her strength, Romy fought the blackness. "Mom?"

All she heard was the rushing of air, the pounding of blood in her ears before finally, the light went out.

Romy didn't realize she was shaking until both Nico and Farron wrapped their arms around her. She had just watched her family die.

"He killed them. Whoever was driving that car intended to kill us." She looked up with haunted eyes as Milo came into the room, saw the confusion on his face as Farron and Nico released her into his arms. "He tried to kill us... he murdered my family, Milo... he murdered my family."

TWENTY-EIGHT

Christmas Eve...

ROMY AND MILO DECIDED not to say anything to Jae and Moon.

"I just want a happy Christmas with you—our first together—and with Jae and Moon."

Milo stroked his hand down her back. "I'm going to give you the best Christmas ever, darling." He studied her carefully. "Are you okay?"

She turned her dark eyes at him, and they were full of unspoken rage. "I'm pissed, Milo. I feel murderous. I'm going to find out who did it and fucking end them."

Milo pressed his lips to his lover's soft skin. "I'm right there with you."

But they still needed to find the connection between the Parks' murder and Sarah's killing.

"But not until after Christmas. I need this. *We* need this."

When Jae and Moon arrived, it was like a shot of pure joy through her veins. Jae, his silky dark hair was becoming shaggy now as he grew it out, and Moon, with newly ash blonde hair, looked healthy and happy.

The boys immediately took over Milo's kitchen, and between teasing Romy and revving Sailor up into an excited doggy frenzy, they made enough food for an army.

Christmas Day dawned, and they all ate their own body weight, exchanged gifts, and lazed around. They played board games, and as they did, Romy marveled that they could all pretend nothing was wrong, that no one had been attacked or threatened, that they weren't dealing with the knowledge that their loved ones had been murdered.

Sometime, cognitive dissonance is a good thing when the truth could drive us out of our minds. Romy chewed on her bottom lip, trying not to let negative thoughts in.

Jae nudged her. "Hey, space cakes, your turn."

In the evening, they ate huge subs filled with turkey and stuffing and laid around on the couches, half-watching a movie, half-talking. Romy fell asleep, her head on Milo's chest, his arms wrapped around her.

Milo kissed the top of Romy's head. Jae smiled over at him.

"You really love her, don't you?"

"More than I can tell you, buddy."

Jae, sitting on the floor, his back against the couch where Moon was napping, looked around at his lover. "I get it."

Milo smiled at him. "I just wish... I just wish I could protect her from all of this bullshit."

"I think Ro feels the same about you. She told me that if she could do anything, she would take your pain away."

Milo chuckled softly. "That sounds like her."

Jae studied his sleeping cousin. "She thinks I don't remember the accident, but I do. I wasn't in the car... Mom didn't think

I should go to Connor's wedding. She didn't want me to see Ro upset, I think, so I was with Moon that day. I remember the police officers coming to the house. They wanted to know if my dad was around—my dad hadn't been around since before I was born. My grandmother flew over from Korea the next day to take care of me and Romy."

Jae's lovely face creased with grief. "I didn't process it. My mom's death, along with my aunt and uncle. I focused on Romy. I didn't understand why she couldn't wake up and talk to me. I used to get into the hospital bed with her and sleep curled up against her."

"Her little koala. She told me."

They both laughed softly. "I can't imagine anyone wanting to hurt her."

Milo felt a pang. They hadn't told Jae about the clip on the video streaming site; Romy hadn't wanted to ruin his Christmas. But the young man in front of him was no fool; he could obviously tell something was wrong.

Romy whimpered in her sleep, and Milo's arms tightened around her. "It's okay, baby." He sighed. "I think I'll take her to bed. She's obviously bushed."

Jae grinned. "Same here. Sleep well, buddy. Thanks for having us to stay—and for loving my cousin. You're a good one."

Milo was touched. "That means a lot coming from you, man. Thank you." He managed to slide off the couch, lifting Romy into his arms. She stirred but burrowed her head into his shoulder. "You guys set?"

Jae was gently shaking Moon, but he turned and grinned at Milo. "We're good. Night."

"Goodnight."

Upstairs, Milo took Romy's clothes off as best he could and tucked her into bed. She mumbled something.

"What's that, baby?"

But she was asleep again. Milo smiled, stroking her hair back from her face. He wished he could feel as peaceful as Romy did, at least right now, but his mind was in more turmoil than he had admitted over the past few days.

The knowledge that Sarah had been murdered and that Romy's family had been intentionally killed was messing with his mind. He had thought he would have felt more vindicated, but the fact that they were somehow linked... it was driving him crazy. How? He thought about calling Sarah's parents, asking them if they had known or were connected to Romy's family in any way, but the way they had reacted to the news that he and Romy were seeing each other made him think they wouldn't be forthcoming.

He couldn't imagine it anyway. He remembered the Parks as being kind and generous with their time and their love. Sarah's family kept to themselves—not that it was a bad thing, they just weren't "people-people."

Milo smiled sadly to himself. *How the hell were you related to them, Sarah? You were the kindest, loveliest...* Shit. He was getting maudlin. He left Romy asleep in his bed and went back downstairs. Sailor got up from his bed, gave an expansive yawn, and came to nuzzle Milo's hand. "Hey, boy."

He fussed the dog for a while before Sailor decided he liked sleep more than Daddy and went back to bed. Milo poured himself a shot of bourbon and took it out onto the deck. Outside it was bitingly cold, but he didn't care. The alcohol slid down his throat, the warmth of it curling in his stomach. It didn't help.

He took out his phone. *Hey, you up? I need to talk.*

A few seconds later, Harper replied.

I'm up. I escaped the fam early, thank god. What's up? Can I call?

Sure.

Harper picked up right away. "Hey, dude. You all right?"

"No, not really. I need to talk about something."

"Go for it."

Milo told Harper everything. "I know you're still raw from Connor, and I really don't want to upset you any, but I've reached the point where I'm too close to this. Can you think of anything from back then you might have heard? Anything?"

He heard Harper blow out a long breath. "Honey, I'm sorry, no. But back then I was just too wrapped up in Connor and the wedding to notice. I knew the Parks, of course, and I remember feeling horrible for Romy that day. She looked so sad. And then we heard about the accident—god, why, would anyone want to kill that lovely family? Or Sarah?"

"Did Connor ever say anything about Sarah to you, back when they worked together?"

Harper gave a little hiss of frustration. "Milo..." Her voice trailed off. "Look, I'm going to tell you something, but I want you to know, I think it's one hundred percent bullshit, okay?"

Milo could tell where this was going, but he needed to hear it. "Just say it."

"During one of our knockdown fights, Connor claimed that he slept with Sarah. I didn't believe him then, I don't believe it now."

"Sarah hated him."

"I know. With good reason."

"Do you think he killed her? Maybe he was working with someone?"

"No and no. I don't, really. Connor was a bully and an asshole," Harper spat the words out. "But he wasn't a killer. What he did was push people's buttons. He loved to do that." She laughed without humor. "I remember he had an argument with my dad a week before the wedding. Dad would never talk about it afterward, but I think some pretty harsh words had been said."

A suspicion began to grow in his mind. "Do you have any idea what it was about?"

"I don't, really." Harper was quiet for a long minute. "Milo, Connor cheated on me right from day one. If he had wanted to have an affair with Romy, I doubt he would have had her run off the road on our wedding day."

"Right." He gave a frustrated grunt. "I just want to figure this all out."

"I know, sweetie. Look… I'll talk to my dad, try and see if he knows anything."

"I appreciate it."

Milo said goodbye, wished his friend a merry Christmas, and ended the call. He went back upstairs and stripped off, slipping between the sheets. Romy stirred, opened her eyes and gave him the sweetest smile. His body relaxed. What could be wrong in the world when she smiled at him like that?

She moved closer, and he wrapped his arms around her, chuckling when she complained about his cold skin. "Sorry, baby. I got some fresh air."

"Your feet are freezing." Romy giggled as Milo blew a raspberry on her cheek. "Silly boy. I'll warm you up."

She rolled him onto his back and straddled him. Milo's hands slid down her sides, tracing the soft curve of her waist as he gazed up at her. Her dark hair tumbled about her shoulders, mussed up from sleep, and her skin was warm and silky as his fingers stroked her belly, cupped her breasts.

Romy was stroking his cock against her belly as it stiffened. Then, as it became hard, she slowly impaled herself on it. They made love slowly, quietly, just enjoying the connection of their bodies. Midway through, Milo flipped her onto her back so he could thrust deeper, Romy hooking her ankles around his back.

He swallowed her cry of release in his mouth, his lips against hers as he too reached his climax. They lay together, panting hard. Milo tightened his arms around her.

"Romy?"

"Yes, my love?"

"There's something I've been meaning to talk to you about."

She looked up, her eyes wary. "If you want to break up, now is not the time." Then she grinned, and he chuckled.

"Never." He brushed her lips with his. "I just wanted you to know that you have brought me back to life. After Sarah died, I thought that was it. I got to be happy for that long and then... I never thought I would be head over heels for someone else. So... thank you. Thank you for loving me, thank you for being who you are, Romy Park. Despite all the crap we're going through, I know we'll make it out the other side."

Romy's face was flushed. "Damn, boy. You really went for it."

Milo laughed out loud this time. "That. That right there. You make me feel like all I want to do is play around with you, laugh every day, all day."

"Sappy fool." But she was beaming, and her eyes were filled with tears. "That's what you wanted to tell me?"

"That I love you, yeah. But also, this..." He drew in a deep breath. "I'm painting again."

He could tell that shocked her. "What?"

"Finding your muse once in life is a special thing, finding her twice... well. I'm painting again. It's nothing much, just a few sketches and experiments, certainly nothing worth showing yet. But the urge is back, the passion. And it's all because of you."

Romy crushed her lips against his, and he could feel the tears on her cheeks. "I can't tell you," she whispered to him, "how much that means to me."

He kissed her again, and they began to make love again, not caring that the night was slowing turning into day...

TWENTY-NINE

HARPER WENT TO FIND her father in his study the next day. Keith Van Warren was one of the few members of her family that Harper could bear to be around for more than a few minutes. When she saw her mother, Esther, and younger brother, Simon, setting up for a mammoth game of bridge with her cousins, Harper took the chance to seek out her dad.

Keith had escaped to his study the second he could get away from 'all the damn relatives,' but he smiled when he saw Harper at the door.

"Come in, love. I smuggled in some of that sloe gin I made." He poured them both a glass, and they sat down on the old leather couch that her mother loathed because it looked 'too hippy.' Keith touched his glass to Harper's. "Here's mud in your eye."

Harper winced at the alcohol in the drink. "Jeez, pa."

"Good, isn't it? Now, what's up?"

Harper took another sip. "Dad, did you know the Park family well?"

"Well enough, I suppose. We invited them to the wedding, didn't we? Terrible what happened to them."

"Yes. Dad, I can't tell you much, but there's evidence that the crash wasn't an accident."

Keith went still. "What?"

"The accident. It wasn't. Someone targeted them."

"God." Keith shook his head. "Why? Jin Park had no enemies that I know of. And Giovanna was very popular."

"That's what we're trying to figure out."

"We?"

"Milo, Romy, and I."

Keith smiled. "You know... for a while there, I honestly thought you and Milo Keys would get together. I would have approved of that, my girl. He's a good man."

"He is. No, that was never in the cards. He's like my brother... except *not* like Simon at all." They both laughed. Simon was okay, but he and Harper had never been close—too much difference in personalities.

Harper looked at her father now. "It seems Sarah Keys was murdered now, too."

"Oh, god, damn. That never sat right, that whole thing." Keith shook his head. "What does one have to do with the other?"

"That's what we're trying to figure out." Harper sighed. "Maybe Sarah found out something about the crash?"

"Like what?"

Harper shrugged. "Maybe... god, I don't know. What if... what if someone wanted the Parks out of the picture for financial reasons? That property Romy's opened her gallery in is prime real estate."

Keith didn't look convinced. "Is that a reason to kill?"

"Who needs a good reason for violence? Dad, I just... I feel for Milo and Romy. They need answers. Is there anything, anyone you can think of back then who would have anything against them?"

"I can't, honey." Keith looked uncomfortable. "Harper, I don't want you getting mixed up with anything dangerous, even if it is to help your friends out. They should be in touch with the police."

"They are, Dad. They have a contact. James Halsey—do you know him?"

"Jim Halsey? Yes, I know him. Well, I hope he helps them out."

Harper sensed that her father wanted to end the conversation, but she wondered at the sudden weariness in his eyes. "Dad, how well do you know Jim Halsey?"

"I know he's well-regarded in the service. Look, I'm hungry. Let's go grab some food."

Keith got up suddenly, and Harper knew the conversation was over. She was frustrated. Her dad was hiding something, but she couldn't tell what it was. She had an uneasy feeling it was about the detective, but she hoped it was nothing bad. The last thing Milo and Romy needed was a bad cop. *He's well-regarded in the service.*

So why didn't her father share their faith?

The four of them took Sailor down to a dog-friendly beach the day after Christmas, and Jae and Moon threw a tennis ball for him, laughing when he would barrel towards them and knock them down on the sand. Romy and Milo walked hand in hand, watching them play. Romy chuckled.

"Why do I feel like a mom with these two sometimes?"

Milo smiled down at her. "Do you want kids someday?"

"If it happens, it happens. It's not something I ever aspired to as desperately as some, but then again, if it happens, that's good, too." She kissed him. "You?"

"I always thought I would be a father, but, same as you, if it happens, it happens." He smiled down at her. "We have time to discuss all that stuff. I just want to enjoy us being together for a while."

"Me too." Romy hugged his arm. "I just wish all this other crap was over."

"We'll go see Halsey after the holiday, and in addition, I'll get my investigator to step up his research." Milo stopped, his eyes serious. "Romy... he can go deep, but if he finds out something you don't want to hear—"

"I want the truth about everything. Nothing can change my love for my mom and dad, but they were human, flawed humans. They made mistakes. What if one of those mistakes cost them their lives?"

THIRTY

THREE DAYS AFTER CHRISTMAS, Romy opened the gallery. There were plenty of people on the streets, even in the cool weather, and there was a steady stream of customers flowing through the gallery.

Jae and Moon hung around, cleaning, taking inventory, and chatting to the customers, while Romy caught up on paperwork and began to call in work from local artists. With Milo's work being front and center, she could afford to give up-and-coming artists a platform.

This was her favorite part of her job. Back in Manhattan, Seb had taught her about the balance between showing established artists to get the attention and also breaking a new artist onto the scene. Sometimes it worked, sometimes not, but when it did, it not only began the artist's career proper, but it was a huge boon to the gallery.

Seb had exquisite taste, and more often than not, his protégées went on to have great success. Romy had found a few young artists for him to consider, and although they hadn't worked out, Seb had encouraged her in her search. "You will know, for sure, when you find a good one, Romy. You have that gift," he had said.

Romy didn't think any of the local artists she was calling now were going to set the international art world on fire, but that was okay. She was just starting out. Giving a voice to them was all that mattered at the moment.

She was so absorbed in her work that she didn't even notice it was getting dark outside.

"Ro?"

She looked up to see Jae in her doorway. "Hey."

"It's after five already."

"Jeez, really?" She sat back in her chair and rolled her shoulders. "Weird. Milo hasn't called."

"Maybe he got stuck in his research."

"Maybe." She frowned as she tugged her cell phone out of her bag. "Or maybe someone forgot to charge their phone." She sighed and plugged the charger into the outlet. Jae grinned.

"Derp. Look, Moon and I thought we might go grab us some pizza and bring some back for you. Will you be okay?"

Romy nodded. "Of course. I'll lock up the gallery, so come in the back when you're done, okay? You have the key, right?"

"Gotcha."

When Jae had left, Romy said goodbye to the last customers and then locked the gallery door. Back in the office, she checked her phone, saw a message from Milo and called him back.

"Sorry, baby, my phone wasn't charged."

"It's okay, sweetheart. Listen, I called Sarah's parents. I think her father is hiding something—he was very cagey when I mentioned your mom and dad. Listen, honey, I have to admit something."

Romy frowned. "What is it?"

She heard Milo sigh at the other end of the line. "I wasn't truthful with you when I said they were happy about you and me. They didn't react well. The opposite, in fact."

"Oh." Romy's heart sank, but she took a deep breath in. "Well, I guess… that sucks, but it is what it is. Not everyone will be pleased for us."

"No." There was a long pause. "Well, look, I'm going over there, and I'm going to get answers. Will you be okay?"

"Yeah, sure. Jae and Moon are just getting pizza, and they'll be back. I'll see you at home later."

"If you're sure. I love you."

"I love you, too."

Romy tidied up her desk, then went out to the main gallery to check that everything was good for the morning. It would be New Year's Eve the next day, and she had decided she would open in the morning but close at lunchtime. Milo had thought ahead and booked a table for five at one of their favorite restaurants in the evening, and afterward, they, along with Jae, Moon, and Harper, would go to a bar and wait for the New Year's countdown.

The gallery was spotless, thanks to Jae and Moon, and so, to occupy her mind while she waited, Romy went upstairs to the bare apartment. She flicked the light on and looked around.

To think I was going to move in here, and now I live in a goddamn mansion. She chuckled to herself, shaking her head. She loved Milo's place, but she could still picture how she would have laid out her home in this small apartment, which room she would choose for her bedroom.

She and her parents had never lived here—Jin and Giovanni kept stock up here, plus a comfortable staffroom for the few workers they employed.

There were a few boxes of papers and old accounts from back then, neatly stacked in the room Romy had initially allocated as her bedroom. She sat cross-legged on the floor and tugged a box over to herself, opening it gingerly, anticipating a spider or a bug. There was nothing, however, except a few dusty receipts. The same for another two boxes, but then on the fourth, Romy hit pay dirt.

And wished she hadn't. Underneath a stack of remaindered books, she found them. Letters. All seventeen of them were addressed to Giovanna. There was no return address on the envelopes, but they had been typed and sent through the mail.

Romy held the envelopes in her hands, wondering whether she wanted to know what they contained. She could feel her heartbeat quicken. Whatever was in these envelopes would change her view of her mother's life, whether it was good or bad. Was she ready?

While she considered whether or not to read them, she sorted them into date order and found herself opening the first one.

My lovely Giovanna,

Forgive me. I would never want to make you unhappy. My love for you prohibits me from telling you that I would do anything for you. I know you love your husband. I don't ask anything from you except to be your friend.

Me.

Me? Romy sighed. "So helpful." She opened the second one. It was more passive-aggressive fawning, telling Giovanna how beautiful she was, how much she meant to the mysterious 'me,' and although it was creepy beyond words, there were no implicit threats.

Until the eighth letter. Romy's stomach contracted when she read the words.

I can't believe I am having to write this down, but this is the only way I can talk to you right now. You and he have broken my heart into a million pieces, and all the while you smiled while doing so. I hate you now as much as I love you, and I will never stop making you pay for what you have done, you bitch.

"Jesus." The tone of the letter made the breath catch in her throat. What was this? Had her mother cheated on her father? Somehow, even setting aside her personal hopes, she didn't think so. This letter, the others, read like an obsession, a deeply disturbing, one-sided infatuation.

She opened the next one, and a small sob escaped her throat. A photograph of herself as a baby with her mother. A candid shot, out on the street—her mother hadn't known it was being taken.

I am always watching over you,.

A flood of anger swept through Romy. "You fucking creep… you utter scumbag…"

A floorboard creaked and made her start. Romy blew out her cheeks. "Jumpy idiot," she told herself. She was reaching for the last letter when she heard the movement again and froze.

She sat in utter silence, the only sound was the faint noise of traffic from the streets.

Something brushed against the wall opposite her. Romy's senses were on alert now, and she got up, her eyes darting around, looking for something to defend herself with. She grabbed the broken leg of a chair and padded quietly around the apartment.

Again, that strange swishing, brushing sound and prickles began to run up and down her spine. It was in the walls… something was in the crawl spaces in the walls. *A bird? A rat?*

Romy listened carefully. Was it her imagination, or could she hear breathing?

Don't be stupid…

But she decided she was going to get out of there anyway. She slowly walked out of the bedroom and towards the stairs.

The door to the empty linen closet was open.

Romy barely had time to suck in a shocked breath before suddenly there were hands on her, and the pain began.

THIRTY-ONE

MILO SAT OUTSIDE SARAH'S parents' house for a half-hour before he psyched himself up to go inside. Penelope and Eben Ingles were the last people he wanted to see, but he was sure Eben hadn't been truthful about his reaction to the fact he was dating Jin Park's daughter. There had been something in Eben's eyes... wariness.

Milo rubbed his face hard, trying to get some blood flowing. *I wish I could just take Romy and Sailor and get away from all of this. Start again.*

But Monterey was Romy's home. They were building a life here, and she was building her business.

And running away was never his thing.

He got out of the car and walked up to the door. Eben opened it for him without Milo having to knock. Eben had the strangest smile on his face.

"I wondered how long it was going to take you to come in." He nodded his head for Milo to follow him in. "So, what is it? You're going to marry the Park girl? You knocked her up?"

Milo gritted his teeth as he followed Eben into his kitchen. "Neither, although both of those things are real possibilities in the future, so you're going to have to get used to it."

Eben gave him a nasty smirk as he pulled a bottle of bourbon out of the cabinet. "Do I care about the whores you bang?"

Milo went very still. Eben was clearly already three sheets. "Where's Penny?"

"Church. Seems my wife prefers imaginary deities to her own husband." He offered the bottle to Milo, who shook his head.

"I'm driving."

"You're welcome to stay."

"No, thanks." It was Milo's turn to smile without humor. "You never liked me, did you?"

Eben sat down. "Not particularly."

Milo studied him. "It wasn't that you thought I wasn't good enough for your daughter, was it?"

Eben shrugged.

"Because you didn't particularly like Sarah either, did you?" Milo spoke slowly, clearly, trying to keep a lid on his anger. "I never knew how the pair of you could raise a woman as strong, as brilliant, as loving as my Sarah."

As he spoke the words and saw the look in Eben's eyes, Milo suddenly realized it, and he groaned to himself. How could he not see it?

"She wasn't your daughter, was she?"

"Give a prize to the man." Eben raised his glass. "No, Milo, Sarah wasn't my daughter. Penelope didn't always take God's word as seriously as she does now."

"Who was Sarah's father?"

Eben smirked. "Hell if I know. All I know is my swimmers haven't ever worked. We tried for years to get pregnant, went to clinics, jerked off into so many little white cups that I felt I should take them out to dinner, at least. But... nothing. And it was all my fault." He sighed, and for the briefest second, Milo saw heartbreak flash across the other man's face.

"So, when she got pregnant by her lover?"

"Easiest thing in the world to do to say it was mine. It. Her. *Sarah.*" He sighed. "It was my mother's name. I thought that if I gave her my mother's name I could learn to love her, that I would be able to trick my brain into thinking she was mine. And for a little while, it worked."

Milo drew in a deep breath. "She was murdered."

If he was waiting for the shock to hit Eben, he was disappointed. Eben nodded. "I thought as much. At first, those first days, I was so crazy I thought it was you. Maybe she'd cheated like her mother, but Sarah would never... I knew it wasn't you. You might be built like a sasquatch, but there's not a violent bone in your body."

Milo half-smiled. "I wouldn't count on it. When I find out who killed Sarah, who's threatening Romy, I—"

Eben frowned. "Someone's threatening your girl?"

"Yes. Do you know anything about that?"

Eben leaned forward, his face clearing now, earnest. "I don't. I swear, Milo, I do not." He sighed heavily. "And I'm sorry for calling her a whore. From what I've heard, she's a sweet girl. Her parents... they were good people, too."

Milo nodded, his mind racing. "Did her real father ever know about Sarah?"

"That I don't know. Penny wouldn't tell me who, what, where, or even why. Ah, screw that, I knew why. She was desperate to be a mother, utter desperate. More than that, she wanted to be pregnant. I couldn't blame her for that." He rubbed his forehead.

"I need to speak with Penelope."

Eben waved his hand. "Feel free. She's kept her secret for thirty-odd years, but Sarah's death destroyed her. She's a husk, Milo. Do one favor for me. Don't tell her Sarah was murdered."

Milo stood as Eben got up, unsteady on his feet. He stumbled, and Milo caught him.

"Where is she, Eben? Which church?"

Eben told him, and then, to Milo's shock, he pulled Milo into a bear hug. "Find him," Eben whispered, his voice breaking. "Find him, Milo. Find the bastard who killed my little girl. Please."

Milo got into his car and waved at Eben as he pulled away. Two blocks later, he stopped the car and let out a long breath, realizing he was shaking way too much to keep driving. He dropped his head into his hands. "Fuck," he whispered to himself. Sarah had always felt disenfranchised from her parents, and now he knew why. It had all been a lie.

His phone bleeped, and he pulled himself together. He frowned when he saw he had thirteen missed calls. He listened to his voicemail, and a cold hand closed around his heart.

Jae's voice, dull, broken. Shocked. "Please, Milo. You have to come. It's Romy."

THIRTY-TWO

Earlier that evening...

JAE SHOVED HALF AN entire slice of pizza into his mouth as he and Moon walked back to the gallery. Moon shook his head, laughing at him.

"There won't be any left for Ro."

Jae kissed his lover's mouth, leaving marinara sauce on Moon's pillowy lips, and Moon groaned. "Absolute vagabond." He licked his lips clean and grinned at Jae.

"Sweet talker."

Jae finished his pizza, then took Moon's hand. He was grateful when Moon didn't pull away. They were still careful about where they showed public affection—not because they were ashamed, but because the world was still how it was, and they'd had their fair share of homophobic abuse.

"I hate to be prosaic, but we could get a place in SF next year."

"Commute?"

"About an hour."

Moon nodded. "That's doable. We'll have to get jobs."

"I got this."

Moon rolled his eyes. "Right, because I'm going to let you pay for everything. Don't be a dick."

"I thought you liked—"

Moon pushed Jae away, grinning. "Stop."

They turned onto the block with Romy's gallery at the end. "All dark. She's probably out back in that little office."

At the gallery, they slipped down the alley at the side, and Jae opened the back door.

"Hey!"

No answer. The office was empty, but Romy's laptop was on, and her coffee cup was still a little warm. Moon looked at Jae. "Bathroom?"

Jae nodded. "Hey, Ro? We're back. Pizza's in the office."

Moon snagged a couple of sodas from Romy's mini-fridge, and they sat down. It was a couple of minutes before Jae frowned. "Maybe she's sick."

He got up and went to the bathroom door, knocked quietly. "Hey, Ro?"

No answer. Jae felt Moon behind him. "Open it."

"Coming in, Ro."

But the bathroom was empty. Jae and Moon shared a glance. Without needing words, they split up and searched the ground floor for the missing Romy.

Jae went out to the main gallery—nothing was out of place or missing, but there was a creeping feeling of dread inside him. Where the hell was Romy?

"Jae!"

Moon's cry of distress sent Jae sprinting to his boyfriend's side. Moon was standing at the bottom of the wooden staircase, staring down at the bottom step. As Jae came closer, he saw it.

Blood. A pool of it.

For a moment, time stopped. All he could hear was Moon's and his own ragged, shaky breath. A drop of blood hit the puddle and broke their trance. In a second, they were both racing up the staircase. At the top, they saw her.

And Jae wondered how he would ever stop screaming.

THIRTY-THREE

MILO COULD BARELY GET the words out to the woman at reception, but she took pity on him and escorted him to the emergency room. He saw Jae and Moon holding each other, both looking so young, so vulnerable, and so broken.

"Where is she?"

They looked up, and then he had his arms around them both, trying to hold himself together as the boys sobbed. When he could finally get some coherent sentences from them, he wished he hadn't.

He didn't want to hear the truth.

"We found her at the gallery, Milo. She was bleeding so much, and she wouldn't wake up."

Jae choked on the words, and Moon looked at Milo, bottomless sorrow in his dark eyes.

"They're operating now, but… but they say she's lost so much blood… we need to… god, I can't say it."

"Prepare ourselves?" Milo's voice was dull and resigned. It had happened. "She was stabbed?"

Both of the boys nodded, and Milo's knees gave out on him. "Oh, Christ… oh, Christ…"

It was Milo who needed support now, and Jae and Moon steered him into a chair before he fell down.

"It's just like Sarah, all over again."

"Not quite."

Jim Halsey was walking towards them. "Can we go somewhere private? All three of you?"

He led them to an empty conference room and closed the door. "To you all, I'm so terribly sorry. We dropped the ball protecting her, protecting all of you."

"No one could have seen this coming. The gallery was secure."

"Obviously not."

Milo was slumped in a chair, his head in his hands. He looked up.

"Why do you say it's different from Sarah?"

Jim Halsey's lips hardened into a tight line. "Because Sarah was stabbed once. Because we couldn't tell whether it was self-inflicted. There were no defense injuries."

Milo felt sick. "What did he do to Romy?"

Jae moaned, and Moon held him, looking away from the detective. But Milo needed to know. "Tell me everything."

"Multiple stab wounds to the abdomen. Defense injuries on Romy's hands and arms. Bruises all over her body. He wanted us to know that he intended to kill her."

Milo slammed his fist down on the table, his pain too much to bear. "He, he, he! *Who*? Who would do this? Why?"

But Jim Halsey had no answers for him. There was a knock at the door, and a doctor, dressed in OR scrubs came in. "Detective Halsey?"

"This is Jae Park, Miss Park's cousin and next of kin, his partner Moon Kim, and Miss Park's partner, Milo Keys. Guys, this Dr. Ramos... he's operating on Romy."

"Not at the moment," Jae said, standing up. "Please, god, tell me she's not—"

For a horrific second, Milo felt his soul flex and shatter, but then the doctor shook his head.

"She's still with us, but I wanted to come and update you. I won't sugarcoat things—Romy is in a very bad way. She lost almost one third of her blood volume, and her injuries are something she's not going to get over in a week. We'll be giving you a full report, detective, but for now, folks, we've stabilized her... as much as we can." He gave them a sympathetic smile. "She's in recovery, but we'll be moving her to the ICU soon, and you can sit with her. Listen... the next few days are critical. If we can keep her with us, the stronger she'll get with time. For now, we're keeping her in a medically induced coma so her body can heal."

"She was in a coma for months ten years ago," Jae said, in a dead voice. "She fought then, she'll fight now."

Milo nodded. There was hope—little—but there was hope. Halsey stepped outside with the doctor, and the three of them sat in silence, their hands linked. Jae looked at Milo.

"She'll make it," he repeated, and Milo didn't know if he was telling him or trying to convince himself.

It was his job now, as the older man, to keep this family—his family—together, even though all he wanted to do was scream.

There were hours before the staff allowed them to see Romy. As he approached her bed, she looked so tiny, so still, that she looked doll-like. Only the myriad of scratches and cuts on her face and arms told her story. The blanket covering her couldn't hide the bulk of the dressing on her stomach, however, and he couldn't stop staring at it. Images of when he found Sarah were haunting him, and he didn't know whether it was a good thing he hadn't seen Romy like that or not.

He could see it in his imagination, and every time the image flitted into his brain, it got more twisted, more violent, more blood-soaked. "Why?" he whispered as he took her hand in his. He bent down and kissed her cool forehead, willing her to open her dark eyes and smile at him, the way she did in the mornings when he woke her and they made love.

This broken girl in the bed wasn't his Romy. Milo felt cold inside. Something switched inside of him, and suddenly all he could think of was running. Getting out of there.

If he couldn't see her, then it wasn't real.

It wasn't real.

Mumbling something about coffee, he stumbled from the room, not hearing Jae and Moon's surprised voices calling him, and then he was running, knocking into staff who yelled at him, but the blood was rushing in his ears louder and louder and louder as he almost fell out of the hospital entrance and into the street.

Milo didn't even realize he was screaming until the hospital staff came to sedate him.

He'd followed the ambulance to the hospital, expecting them to bring her out of the rear of the truck already covered or at least past the point of no return. He reeled in the disappointment when he realized they were trying to save her, that they thought it was worth trying.

How?

When he'd left her at the top of those stairs, her blood pouring out of her, he'd been certain she was already gone. Her body had gone limp in his arms, all the fight gone as her body betrayed her.

Romy had fought for her life. He'd stepped out of the darkness behind her, clamped his hand over her mouth and thrust the knife into her soft belly before she reacted. Then, hell, she had *fought,* bucking and kicking, even as she bled profusely.

She'd even gotten away at one point, staggered towards the stairs, but he'd grabbed her hair and yanked her back violently, slamming her against the wall. It had knocked the wind out of her, and he'd stabbed her over and over until she went limp.

He laid her across the top of the open banister so her blood would pour down on anyone walking up the stairs.

Oh, the theatre of it. Goodbye, Romy Park. It had been as delicious as he had anticipated.

But, somehow, as far as he knew... she was still alive in there, and he had failed. He cursed and banged on the wheel in anger, but then...

Then...

Milo. Milo Keys staggered out of the hospital, screaming, an animal in pain, and his heart lifted. She was dead—she had to be for Milo to be reacting like that... right?

He watched in fascination as orderlies wrestled the big man to the ground and a nurse rushed out. They sedated Milo and wheeled him, slumped over in a wheelchair, back into the hospital.

Destroyed. She's dead. I killed her.

A smile spread across his face, and he started the car. Now, there was only one more thing left for him to do.

He could hardly wait.

THIRTY-FOUR

THERE WAS PAIN, AND then there was *this*.

"Romy, it's okay. We want you to open your eyes now, sweetheart."

The woman's voice was warm, with an accent. Italian, maybe. *Mom?*

I'm dead, right? So... maybe you are my mom, and maybe this pain is just an echo of that knife inside me. Not reality. She sighed.

"Ro? Ro, please open your eyes."

She knew that voice. *Brother.* The word came to her. *My brother.* She felt both of her hands being held, soft lips being pressed to her right hand as she heard Jae's voice again.

"Please, Ro-Ro. Open your eyes."

She hated the way his voice broke. That more than anything made her comply.

"Oh, oh, god, oh god, hi Ro, hey..."

Jae's cheeks were drenched in his tears, and she freed her left hand to wipe them from his face. "Don't cry."

He closed his eyes, nodding, trying to smile. Romy heard soft weeping from her other side and turned her head, wincing at the pain to see Moon kissing her hand and crying. "Hey, Moonbeam."

Moon just nodded, unable to speak. Romy blinked, her eyes gritty and sore.

"Close your eyes, sweetie, and I'll clean them for you."

She felt a cool pad being swept over her lids. "You're good."

Romy looked up to see the kind smile of the nurse. "How long have I been out?"

"Three days. You remember what happened?"

She nodded grimly. "Stabbed in the gut."

She regretted her words when she saw Jae wince and Moon shake his head. "And before anyone asks, no, I don't know who it was." She looked around the room, then back at Jae. "Milo?"

Jae's expression grew hard. "He's not allowed to be in here."

"Jae, what the hell?"

"After what he—"

"Jae, stop." This was Moon. He swept his hand onto Romy's forehead. "He broke down. When he saw you, he completely broke down, and they had to sedate him. They had to put a five-one-five-oh hold on him. He's in the psych ward, but he's getting there, he's cooperating with his treatment, but his psychiatrist won't let him see you until both you and he are ready."

Jae made a disgusted noise, and Moon shot him an annoyed look. "What?"

"You seem to know a lot about him."

Moon ignored his boyfriend. "Romy?"

"It's okay, Moon, I get it. Jae... Milo found Sarah stabbed to death. He saw me in this hospital bed. Imagine if you saw me dead on the side of the road after a car wreck, having lost your mother in the same way."

Romy could see Jae struggling with it. "He's a good man, Jae. This must have broken him."

"He's not the one who was almost disemboweled."

Romy half-smiled. "Thanks for that."

Jae's face softened. "Sorry. Does it hurt?"

"Yes. Like a mother."

The nurse was back then, fiddling with the tubes on the IV. She handed Romy a button.

"Press this when you need more morphine."

After an hour Romy felt wide awake, and now she was becoming used to her surroundings. She saw a young doctor sitting across the room making notes. He looked up and smiled.

"Hey, Romy. I'm Dr. Ramos."

"Oh, I'm sorry, doc, we've kept you waiting."

Ramos got up and came over to her. "Please, you needed to see your loved ones first. Having said that…" He smiled at Moon and Jae, who both nodded. Jae kissed Romy's cheek.

"We'll be right outside, Ro-Ro. We love you."

"I love you, too."

When they were alone, the doctor's expression become more serious.

"Well, now. That I'm talking to you is a great sign."

Romy swallowed hard. "Can I sit up? It's really weird talking to you laying down."

"Well… I'll raise the bed, but it might be a little sore. Your abdominal muscles have been…"

"Shredded?"

"That's one way of putting it." Ramos half-smiled. "I might have put it less viscerally."

"So to speak. I have to make jokes, doc, because I'm beyond angry, and if I don't deflect, I might lose it." Romy winced a little as the doctor pressed a button, and the upper part of the bed raised a bit.

"Okay?"

"Painful, but preferable. Now… don't sugarcoat anything, doc, please. How bad is it?"

Doctor Ramos hesitated. "Romy, we had to perform a hysterectomy. The knife damaged your uterus, sliced through your intestines. We also removed your spleen. The blade missed your liver and kidneys, which is one good thing. And…"

"I have pins and needles in my legs, and I can't feel my feet," Romy finished in a resigned voice. "I can move my legs, but my thighs are numb to the touch,"

The doctor nodded. "Nerve damage. It's not something the movies and TV shows ever mention in a traumatic injury."

"Worst case?"

"It might never get better."

Romy blew out a long breath. "I'm avoiding the hysterectomy thing. I don't want to think about that just yet." Her voice broke at the end of her sentence, and she looked away, out of the window. "Doc, the police?"

"They'll want to talk to you, but not today."

"I don't mind."

"I do. You're just coming out of a coma, Romy."

She gave him an exhausted smile. "Been there before."

"I know." He sighed. "And I'm sorry you're back here again, but I'm very glad you decided to stay with us."

Romy chewed her lip. "Dr. Ramos, can you tell me how Milo is? In a way, he's got it worse than me. I can get morphine for physical pain."

"And he's getting treatment for his mental health." Ramos smiled at her. "And he asks about you all the time, but he's determined to get strong so he can be there for you. It's a delicate balancing act for both of you."

"Doc?"

"Yes?"

"Would you give him a message for me?"

Ramos hesitated, but then nodded. "Would you tell him that I love him, and I'll be right here waiting when he's ready? That he should..." Her voice broke, and a tear dropped down her cheek. "I want to hold him so badly, but I get it, I want him to get the help he needs. How he hasn't broken down before is incredible." She took a shaky breath in and tried to smile at the doctor.

Ramos patted her hand. "Look, of course. And I'll talk to my colleagues in psych. Maybe we can work something out. But for now, I want you to rest, and I mean *rest*. I'm ready and willing to pop you back into that coma if you do too much."

He grinned to show he was kidding, and Romy laughed, wincing as the movement pulled on her wounds. "I promise."

"I'll send your brothers back in, but I don't want them to stay too late, okay?"

"Sure. Thanks, doc. For saving my life."

He chuckled. "Well. I like a challenge." His smile faded. "I've seen horrific injuries before, Romy, but never, in my life, that level of violence. I hope I never see it again."

"Me too, doc."

Jae and Moon, both of whom looked absolutely drained, stayed until Romy insisted they go home and get some rest. They were loathed to go but relented eventually.

Romy lay back against the pillows and closed her eyes. Fatigue took over, and she fell into an uneasy sleep, filled with shards of memories, pain, fear, and terror. Worse, when the fog cleared and she relived the stabbing, her subconscious made her would-be killer have the faces of those she loved: Jae, Moon, Harper... Milo.

She didn't know she was whimpering in her sleep until she felt a cool hand on her forehead and a familiar voice.

"It's okay, Ro, take it easy. Hey, Harper, I think she's waking up."

Romy felt her skin wash with sweat, and her wounds throbbed with pain as she opened her eyes to see Nico Fleming smiling down at her.

THIRTY-FIVE

MILO KEPT RELIVING THE moment when the doctor told him, "She's awake. She's getting strong."

He savored the words, rolling them around his mouth when he was alone. *She's going to be okay.* Of course, he had wanted to go see her right away, and he was grateful that Dr. Ramos argued his case, but his psychiatrist was adamant.

"A couple more days, Milo. Romy needs to rest, and you need to complete these six sessions. You're doing so well, and I know you'll want to be at your strongest for Romy."

He couldn't argue with that. They, at least, let him write her a note.

> *My lovely Romy,*
>
> *I'm so sorry, I miss you and I love you. I will be with you soon, and we will get through this together, I promise. I hate that I wasn't strong enough for you. Please forgive me.*
>
> *Always yours,*
> *Milo.*

She'd sent a note back right away.

My darling Milo,

There's nothing to forgive. We are already together—the rest is geography.

I love you with all my heart,
Romy.

He kept her note in his shirt pocket, next to his heart. He'd had visitors. Harper came almost every day. She had been taking care of Sailor and liaising with the police at the gallery for them. Nico and Farron Lee stopped by, and, of course, Moon, relaying messages back and forth between Romy and himself. Only Jae didn't come, but Moon told Milo not to worry about it.

"He knows it's not your fault, but he needs someone to blame for this."

"It's okay, Moon, I'm pissed at myself, too."

The last session with the psychiatrist was this afternoon, and then, tomorrow, he would be discharged. Milo was annoyed at himself that he hadn't attempted therapy before, when Sarah died. Maybe then he would be able to be with Romy when she needed him the most.

Jeez... he had messed up. But now that his mind was clearer, he was remembering what Eben had told him. He wasn't Sarah's biological father. Milo held onto that, the only thing he could find that they didn't know. If Sarah's biological father had something to hide... but what did that have to do with the Parks?

He gave a hiss of frustration. He needed to talk to Penelope, get the truth of Sarah's parentage from her. There was a knock at the door and he turned, his eyes widening in surprise when he saw Keith Van Warren at the entryway.

"Hey... Keith, what are you doing here?"

Keith looked uneasy. "Harper tells me you've been going through a hard time. Your girl, Romy, is she doing okay?"

"Yes, she's getting stronger, thanks."

"Terrible thing."

Milo nodded. "Keith...?"

"Penny Ingles came to see me. She's... a little scared."

"Of what?"

Keith nodded to a chair. "May I sit?"

"Of course."

When they were seated opposite each other, Keith held Milo's gaze steadily. "She's scared of you, Milo. Because of what Eben told you."

There was a long silence as Milo processed what wasn't being said. "You're Sarah's father."

"Yes. And as proud of her as I was, I'd rather people not find out. Especially my wife."

Milo sighed. "Keith, I'm not going to tell any secrets unless it means protecting Romy. I already failed her. I just don't get why anyone would want to hurt her. Keith, tell me you had nothing to do with Sarah's death."

"Of course not... God, Milo. I may be an unfaithful husband, but I'm no killer. I was devastated, and worse, I wasn't allowed to express it."

"Did Sarah know you were her father?"

"I don't think so."

Milo was quiet for a while. "Do you think... maybe she found out, told your wife? Maybe someone connected..."

"My wife isn't the most sensitive person, but she would never hurt anyone. No one in my family would. And it wasn't as if Sarah was any threat to her or my children."

"Does Harper know?"

"No one knows except Penny and I, and now you. I'd like it to stay that way."

"As long as it doesn't impact Romy's safety, it will." Milo sighed. "I'm just trying to figure out the connection."

"What if it isn't the same killer?"

"I just don't know what the hell is going on, Keith, but I'm damn determined to find out."

The psychiatrist, Emily Harris, sat back and smiled at him. "You're done."

"All cured? That was easy."

She laughed at him. "If only, huh? You know as well as I do that this is just the beginning, but it's a solid foundation, Milo. What comes next is up to you."

"All I care about is being the best person I can be for Romy."

Emily shook her head. "Be the best person for you, Milo—the rest will follow naturally." She got up and shook his hand. "Listen, you have my number, but I suggest you find someone private. I can give you some names. Build a relationship with a therapist. These things take time."

"But I can see Romy now, right?"

Emily laughed. "If she's ready to see you, yes. Try not to get too emotional."

"Yeah, I'll give that a try."

Emily grinned and scribbled on her prescription pad. "Mild antidepressants. We'll keep you on them for a few months while you process things. I'll see you in a month, Milo, but do find a good therapist."

"I promise."

Milo felt strangely nervous as he walked slowly down the hallway to Romy's room. He texted Moon to see if Romy was ready to see him—he felt like a pussy for avoiding Jae—and Moon texted him back.

Ro says to get your sweet ass to her room. Stat!

Milo grinned. Thank god for Moon—the gentle boy was the perfect go-between. Milo knocked at the door.

"Come in."

Just hearing her sweet voice made his pulse quicken. He pushed open the door and stepped in. Romy was sitting up, her long dark hair clouding around her shoulders, her lovely face pale and tired but more beautiful than he had ever seen her. Milo had wanted to play it cool and calm, but the second he saw her and she held out her arms to him, he went to her, wrapping his arms around her.

"Oh, god, Romy…"

They held each other for the longest time before Milo pressed his lips to hers and kissed her until they had to break away for oxygen. He leaned his forehead against hers.

"I'm so sorry, my love, I'm so, so sorry."

"It wasn't your fault. None of it. If there's something good to come out of this, it's that you're finally dealing with Sarah's death."

"Not just that. When I saw you in recovery, you didn't look like you. I couldn't believe you would make it." He sighed heavily and sat back in the chair by the bed, taking her hands. He couldn't stop staring at her. Yes, she looked sick and in pain, but she was here, alive and getting stronger. Romy smiled at him, reading his mind.

"I'm not going anywhere, baby. At this point, I'm pretty much invincible." She laughed, then winced as the movement pulled on her belly. Milo laid his hand gently over her abdomen.

"What did the doctors say?"

Romy's smile faded. "Mostly good news. No damage to my liver or kidneys. They repaired what they could." She bit her lip. "But... Milo, they had to remove my uterus. I can't carry your child."

Milo could tell she was on the verge of tears, and he lifted her hands to his lips and kissed them. "Darling, there are thousands of kids who need loving homes. Doesn't matter if they don't share our DNA. When we're ready, we have options. All I care about right now is that you heal."

Romy nodded, but there were tears in her eyes and carefully, Milo sat next to her and held her as she cried quietly. Eventually, she looked up, wiping her eyes.

"Sorry, hormones. I'm essentially in menopause right now."

"Hot."

"Literally." She chuckled as he grinned at her. "Still, as you say, I'm here, I'm alive."

She shifted in the bed, her face wracked with pain, and Milo sat back down in the chair to give her some space. Romy settled herself and then looked at him.

"So... has Det. Halsey talked to you?"

Milo nodded. "His team have gone over every inch of the gallery. They found the letters you were looking at before. Halsey says they're testing them for fingerprints and DNA. It should give us another lead."

"I talked to Farron."

"Was it him?"

Romy shook her head. "No, he said although he adored my mom, he would never have intruded on her and my dad's marriage. I believe him. But he did bring me something interesting."

She reached out towards her purse on the nightstand but groaned. "Ow."

"Ro, just ask for help." Milo grinned, handing her the purse. "I can see what it's going to be like, trying to stop you from doing too much."

Romy stuck her tongue out at him, and he laughed. It sounded strange to his ears—there was a time very recently that he had thought he would never even smile again.

But despite everything... they had *this*. *Them*. Their relationship, their laughter, their teasing. No psychopath's knife could take that away from them, and he felt absurdly proud.

Romy rummaged in her purse, then pulled out a photograph. "Farron debated showing me this because, well, obviously, it was taken at my parents' funeral. But he thought seeing who the mourners were might help." She handed the photograph to Milo. "Obviously, I don't know who most of these people are, except Connor and Harper, of course."

Milo leaned in. "That's Harper's mother and father. Her younger brother Simon... I think he was about fourteen at the time. Huh."

"What?"

"That guy, the one behind Simon. Pretty sure that's Nico. I didn't know he knew your parents."

Romy squinted at the photo. "It *is* him. He did mention knowing of them, at least. He used to go to the bookstore. Who's the older guy?"

"Quintin, Nico's dad. His mother died a few years before."

"I don't know him. Who's that woman there?"

Milo sighed. "That's Penny Ingles. Sarah's mom." He argued with himself for a moment, then decided he didn't want to hide anything from her. "Sarah's dad is there, too."

Romy looked around the remaining mourners, but then Milo pointed to Keith Van Warren and Romy's eyes widened. "*No.*"

"Yep."

"Sarah and Harper were half-sisters? Oh, Milo… I bet Harper will want to know."

Milo shook his head. "I promised Keith that unless it impacted our case, I'd keep his secret. I think he's been unhappy in his marriage right from the start. I've heard rumors before of his wandering eye."

"Can't keep it in his pants?"

"Nope. But it's that old cliché… if I was married to Harper's mom…"

Romy grimaced. "Harper's mentioned she and her mother don't see eye to eye much."

"I honestly can't believe she gave birth to Harper. She favors Simon, always has." Milo pondered for a moment. "There's someone we haven't considered in all this."

"Who?"

"Connor's mother. The social climber of social climbers. She's still in a world of pain over Connor's death, and from what I hear, she blames Harper, she blames you… everyone but herself."

Romy rolled her eyes. "She never liked me, thought I wasn't good enough for her son. I used to think it was because I was biracial, but then I realized it was because my family weren't Van Warrens." She looked at the photograph again. "I notice she wasn't there. It was good of Connor to go."

"If you say so. Did he visit you in the hospital?"

Romy frowned, trying to remember. "I'm not sure. Grandmother was pretty fierce about who she let in to see me." She sighed in frustration. "None of this is getting us anywhere."

"I have a private detective looking into the other victims in the crash. Maybe someone wants revenge, you know. The killer was after you, and the other victims were collateral, and they want payback on someone."

Romy nodded slowly. "Maybe. But that doesn't explain Sarah."

"No."

Romy tapped the photo. "I wonder why Nico never mentioned he was at the funeral. He's coming to visit this afternoon." She hesitated as Milo raised his eyebrows. "That's okay, right?"

"Of course, it is. He's been a real friend in all this."

Romy nodded, and Milo leaned in to kiss her. "You need to get some rest, sweetheart. Enough detective work for today."

"We didn't get very far."

He leaned his forehead against hers. "There's time."

THIRTY-SIX

BUT AFTER ROMY HAD fallen asleep, Milo went to call his investigator. "Another lead... would you look into Quintin Fleming?" He gave the detective Quintin's details and his connection to Nico and to Sarah. It bugged him as to why Quintin had been at Romy's parents' funeral when there seemed no connection. Nico had never mentioned he had been there, nor that he had known Romy's family. Milo liked and trusted the other man, but his father was a different prospect.

For one thing, Quintin had been a senior partner at Sarah's architectural firm before he was 'retired' due to personal reasons. Sarah had told Milo all about it—Quintin had been awarding contracts to businesses from which he received kickbacks. The partners at the firm had been very kind under the circumstances and allowed Quintin to retire, but gossip spread quickly, and the truth came out.

Quintin had kept to himself after that, humiliated and angry. Milo had seen him around town occasionally. Nico had built up his business quietly and efficiently, and many people didn't even connect the two when they hired Nico to remodel their properties.

Not surprising, Milo thought now. Nico was a wildly different person to his father. Milo remembered Nico's mother vaguely, but he hadn't know her at all.

Yeah, Nico was the antithesis of his father... but there was one thing Milo had noticed and, god help him, he was bothered by it.

Nico was crazy about Romy.

He kept it hidden, and he was always respectful of her and Milo's relationship, but Milo knew love when he saw it. Milo wasn't a jealous person, but he was torn with feeling bothered by Nico's attentions to Romy and being grateful that she had another ally.

So, he said nothing. He trusted Nico not to overstep the mark, but he hoped Nico's crush would subside over time. It was a complication they didn't need.

Leaving Romy asleep, he went down to the cafeteria to grab some coffee. It was late, and he felt drained, the exhilaration of earlier slipping away. Now that he knew Romy would be okay—relatively speaking—he knew they had to face whoever was targeting her. The horror Milo felt was for the fact that they might never know, that their future together would be blighted forever by someone who wished to cause Romy harm.

His cell phone buzzed. A message from Harper.

How is she? How was the reunion?

Milo called Harper back and updated her. Harper let out a long breath.

"That's good news. Holy crap, Milo, doesn't it feel like things are spiraling out of control?"

Milo gave a humorless laugh. "And I am at a loss for how to stop it."

"Jim Halsey's been around, talking to my dad. Do you know what that's about? Dad won't tell me."

"I really don't." Milo frowned. "I can't see how this is related to Romy."

"Yeah, me neither. Everything's all fucked up."

Milo was surprised to hear Harper so down. "What is it, love?"

She sighed. "I don't know. Just… I'm sick of all the violence. Sarah, Romy… Connor. What the hell is wrong with this world, Milo?" Milo was shocked to hear her start to cry.

"Oh, sweetheart, I know."

"It's just… I know he was an asshole of a person, I do, but everyone seems to have forgotten about Connor in all of this. He was my husband for a long time, and there were good times, too, and I…" She choked off. "Sorry, I know this isn't the time or the place. Just… what happened to Romy brought it all back."

"Are you okay? Do you want me to come over?"

"No, you should stay with Romy. I'll be okay. Sailor's being good company." She sniffed and chuckled softly. "Sorry, Milo. I didn't mean to freak out on you… hang on, someone's at the door."

Milo waited a few beats before Harper came back on the line. "Sorry, it was Dad. He likes to walk Sailor in the evening."

They chatted for a few more moments, Harper assuring Milo she was okay, and then they said goodbye. Milo went back up to Romy's room and sat in the chair next to her bed as she slept. He leaned his head on the bed, tucking her hand under his cheek, wanting to feel close to her. He couldn't shake the feeling that all of this was far from over, that Romy was still in terrible danger, but eventually, in the early hours, he fell into a fitful, nightmare-filled sleep.

In the morning, both he and Romy woke up to the news that Keith Van Warren was dead.

Milo wrapped his arms around Harper and held her tightly. She was trembling violently.

"God, Harper, I'm so sorry."

"Why is all of this happening?"

Milo could hear Esther Van Warren's high-pitched voice from the other end of the house. Harper wiped her eyes. "She's playing the devastated widow, but really she's counting all the money that's now hers." She sniffed and smiled ruefully at Milo. "Sorry, excuse my bitchiness."

"It's understandable. Harper... what happened?"

The news said that Keith had been found on the beach where he'd taken Sailor to walk. The dog had been sitting dutifully by Keith's body, barking for attention until another dog walker found Keith's body.

"They think heart attack, but there's an autopsy this afternoon."

Sailor nudged Milo's hand, then rubbed his head along Harper's knee. She chuckled through her tears. "Thank you, buddy. Thank you for staying with my dad." She leaned down and hugged Sailor to her, kissing the top of his furry head.

Milo kept an arm around his friend. "Look, anything you need, I mean it. If you need to get some space, you can come stay with us. Well, just me, really. Romy argued like hell with the doctors to let her come see you, but they wouldn't let her."

Harper rolled her eyes. "Good. Jeez, will that girl just let herself get better?"

"She hates being there. She says it gives her nightmares, reliving the accident and the aftermath. She's itching to get out, but she's still too sick. Her wounds are healing, but any strain and she could open them up, get an infection."

Harper waved her hand. "Tell her I'm ordering her to stay in bed. This thing with my dad... we'll get through it. It's just... I was unprepared."

"How do you get prepared to lose someone you love? Give yourself time."

Harper nodded, looking exhausted. "I know. Look, I have to deal with my mother, but you don't have to. Go back to Romy. Tell her I love her, and I'll come see her when I can."

Romy was antsy and frustrated. Her wounds were bothering her, but what was worse was the numbness and pins ands needles in her legs. The doctor had reassured her she would be able to move around, but that she might never get the feeling back in certain parts of her body.

And… she would never be pregnant now. The pain of that realization had slowly turned to anger and resentment, and the doctors were worried about her stress levels. "It won't help your recovery," they had repeatedly told her.

Yeah, no shit. Romy sighed and pressed the button for the nurse.

"What's up, honey?"

"Can I shower? I feel so gross."

The nurse helped her in the shower, and Romy discovered just how weak she was, having to cling onto the other woman, trying not to get her dressings wet. Her core muscles had been so badly damaged by the knife that she had trouble standing, and, in the end, the nurse had to sit her down to help her shower.

But being clean made her feel a million times better. She ate nearly all of her supper, and with a shot of morphine, Romy decided she finally felt human again. Jae and Moon were due to come see her in a few hours, and Milo was coming back to spend the night again, although she had urged him to get some rest himself.

Romy had no idea when she fell asleep, but when she woke, the hospital seemed unnaturally quiet. She checked the clock.

Six p.m.—Jae and Moon would be here in an hour. Romy shifted uncomfortably in the bed and pressed the call button.

No one came. Romy frowned. That was unlike this place— the staff were incredible and super-attentive to all their patients. *Maybe there was a crisis with another patient*, Romy thought, and laid back, closing her eyes. She felt herself slipping back into sleep again.

Then she had the sensation that she couldn't breathe, like something was being pressed down over her face. Romy panicked, her lungs feeling like they would explode, and she struggled against the pillow being rammed down over her face. Agony ripped through her body as she bucked and writhed to get away from the constricting grip, and she felt herself sinking, sinking…

A hand was tangled in her hair, and as the pillow was removed, she was dragged out of the bed. Romy fell to the hard floor with a thump, her eyes streaming, gasping for the precious oxygen that filled her lungs.

Even through the searing pain and the need for air, Romy tried to see who her attacker was, but as darkness gathered in her vision, all she saw was the attacker's legs retreating from the room as the machinery monitoring her vitals went crazy. She heard shouts and people approaching.

The last thing she heard before she passed out was one of the nurses gasping and her doctor shouting.

"She's bleeding out… she's bleeding out."

THIRTY-SEVEN

MILO HAD FINALLY HAD enough. "Where was her protection? Where was Romy's care?"

The doctor let him get his frustration out before raising his hands. "I hear you, Mr. Keys, but there's a limit to what we can do. Our security cameras were disabled, her call button was vandalized, and whoever wanted to hurt Miss Park created a diversion. We dropped the ball, no doubt, and I sincerely apologize."

Milo struggled to keep his temper, but he knew it wasn't this man's fault. It was down to him. He should have hired private security, or the police should have done more. Romy was the victim of now of three separate murder attempts. The simple fact that she was still alive was a miracle.

They'd had to operate again, stem the bleeding from her reopened wounds, but she'd pulled through. What was troubling was that since she had regained consciousness, she had been almost catatonic.

"It's the shock. Her brain is shutting down so her body can heal. She'll get there."

But it was disturbing to see his love so silent, so dead behind the eyes. Her spirit had been crushed, Milo knew, by this further assault, and he was in agreement with Jae and Moon that they needed to rally around Romy even more now. Jae and Moon had taken a sabbatical from Berkeley and were staying at the mansion, looking after Sailor. Milo had hired protection for them, as well as for Farron, who had kindly offered to look after Romy's gallery for her.

And then there was Keith Van Warren's funeral. Milo went to support Harper, and she was grateful to him, but strangely distant. Esther Van Warren garnered all the attention, but Milo had the sense that Harper just wanted to disappear. The local press was there, and Harper slid out of view as Esther played to them.

At the wake, Milo found Harper outside in the lush gardens of the Van Warren estate. She smiled at him wanly.

"What a circus."

Milo hugged her. "It's almost over."

"Is it?" She laughed harshly. "It doesn't feel like any of it is over. It just keeps getting worse."

She leaned her head against his shoulder. "Thank you for coming, though, Milo. With you here, I feel like I can deal with anything."

Milo kissed her temple. "Always, honey. You're my family, you know?"

She looked up at him, sadness in her eyes. "Sometimes I wonder if you hadn't met Romy, whether we missed a chance for *us*... no, sorry. That's inappropriate. You and I were never in the cards." She held up her glass of champagne. "I'm rambling, and I'm drunk. Forgive me, Milo. It's been a difficult few days."

"It's okay, honey." Milo didn't take her confession seriously. He'd wondered, too, before he had met Romy and fallen so deeply in love, whether he and Harper would make a good couple. It was just that the physical attraction had never been there, as beautiful as Harper was.

Harper stared into the garden. "They sealed the records of the autopsy. Mom's request. And the Van Warren money goes further than you think. She wouldn't tell me the results."

"I thought it was a heart attack."

"That's the official line. Forgive me, but given what's been happening…"

"It *was* a heart attack."

They turned to see Nico Fleming behind them. Milo was surprised; he hadn't seen Nico at the funeral. Nico nodded at him, then smiled kindly at Harper. "You know it was, Harper, come on. Don't do this to yourself."

He looked at Milo. "How's Romy?"

"Getting there. She's desperate to get out of the hospital."

Nico nodded, sitting down next to them. "Can't say I blame her. Look, the police have finished up at the gallery, and I thought I might go through it, really ramp up the security." He sighed, running a hand through his hair. "I blame myself. I thought we had it covered, that the place was locked up tight. How the hell he got in—"

"If it was a *he*." Harper shook her head. "We're assuming an awful lot here."

Milo frowned. "What do you mean?"

Harper's mouth set in a grim line. "Connor's mother. She's an active, fit woman. She rides horses, does cardio five days a week. And she has motive."

"Did you tell this to Halsey?"

Harper nodded. "I did. He seemed to take it seriously. After all, she's looking for someone to blame for Connor's death, even if his killer is unknown."

"Which means she might come after you as well."

Harper looked at him. "I can deal with that bitch. I did it my whole marriage."

Milo looked unhappily at Nico. "And what about you?"

"What about me?"

"How are you involved in all of this? I didn't even know you two knew each other that well."

Nico chuckled. "We've been spending some time together at the gallery. I thought maybe Harper could do with some protection. Like you said, Connor's mom is a vindictive bitch."

Milo sighed, smiled wanly. "Seems you're more a bodyguard these days."

"I didn't do so good protecting Romy, did I? I have a lot of making up to do. Hell, I'm just a contractor, Milo, but I should have thought about the crawlspaces in the apartment upstairs. I never thought someone could break in and hide in them."

"Who would?" Milo scratched his head. "What I can't figure out is how they got up there."

"And that's down to me, too."

Milo shook his head. "The only person at fault here is the psychopath who stabbed Romy. That's it. And, with or without the police's help, I'm going to find him or her and make them pay." He looked at his two friends. "You with me?"

"You know we are." Harper kissed his cheek, and Nico nodded.

"Damn right."

And for the first time in weeks, Milo felt some hope.

THIRTY-EIGHT

ROMY'S EYES LIT UP as Doctor Ramos came into the room and laughed at her.

"Today, doc?" She'd been asking the same question for days, itching to get out of bed and go home. She missed her things. She missed Sailor. She missed waking up next to Milo.

Her wounds were healing again, and since the second murder attempt, security had been ramped up, both at the hospital and with the private team Milo had hired.

But she wanted desperately to go home. She looked at Ramos hopefully.

"Please, doc? I've been *really* well behaved. I walked three times around the floor this morning, my bodily functions are regular..." She trailed off, grimacing. "Ugh, I hate that that phrase has become so normal to me."

Ramos laughed. "Well... okay then. With all the warning I can muster for you to take things easy, you can go home. I assume Milo will be there to take care of you?"

Elated, Romy nodded. "You're really discharging me?"

Ramos sat on her bed. "Your recovery, albeit with the... setback... has been remarkable."

"Told you I was immortal."

"Ha. Well, I mean it when I say to take it easy. Even when the wounds are scarring over, you can still damage them if you do too much. So, no work."

"Sure."

"Romy."

"I promise," she chuckled at the skepticism on Ramos's face. "I have a friend looking after the gallery, and I can always keep in touch via the internet."

"Rest." Ramos shook his head, laughing. "Just keep saying that word to yourself."

Romy called Milo with the news, and he was delighted. "I'll be right there, darling," he said on the phone.

Romy moved slowly around her room, using a stick when she needed to, but otherwise her adrenalin kept her going as she packed her stuff. While she waited for Milo, she went to thank the staff that had looked after her so well. Then she went back to her room to rest.

As she walked into the room, there was an orderly standing at the window, but when she turned around, Romy drew in a breath.

Wendy Small. Connor's mother. The older woman smiled, but there was no friendliness in the expression.

"Hello, Romy. I think it's time we talked."

Milo saw the security guard outside Romy's room looking uncomfortable as he approached. The man—Jeff—stood when he saw Milo.

"Mr. Keys, I was with Miss Romy earlier, we were walking around and when we got back to the room, she was there. Miss Romy said it was okay, but—"

Milo looked past him into the room, and his heart went cold as he saw Wendy Small talking to Romy.

"What the fuck?"

He pushed past Jeff, whose mouth flapped ineffectually, but Milo ignored him. He opened the door, his gaze fixed on the older woman.

"What the fuck are you doing here? Get out, before I have you arrested."

"Milo, it's okay."

"No, it *fucking* isn't. You realize she's a suspect, right?"

Wendy lifted her chin. "Yes, I am. I know you think I have the motive, and the desire for revenge. I can assure you about the latter… but it's not true."

Milo moved between Wendy and Romy, ignoring Romy's hand on his back. "The police will have questions about that, I'm sure."

"Please, feel free to call them. I'm happy to talk to them."

"Why are you here?" Milo's anger was a roiling under the surface, threatening to burst out.

"Wendy came to see me to tell me she was sorry."

Milo laughed without humor. "For what?"

"For telling my son to marry Harper Van Warren back then. For my insisting on it." Wendy sighed, suddenly looking much older than her fifty-seven years. "I was an idiot, a greedy idiot. I didn't know the viper's nest I was sending my son into."

Romy stepped around Milo, ducking the arm he put to stop her.

"It's okay, Wendy. With respect, I think you did me a favor. But you're wrong about the Van Warrens, Harper especially. She was devastated when Connor was killed."

Wendy snorted. "Only because it might ruin that perfect image she likes to put out to the world."

Romy sighed, but Milo stared at the other woman. "Harper is one of the best people I know. This attempt at... whatever it is you're doing, won't work, Wendy. Now... please leave."

Wendy nodded. "Fine. As she passed, she looked at Romy again. "Don't trust them. Don't trust any of them."

As soon as they were alone, Milo raised his eyebrow at Romy. "Well?"

"I gave her time to say what she wanted. Doesn't mean to say I believed her entirely, but I appreciated her apology."

"You realize she could have hurt you? That she may well be the person who attacked you?"

Romy shook her head. "My gut says no. It was a man, I'm absolutely sure."

"What makes you say that?"

"Because of how he hurt me. He got off on it. I would think a revenge kill would have been swifter, final. He *enjoyed* stabbing me." Romy shivered, then grinned sheepishly. "I've been watching a lot of true crime shows while I've been in here."

Milo made a mental note to remove the television set from their bedroom. For now, he drew in a deep breath. He was taking her home. That was all that mattered right now. He drew her close and wrapped his arms around her, burying his face in her hair.

"I love you so god damn much, Romy. I'm so glad you're coming home to us." He tipped her chin up so he could kiss her. His lips moved slowly over hers. "God, I missed you."

"You keep talking like that, I'm going to have to break all my promises to Dr. Ramos not to overexert myself." Romy chuckled, and Milo smiled. "And despite how much I want you, I don't think sex will be on the menu for a while."

"You and I were never just about sex."

"Great sex."

Milo grinned, relaxing. "Of course. But there's so much more to us."

"I agree. For one thing," Romy said while raising an eyebrow at him, "there's the dog."

"Sailor is desperate to see you. Come on, let's go home."

In the car, Romy opened her window and breathed in the ocean air as Milo drove along the coastal road to Big Sur. Although the movement of the car jostled her sore body, the fresh air streaming through her hair made her feel clean again for the first time in weeks.

She reached over and put her hand on Milo's hard thigh, and he looked over at her, smiling.

"Hey," he said.

"Hey. You seem deep in thought."

"Just trying to figure out stuff."

Romy nodded. "Maybe we should just step back, leave it to the police."

"We were doing that, and then this happened." He slid his hand gently onto her belly. "I just get the feeling this is going to get worse before it's over. I'm scared for you."

"Didn't you hear? I'm invincible." But Romy could tell her lover was troubled. "What we're not going to do is let it stress us the fuck out so much that we can't enjoy being together. Especially tonight."

Milo smiled at her. "You're right, of course."

At home, Milo had to hold Sailor back as the excited dog tried to leap up at Romy. "Gentle, boy, gentle."

When they finally managed to calm him down, Romy hugged the dog tightly as he covered her face with kisses. "I love you, too, boy. I've missed you so much."

Milo took her case up to their room, and when he came down, Romy had already set up camp on the couch. She grinned at him.

"I know you want me to rest, but there's no way I'm getting into that bed until tonight." She patted the couch next to her. "Come sit with me."

"My pleasure."

They spent a lazy afternoon talking and watching movies, and later, when Romy fell asleep, Milo covered her with a comforter and went to grab Sailor's leash. The dog seemed reluctant to leave Romy's side, which made Milo's heart pound with love, but he knew he had to walk Sailor now, since he wouldn't want to do it later. Milo left a note for Romy along with a fresh bottle of water and an apple on the table in front of the couch. Leaning down, he kissed her cheek. "I'll be right back, baby. I love you."

Outside, he nodded to the security guard sitting in his car in the driveway. "I'm just going to walk the dog on the beach. I've left Miss Park inside, asleep. You hear anything, you go in, understand?"

"Yes, sir, of course."

Once down on the beach, Sailor perked up, bounding along the shoreline, ducking in and out of the waves. In late January, the water was cold, the breeze picking up spray, and Milo winced as the icy salt water dusted his skin.

It wasn't until he turned back for home that he saw him. A lone figure sitting at the edge of the cliffs, watching the house. As Milo got closer, he saw who it was. Quintin Fleming. Nico's father.

"Quint?"

Quintin turned and saw Milo, his expression changing from confusion to recognition.

"Hey... hey, Milo. Good to see you."

Quintin bore little resemblance to his son. Thinning sandy blonde hair and dark brown eyes, Quintin's eyes were rimmed with red—exhaustion, Milo guessed. Quintin was a staunch teetotaler and a devout Christian, but there had always been something about the man Milo never liked. He realized he thought of the other man as weak, perhaps unfairly so.

"What are you doing here, Quint? Looking for me?"

Somehow he knew he wasn't. "No, I... I wanted to come pay my respects. To Giovanna's daughter. My boy told me to stay away, but I heard what happened—well, who didn't?—and I wanted to come see if there was anything..." Quintin trailed off, and he sighed. "Hell, Milo. Giovanna was always kind to me. Terrible what happened to them. I... just wanted to meet her daughter."

Milo was silent for a moment. "Quint..."

"I know I shouldn't just show up here. I guess I thought there would be less chance of her saying no." He broke off again, shaking his head. "I know, that's real manipulative of me, but..."

"Give me a few minutes. I'll ask Romy, Quint, but if she says no, that's an end to it, and you don't come around again without permission. Agreed?"

There was a light of hope in Quintin's eyes, and he nodded. "Of course."

"Okay... wait here."

Milo patted Quintin's arm, but as he passed by the security guard inside the gate, he nodded back at Quintin. "Keep an eye out. I'll be right back."

Inside, he told Romy that Quintin was waiting. Romy nodded at him. "Of course he can come in, I'd like to meet him."

"You sure?"

Romy laughed. "Of course, he's Nico's dad."

247

Milo nodded and turned to go back outside. At the door, he paused, looked at her. "Romy... don't expect Nico 2.0. They're very different people."

Romy frowned. "You don't like Quintin?"

"It's not that, it's just...ah, nothing. Make up your own mind—I trust your judgement."

She nodded. "That's a nice thing to hear, thank you."

Milo beckoned Quintin in, and the older man followed him to where Romy was waiting. Milo watched as Quintin saw her for the first time. The color drained from Quintin's face as he looked at Romy. She was leaning on her stick as she waited for him to say hello, and her eyes flicked to Milo's, confusion in them as Quintin just stared at her. Eventually she held out her hand.

"Hi, Quintin. It's good to meet you."

Quintin stepped towards her, then seemed to stumble and fall to his knees in front of her. He began to sob as Romy and Milo rocked back in surprise.

As he heard Quint choke out the words, "Oh, Vanna... Vanna..." Milo shared a glance with Romy, realizing they both now knew exactly who had sent the love letters to Romy's mother, the letters she had found on the night she was attacked and stabbed.

As he watched, Milo saw Romy gently bend down and put her hand on Quintin's shoulder to comfort him as he sobbed his heart out for his lost love.

THIRTY-NINE

MILO CALLED QUINTIN A cab, and Romy hugged the older man tightly before he left. When the cab had pulled away, Romy's body sagged, and Milo helped her back to the couch.

"Do you want some painkillers, my love?"

He brought her some aspirin—Romy was refusing anything stronger—and a hot pad for her belly.

"All I want is you," Romy told him, and he sat next to her, cradling her in his arms as they both silently processed the conversation with Quintin.

After he'd calmed himself, Quintin had sat down with them, gratefully accepting the glass of scotch Milo offered him.

"I'm sorry, Romy, I didn't know I would do that." His hands were trembling.

Romy smiled at him kindly. "It's really okay." She exchanged a glance with Milo. "You loved her, then?"

Quintin nodded. "I want you to know I never made any moves on your mother. I had too much respect for Jin… he was a wonderful man."

Romy looked at Milo. "Milo, could you get the…?"

"Sure."

Quintin looked confused, and when Romy handed him the letters she had found at the gallery, he smiled. "Ah, the ramblings of a lovestruck fool." He read a couple. "Lord, it was a different time. I would never write this now, hell, I would never send this now. The world has moved on, I know, and these seem... ugh... I sound like a creep."

Romy felt her face redden, remembering she'd thought the same thing when she'd found the letters. "Like you say, it was a different time."

"I'm sorry, Romy. God, what you must think of me... wait." He held up the letter she had found last. "This wasn't from me. I did not write this one." Quintin read through it with confusion as Romy felt a jolt. "Jesus... who would write this?"

Milo took the letter gently from him and read it. "Quint, I have to say... it's typewritten, just like yours."

Quint nodded, then groaned. "Oh, darn it. *Caroline.*"

"Your wife?"

Quintin sighed. "It was my fault. I didn't exactly hide my love for Giovanna, did I?" He looked down at the note. "Nico would have been only a few years old, and Caroline wanted another baby. It wasn't happening. We tried, but we couldn't get pregnant again. We drifted apart." He sighed, shaking his head. "I'm sorry, Romy. What you must think of me..."

Now that Quintin was gone, Romy leaned against Milo.

"All of this is such a mess. And we're still no further on finding anything out."

She sighed heavily. Milo kissed her temple. "Baby, I think you need some sleep. Playing detective was not part of Dr. Ramos' instructions."

Romy grumbled, but by the time Milo had carried her

upstairs—much to her disgust—she could barely keep her eyes open. She was asleep by the time Milo left her side and went back downstairs.

Milo waited for a half hour to make sure Romy was asleep before he picked up his phone. The seed of an idea that had been brewing inside him since Quintin Fleming's visit was now fully in bloom, and his mouth set in a grim line as he called his private investigator.

When the man answered, Milo told him what he wanted. "And, listen, no expense spared. You need extra funds to find out that information, you call me straight away." His jaw flexed as he clenched his teeth. "I want you to find out everything you can about Nico Fleming... and who his real father was."

Harper came over later, and she and Milo prepared a meal for the three of them while Romy grumbled about being sidelined. Harper chuckled at her friend's sulky face.

"Lady, just get used to it. Enjoy being pampered."

They ate out on the balcony, Romy's hot flashes making her oblivious to the cold bite of the ocean air. Milo and Harper wore thick sweaters, but neither moaned about the cool air. They enjoyed their meal and went inside afterward.

Harper told them she was checking in at the gallery. "Farron is loving showing your work, Milo. You might have to share your gallery, Ro."

"I really want to go in, soon. Farron's gone way beyond just doing a favor now." Romy sipped her coffee before dumping another sugar cube in it, making Milo smile. She always hated strong coffee without sugar. "I would really like to do something for him... maybe we can talk about merging our galleries?"

"Wow, really?"

"I owe so much to so many of you." She looked at Milo.

"Maybe we could split your work between the galleries?" She looked at him hopefully, and he laughed, leaning over to kiss her.

"We have plenty of time to discuss our future, sweetheart."

Milo told Harper about Quintin Fleming. "He was in love with Romy's mother all that time. Do you remember Nico's mother?"

"Caroline? Yes, of course. She worked for my dad for a long time, just some secretarial work, before she got married. I think she was still friends with him and my mom. I mean she came to the house a lot. Nice woman."

"How did she die?"

"Cancer, I believe. She held off on getting a pap smear, and the next time she did, they found a tumor. It went very quickly after that." Harper's face creased a little with distress. "To be honest with you both, I think she might have hastened her end. She started drinking and taking Vicodin."

"Damn."

"I know. I think it's funny how I never really got to know Nico properly until this year, until you started working on the gallery. Shame, he's a good guy."

Romy noticed Milo was very quiet. "You okay?"

"Yeah, sure. Just tired."

Harper smiled at them both. "And that's my cue to go."

"Thank you for the meal, it was spectacular."

Harper leaned down to hug Romy. "You're welcome, darling,"

Milo walked Harper to her car. She nodded at the security guard sitting quietly in his vehicle.

"Must be weird."

"Surely the Van Warren estate has its own security?" Milo grinned down at her, and Harper laughed.

"I guess so. Bet Romy hates it, though."

"Anything to keep her safe. Until they catch the asshole who's doing this."

Harper sighed. "I know. The one thing that kept me going through my dad's passing was the knowledge that it was a natural death. Look, anything you need, just ask. You know that, right?"

"I do… and thank you. I would not have gotten through the last few years without you."

"Anytime." She looked over to the bodyguard. "If Romy needs a break from him, I can always come over and sit with her. I have a gun, and I know how to shoot."

"Like our very own Avenger."

"You know it. Night, Milo."

"Goodnight."

FORTY

HE WENT BACK UPSTAIRS and found Romy had already made her way to their bedroom. She winced a little as she sat on the edge of their bed and made a face at him.

"Don't be mad, I'm just a little tired of not being mobile."

Milo thought about remonstrating with her, then changed his mind. He knew how frustrated she was. "May I help you get changed at least?"

"Yes, please." Clearly the stair climbing had taken it out of her.

The dressings on her belly were smaller now, the bruises from the attack had faded to a dark yellow, and some of the smaller cuts had healed over, but the scar was still a vivid pink on her dusky skin.

She still had scars from the car accident, but they were on her hips and legs mostly and faded now, a dark greyish brown. *What this girl has been through in her life...* Milo felt a great sadness come over him.

"What's that face for, Keys?" Romy grinned, but her smile faded when she saw how serious he was. "What is it?"

He took her in his arms. "I just want to wrap you up in

cotton wool and never let anyone hurt you again." He kissed her, lingering over the embrace. "Have you got any idea how much I love you, Romy? More than my own life."

Romy's eyes filled with tears. "And I love you, Milo. So, so much."

They kissed again, and Romy gave a soft moan. "If only I could show you how much."

Milo chuckled softly. "I'm not risking your health, baby."

"Dang it." She slid her hand down to his crotch and cupped his cock through his jeans. "I could touch you... I could make you come, darling."

"That goes for both of us," Milo's voice was thick with desire. He stripped off quickly and they laid down carefully together.

Romy was trembling, and he frowned, but she grinned at him.

"Pure desire, I promise. It's been too long."

He chuckled. "It has, but I need you to swear that if you have pain or discomfort, you will tell me immediately."

"Don't you know orgasms are nature's most potent painkiller?"

"Romy."

"I promise, I promise. Now, damn well touch me, Keys, you're driving me crazy."

Milo smiled and kissed her lips, then moved down to her throat, then her breasts, taking each nipple into his mouth in turn and swirling the nub with his tongue until they were rock hard and sensitive.

Romy moaned and Milo looked up. "Don't stop," she whispered, "that's heavenly."

He grinned at her and dipped his head again, careful not to press down on her wounded abdomen as he stroked her body. His hand slipped between her legs and began to stroke, and Romy shivered, sighing happily.

"God, I missed this."

He made her come twice, and then Romy stroked his cock and massaged him until he too released his tension and came. Afterward they held each other, kissing slowly, enjoying every moment of their lovemaking.

Milo tucked a strand of her hair behind her ear. "Romy?"

"Yes, my love?"

"Through everything that has happened, the one thing I kept coming back to is that you and I are so right for each other that it seems almost comical."

Romy chuckled. "Right? I never thought I would fall in love so entirely. It's quite revolting how mushy I've become."

Milo laughed. "Listen… I actually have something to show you. You know I've been painting?"

"I do, Secret Squirrel. Does this mean you're finally going to let me see something?" Romy pressed her lips against his pec then grinned up at him.

"I think it's time. But I'm carrying you up the stairs to the attic."

Romy rolled her eyes. "If you insist."

Upstairs Milo set her down in the chair and brought out three canvases. The first one was of her in the doorway of the gallery, looking to the side, her dark hair tumbling around her shoulders. Milo had captured an expression of excitement in her eyes that made Romy's chest hurt.

"Oh, Milo."

The next canvas was of the front of the gallery itself, but somehow Milo had incorporated the essence of her parents' bookshop into the image so that it had a sense of now and then. The signage was Romy's, but the interior showed ghost images of bookshelves. Romy's eyes filled with tears.

"You know you're a damn genius, don't you?"

"I have the best muse." Milo's voice was quiet, and he brought out the third canvas, still covered in a dust sheet. "Why don't you unveil this one?"

Romy heard the emotion in his voice and slowly pulled the dust cover off. No image this time, but just a few simple words.

Romy chuckled through her tears as she read them aloud. "Romy Park, you are the love of my life... I want to spend the rest of my days with you, laughing, loving. Would you do me the honor of becoming my wife?"

She looked up at Milo, tears flooding down her cheeks as he dropped to his knees beside her chair and took her hands. His eyes were serious, full of love. "Will you?"

"Yes," she said without hesitation. "Yes, Milo, I will marry you."

She went into his arms, and he held her as they kissed tenderly. For some reason, Romy felt a peace descend on her, despite everything. If they were together, then nothing could tear them apart... could it?

She would find out sooner than either of them realized.

FORTY-ONE

MOON THREW HIS ARMS around both Milo and Romy when they told him and Jae the news.

"God, I damn well knew it! Didn't I say, Jae? I said they wouldn't wait to get married." He beamed at both of them, his beautiful face glowing. "I'm so happy for you guys. After everything, you deserve this."

Romy kissed Moon's cheek. "Thank you, darling." Her eyes slid to Jae and she could see the conflict in his eyes. He wanted her to be happy but he hadn't quite forgiven Milo for breaking down when Romy had needed him the most. Romy felt nervous. "Jae?"

"Are you happy, Ro?" His voice was quiet and steady, and Romy nodded, her eyes serious.

"Yes, Jae. More than anything."

"Then that's all I need to know." Jae put his arms around her, and they hugged for a long moment. "Congratulations, darling."

When they broke apart, Jae offered his hand to Milo, who smiled and shook it.

"Your blessing means everything, man."

"Just do right by her, is all I ask." Jae smiled then. "God, are you two going to be extra cheesy now?"

"Yep. Deal with it."

Harper was equally delighted when she came over to see Romy later that day, remarking, "Oh, loves, that's the best news!"

Romy had insisted on going to the gallery, and Milo had wanted as many people around her as possible—it wasn't just the risk of her overexerting herself, but also the psychological trauma of going back to the place where she had been stabbed.

Romy and Milo talked it over the night before.

"More good things happened in that building over the years, than bad." Romy said, determinedly, when Milo expressed doubts. "And it's my business. No stabby a-hole is going to scare me off."

"Don't joke."

"No, it's better to laugh about it. It helps."

And finally, he got it.

Still, Romy felt nervous as they drove into Monterey and onto her street. A jolt of adrenalin shot through her when she saw the gallery, but then, as they pulled up outside, the door opened and Farron Lee stepped out, smiling and waving. Romy felt her tension release.

"My dear." Farron kissed her cheek, and she smiled at him. "It's so wonderful to see you. How are you?"

They went inside, and Romy noticed that Farron hadn't changed the exhibit since the opening. She had almost expected him to put his own mark on the place, given his wealth of experience, but he had left it exactly how she had placed every painting.

He saw her surprise and smiled. "My dear, you should be proud. It takes years for a curator or a gallery owner to trust their own vision. You hit the jackpot right away."

Romy couldn't help but hug him. "You have been such a friend, Farron."

Romy insisted on going upstairs to where the attack happened. Jae and Moon had scrubbed the blood from the stairs and the floor above, but Romy noticed a new rug that had been put down to cover some of the stains they couldn't remove.

Her hands flexed with tension, but she took a deep breath in. This was her building, her legacy, and she wasn't about to allow her attacker to scare her away.

Milo put his hands on her shoulders. "Are you alright?"

"I'm fine, baby."

"Hello?" Harper's voice drifted up to them, and she appeared at the bottom of the stairs. "Hey, you guys."

"Come up, honey."

Harper hugged them both. "Listen, I have an idea, but tell me if I'm overstepping."

"Go for it."

"This may be fast, but I was wondering if Romy would like to go wedding dress shopping?" She looked between the two of them, her eyes hopeful. Romy grinned.

"Well, we haven't really discussed what kind of wedding…"

Both she and Milo laughed as Harper's face fell, and Romy glanced at Milo, who shrugged good-naturedly. "But I suppose…"

"Great. I know the exact right store for us to look, but it is in San Francisco." She looked at Milo.

"Hey. Ask Romy, I'm not her keeper."

Romy was suddenly excited at the thought of a day trip. "Are you sure you don't mind?"

Milo rolled his eyes. "Of course not." He kissed her tenderly. "I can't wait to marry you, however you want, big blowout wedding or ten minutes at city hall. So, whatever you want is fine by me."

"The idea of a girl's day out appeal to you, Ro?" Harper grinned at her encouragingly, and Romy laughed.

"If you don't mind stopping frequently to rest, then I'm in."

Harper tucked her hand under Romy's arm. "Of course. So... tomorrow?"

"Sure thing."

Milo's detective came back to him later that afternoon, and Milo excused himself from Romy and Farron to step out onto the street.

"What did you find?"

"Well, for one thing, Nico Fleming's supposed father was an absentee father for most of his life. All I could find out was that his mother, Caroline, didn't think much of her marriage vows, but then again, the father was a drunk. Nico spent a few years in and out of foster care while they sorted themselves out. But he stayed out of trouble, which seems odd to me. Like he wasn't affected in a negative way by the lack of care."

"That's a good thing, surely?"

"Hmm. There's usually some fallout, like petty theft or fighting, but this kid... there's something hinky. Everything is smoothed out with him. No records, not even a traffic violation."

Milo frowned. He didn't get where the detective was coming from. "Again, I have to ask... why does he ring your bell?"

"Why did you ask me to investigate his family? Somethin' ain't sitting right. Guy's too clean, too helpful. I hate to say it, but even the greatest person has some skeletons. This guy? Nothing. It's just a gut feeling I have... and I'm guessing you do, too."

Milo sighed. He couldn't argue with that. After all, he'd asked this guy to look into Nico. "And you couldn't find out his real father?"

"Nope. Could have been anyone."

Milo was about to say goodbye when he saw the man himself walking toward the gallery. "I'll call you back."

He met Nico at the door. "Hey, man."

"Hey yourself. Heard you and Romy were in town. Thought I'd come say hi."

"Sure."

Romy greeted Nico with a hug, and Milo watched him carefully. There was definitely something in Nico's eyes when he held Romy—but did a crush really make him suspicious? Milo sighed to himself. Was he clutching at straws because he was frustrated the investigation was going nowhere?

Romy released Nico and smiled at him. "It's good to see you, buddy."

"You're looking well. Look, I was thinking... I could replace the flooring where... you know. Free of charge as a gesture of, heck, I don't know, I just feel useless. I was supposed to protect you." Nico looked miserable.

"Nico, you're not my bodyguard. It wasn't your fault. Whoever it was got in somehow, we don't know."

"That right there *is* my fault."

Romy sighed, shaking her head. "Nico..."

He looked down, then back up at her. "Can I talk to you? In private?"

Romy was surprised, and when she glanced at Milo, he didn't look happy. But Nico had been a good friend. "Sure. Give us a few, will you, guys, please?"

"Of course." Farron melted away, and, hesitating for a second, Milo followed him, shooting Nico a concerned look.

Romy closed the office door after them and turned to her friend. "What is it, Nico?"

He gazed at her for a long minute. "I think you know."

Romy sighed. She had known, of course, that Nico had

feelings for her, but she hadn't wanted to confront them. There had been too much going on, and she knew in her heart that Milo was her destiny.

But she also knew that if she said the words aloud, she would lose Nico as a friend.

"Nico…"

"I know you're with Milo. I know that. But it's killing me not to say it aloud. I love you, Romy Park, I'm in love with you. There hasn't been anyone else for me…"

Then she realized. "Nico?"

He slowly looked up at her. "We didn't know each other well back then, but I used to come in here all the time. Your mom and dad, they were so kind to me, but the real reason I always wanted to come was because you might have been here. But I knew you were with Connor, and I didn't stand a chance." He chuckled sadly. "Like father, like son, I guess. My dad was crazy about your mom."

"I know. I found his letters."

Nico nodded, letting out a long breath. "But I'm not here to talk about my dad. Look, I know there's no chance for us, and hell, I really like Milo. You two make a great couple, but I didn't want this hanging over us. I want to be your friend, Ro, but if you feel it would be too awkward…"

"No." Romy drew in a long breath. "I don't want to lose you, Nico. But I don't want to hurt you, either. Yes, I'm with Milo. He is the love of my life, of that I have no doubt, Nico." She hesitated. "And last night, I agreed to marry him."

Nico nodded slowly and smiled wanly. "I thought that might be in the cards. Congratulations, and I mean that."

Ro went to the man and hugged him tightly. "You mean so much to me, Nico, as a friend… as a kind of brother, and I owe you so much. Can we get past this?"

"Of course, we can. You don't owe me anything, Ro."

He gave her a genuine smile then, and Romy grinned. "Of course, now I'll be trying to set you up with my friends... Harper, for one."

"Ha, me and Harper will always be just friends, Ro. Look, I appreciate the offer, but—"

"I know, I'm just kidding." Romy felt a weight lift off her shoulders. She hadn't realized this needed to be said aloud until now, but it had always been there in the back of everything. Now they could move past it.

She opened the door and said, "Let's go join the others."

Romy ordered in food so they could all share lunch together. The gallery was attracting a lot of visitors now, but Romy knew some of them were looky-loos who wanted to see the place where an attempted murder had happened. She fielded the questions politely but shut the inquisitions down quickly.

Milo watched her, pride burning in his eyes. At the end of the day, he drew her into his arms.

"You're amazing, you know that?"

"I'm just me. I have to say, I'm bushed."

"Then we'd better get you home if you're going on this road trip in the morning."

At home, they ate a hastily made pasta dish, then curled up on the sofa. Romy told Milo what Nico had said. As she did so, she studied his face.

"You know that I shut it down, right? I made it completely clear that it was never going to happen."

"I know, I trust you." Milo was quiet for a moment. "How did he seem? Was he upset? Did he creep you out?"

Romy frowned. "No, not at all. Why?"

"I'm looking at everyone with new eyes, Ro. I have to because we're getting nowhere. Before Connor died, I would have sworn *he* was behind everything. He had reason, motive, and certainly the psychopathy to hurt you once you rejected him."

"And now you think... Nico?"

"Wouldn't be the biggest leap, would it? And now you tell me his crush, or whatever you call it, has lasted since before your parents died? Yeah, I'm looking at Nico Fleming."

There was an edge to his voice that made a cold ribbon of fear curl through Romy.

"I just can't see it."

"I've been thinking about those letters to your mother. What if the final one, the threatening one, wasn't directed at her, but rather you? And what if the reason you found them wasn't that you hadn't noticed that box, but because that box had been placed deliberately for you to find? Who had access? Who else had the ability and means to know the layout of the building that well?"

Romy sat up, feeling sick. "No, I won't believe it."

Milo rubbed her back. "Ro... Detective Halsey agrees with me. Nico has motive, the means..."

"But he wouldn't—" Romy's words caught in her throat. "What about Jae? Why would he hurt him?"

"To hurt you. To deflect from himself. Nico didn't have an alibi for that night, but why would he need one? Who would suspect him when Connor was around?"

Romy was silent for a while. "Then why hasn't Halsey questioned him?"

"He has. Nico admitted he was in love with you, readily, in fact, but there's the small fact of evidence, and Nico cooperated with the police fully and without argument. His record is spotless."

"So, why?"

"Because something is off. I don't think Quintin is his biological father, and I think the story is there."

Romy thought of Nico's dark hair. "You don't think... my father?"

"I considered it, but I don't think so. Caroline had a darker complexion like your mother, and I think the resemblance between you and Nico would have been too marked to ignore."

Romy shuddered. "I'm glad because that would be too icky for words."

Milo chuckled softly. "Like the rest of this isn't already disturbing."

"I don't want to believe it's him... but like you said, I'm running out of ideas."

She leaned back into Milo's arms, and he kissed her temple. "Don't worry about it for tonight, love. Tomorrow you can get out of town for a day with Harper and forget all of this."

"A girl's day. I haven't had one of those since I was in Manhattan." Romy chuckled softly, then kissed him.

They held each other for a while, watching Sailor sleep on the rug in front of the fire. After a while, Romy looked up at Milo with troubled eyes. "Milo, tell me everything will be all right."

He pressed his lips to hers before speaking. "I promise, this will all be okay in the end."

But, of course, he was wrong.

FORTY-TWO

THE NEXT DAY DAWNED bright and sunny, and as Harper pulled her car out onto the coastal road, Romy felt her spirits lift. Yes, Milo's security team might have to follow them into the city, but it still felt like they were free to enjoy the day without restriction.

She said as much to Harper, and her friend laughed.

"Doesn't it? I promise, we're going to have an exciting day, Ro, but you will tell me if you're in any pain at any time, right?"

"Yes, mom."

Harper grinned. "Brat."

They chatted easily as they drove towards the city. "The place I'm taking you is a little outside of San Francisco, out near Palo Alto. It's a bespoke wedding dress designer, an old college friend."

"Okay, cool. I don't want anything too... meringue-y."

"Fair enough."

They were still on the coastal road when it happened. Romy had glanced out of the window when she heard the screech of tires behind them and a loud crash. Turning, she saw that the security team's car had been sideswiped. In horror, she watched as the car smashed through the barrier and tumbled down the cliffside.

"Jesus, no! Harper, we have to stop…"

"We can't—look." Harper sounded calmer than Romy would have expected, especially when she realized the car that had swiped the security vehicle was now following them. "I have to concentrate, Ro…keep calm."

"Is he going to run us off the road, too?"

"Quiet, Ro…"

The next few minutes were terrifying. The car chasing after them ducked and weaved behind them but made no attempt to actually run them off the road. Romy's chest was tight with tension. She looked over at Harper. Her friend was pale, obviously scared, but Romy couldn't believe how calmly she was handling it all. The car sped up, and Romy grabbed her bag, searching through it for her cell phone.

"I'll call the police."

The car behind them accelerated past them. "Shit!" Harper tried to angle past them, but the car swerved across the road, blocking their passage, and Harper hit the brakes. The cell phone flew out of Romy's hands before she even had the chance to call 911.

"Brace yourself, Romy!" Harper screamed at her, and Romy's heart almost stopped when she saw what was inevitable.

"No!"

They smacked into the car and flipped over, and Romy heard the agonizing crunch of metal. Her seatbelt tightened across her chest, but then somehow, it came loose, and she was flying forward. Her head connected with the windshield, and everything went dark.

Milo went into town to see Det. Halsey, but before he did, he ducked into the coffee shop to grab a flat white. He thanked the barista as he handed him his drink, then turned. He looked up to see Simon Van Warren walking in.

"Hey, man." The other man nodded to him.

"Simon, how are you?"

Simon looked tired and drawn. "I'm okay. I miss my dad."

"I know. I'm sorry, man. Listen, you want some coffee?"

"Yeah, actually, that sounds good."

They found a table in the window and sat down. Milo studied Simon, noting his disheveled hair and dark circles beneath the eyes. He'd never been overly fond of the other man, thinking him weak and spoiled, but he felt for him now. Simon was devastated.

"Do you need to talk about it, Simon?"

Simon sighed, rubbing his face. "Man, I just... I wasn't prepared, you know? And he was so healthy. He worked out, he ate right."

"It can happen though."

"I know, but... jeez, Mom and I, we want to know what killed him, but Harper... she's burying her head in the sand."

Milo frowned. "What do you mean?"

"She paid someone off to seal the results of the autopsy, said it would be better for the foundation."

"Harper? She said it was your mother who didn't want the results known." Milo was shocked—*Simon must have it wrong in his grief, right?*

An image flashed across his mind of this morning, seeing Romy off with Harper. Both smiling, looking forward to their girl's day. No, Simon was wrong...

"Simon—"

"She's always pulling crap like this," Simon blurted out, interrupting him. "She rules our family, Milo, and yet everyone always falls for the sweet as sugar bullshit." He shook his head.

Milo felt uncomfortable. He knew there had always been rivalry between the two Van Warren siblings, but he'd never heard Simon sound so bitter before.

Everyone in the coffeehouse started as outside on the street, the sudden wail of a police cruiser ripped through, and Milo and Simon watched as more emergency vehicles followed close behind.

"What the hell?"

Milo's heart began to beat unpleasantly. His phone buzzed. His security chief.

"Bill?"

Bill's voice was shaken. "Milo... there's been an accident."

In less than two minutes, he was out of the coffeehouse and in his car, following the emergency vehicles out to the coastal road. It was all he could do to stop himself from throwing up. Bill had told him the news in a dulled, shocked voice.

"They ran my guys off the road, Milo. They're dead. Dead. One of them, Hal, just had a baby. I know it's a high-risk job, but..." He took a shaky breath in. "Whoever did this took the girls, Milo. I'm so sorry. They have Romy and Harper."

Milo felt an icy hand squeezing his heart as he sped out to the scene of the accident. As he approached the police cordon, he slowed down and stopped his car. Traffic was building up on both sides, and the traffic cops were struggling to cope.

Milo got out and ran down to the police tape. A police officer stopped him.

"Sir, please, get back in your car."

"It's my fiancée's car," Milo tried to keep his voice calm. "She's missing, please, I—"

"Let him through."

Milo saw Det. Halsey then, his face grim. "Jim..."

"Milo, I'm sorry. There's no sign of Romy and Harper."

He beckoned Milo closer, and Milo saw Harper's car on its side. The windshield on the passenger side was smashed, and

Milo wanted to throw up when he saw blood and hair on the shattered glass.

Oh my God, Romy...

He looked at Halsey. "Nico Fleming. He's the only one left who has any reason..."

"Way ahead of you. We've been looking into him since the stabbing and found nothing, until one of our researchers came up with a still from a security cam the night Keith Van Warren died." Halsey got out his phone and flipped to the video. "Here."

Milo looked at the shot. Keith Van Warren was holding Sailor's leash as he walked down the cliff stairs to the beach where he was found dead. The next still showed a shadowy figure following him.

Milo frowned. "How do you know that's Nico? And weren't Keith Van Warren's records sealed?"

"They were. But I have friends in the coroner's office. I got the news this morning. He was killed by an air embolism. Someone injected him with an empty syringe. Went straight to his heart."

"Keith was murdered."

"Yes. And to answer your question about Nico, we tracked back all the security cams we could find and got a lock on his movements for the night. Can I prove it conclusively? No. But we have people looking for him now, and he's AWOL. None of his construction guys have seen him, and he was supposed to be out at a job in Carmel. Never showed."

Milo felt panic rising inside him, but he tamped it down. Panicking wouldn't help Romy right now. "You think he took them?"

"I can't say for sure, but that's what we're working on right now. Listen—" He nodded away from the other investigators and lowered his voice. "The letters Romy found. The last one, the threatening one, was written after the others, and by that, I mean it was written *recently*. We tested the paper. The older ones were typewritten, and we know they were from Quintin's old Smith Corona. He still has it."

Halsey let this sink in to Milo's mind. "Fuck."

"Right. So, for now, we're looking at Nico Fleming for this. We think his… *fondness*… for Romy goes way past that. But we think he had help."

Milo closed his eyes. "Please don't say it." Keith Van Warren had been murdered, and Harper had the records sealed. *Harper.* No, he wouldn't believe it.

They were interrupted then, and Halsey was called away for a moment. Milo felt utterly hopeless. *I failed you, baby, I failed you again.*

He pulled out his phone and called his investigator. "Please tell me you have something, anything."

"I was going to try and get into Fleming's place today, but the police are all over it. I did get hold of some of the senior Fleming's medical records, something from an old blood drive back when the Parks were killed. Someone arranged for a blood drive to help the hospital that was looking after Romy. I can't say for sure who Nico's father was, but it ain't Quintin Fleming. Wrong blood group."

Milo thanked him and went to find Halsey to tell him.

"We suspected as much." Halsey nodded.

"Did he kill Connor?"

"Possibly. I'm surprised he didn't go after you if he really is obsessed with Romy."

Milo shot a look at the wrecked car again, the blood— Romy's blood—making him want to scream. "Why would he try and kill her if he was in love with her?"

Halsey gave a humorless chuckle. "I don't think trying to look at this in a sane manner is the way to go. Look at the evidence: he had access, we know he had asked her out before and been rejected. He used his 'salt of the earth' reputation to get close and fool us all."

"I just... I had a hunch, but this is all conjecture. Until we can find something concrete, we're shooting in the dark." Milo looked at Halsey unhappily. "Do you think she's already dead? Harper, too?"

"I don't. At all. If they were already dead, their bodies would be here."

Milo felt useless hanging around, so he went back into town and called Jae.

"I'm so sorry, man."

"We're coming down. Right now." Jae sounded shocked and terrified, and Milo empathized.

"I know, I failed her again."

"No," Jae said, surprising him, "this isn't your fault. It's the psycho's fault. Somehow, I feel like this was always inevitable. Romy's tough. She's a survivor. We have to believe that. She'll find a way to come back to us."

Milo could only hope he was right.

FORTY-THREE

ROMY'S EYES FELT STICKY as she opened them, and her vision was blurry. She felt a cold compress being pressed against her forehead. "Don't try to speak."

She recognized the voice. "Harper?"

"Ssh, it's okay, I'm here."

Despite Harper's warning, Romy sat up, her head screaming with pain. "Where are we?"

"I don't know. I woke up, and we were here."

Romy blinked and looked around. There was sunlight coming into what looked like a basement, but the room was bare, apart from the mattress both women were sitting on and a bucket of water. Harper wiped Romy's face, and Romy saw blood on the cloth.

"What the hell happened?"

"We were taken. He ran us off the road." Harper's hair was mussed, and there were cuts on her face and arms, but she didn't look as hurt as Romy was.

"Who?"

Harper shook her head. "I don't know. Romy, you're hurt. Please lay down and rest."

"I'm okay." Romy gently pushed Harper away and got unsteadily to her feet. She walked over to the door and banged on it. "Hey! Hey, asshole!"

"Ro…"

"*No.*" She turned on Harper. "No, I've had enough of this. I want to know who the hell thinks he can fuck with my life like this. And if it's between me and him, then so be it, but there's no way I'm going to let him hurt another person I love."

"Ro…"

Romy banged harder on the door. "Hey! *Motherfucker!* Come get me!"

She was beyond angry now. *I want this to be over, one way or another.* She would offer him anything if he would just let Harper go. Harper tried to pull her away from the door, but Romy resisted. Her battered body was in agony, but her rage damped the pain into background noise.

She was still yelling when the door opened. Romy stopped, then gave a humorless laugh.

"So… Milo was right."

Nico Fleming smiled at her, levelling a small handgun at her. "Hi Romy. How does it feel knowing you're going to die today?"

Halsey called Milo. "Milo, we got a court order to go to Fleming's apartment. I'll let you know what we find."

Milo had decided to wait for Jae and Moon at the gallery. Farron sat quietly with him, shellshocked from the morning's events. Milo was going crazy.

"I don't know what to do, Farron."

Farron watched him, his face pale. "I was never keen on the Flemings."

Milo gave him a wan smile. "Quint—"

"Was in love with Giovanna, too, I know. But it wasn't him I disliked. The mother... Caroline. If you think Wendy Small was a social climber, she had nothing on Caroline. That boy of hers, he fooled us all, I think."

"Do you remember him from years ago?"

"He was always in the bookstore. I think he had a thing for Romy, but she was so tied up with the Small boy before the wedding."

Milo sighed. "So he had motive?"

"More than you think. Quintin was never around, never paid much attention to him. When he realized Caroline wasn't faithful, he spent all his time mooning after Giovanna. Jin... he was rattled about it, but Giovanna told him it was just a harmless crush. But it meant Quintin was never home for the boy."

"You have any idea who Nico's biological father could be?"

Farron shrugged. "Anyone with more than a million in the bank? That was Caroline's thing."

"Like... Keith Van Warren?"

"Maybe."

"Jesus." Milo shook his head, almost blurted out the truth about Sarah, then remembered his promise to Eben. No, this was about Nico.

And rejection, he realized. All his life, Nico had been second best. To his mother, who wanted social status, to his father who wanted another woman. To Romy, who chose Connor first, and then Milo.

What if Nico had known Keith was Sarah's father? What if Keith had known he was Nico's father and rejected him, too? Would that be motive enough to kill Sarah and Keith?

Everything was slotting into place now. *Nico Fleming is a sick fuck, a poor little lost boy who resented the fact he was always second choice, at least in his own mind.* Milo looked at Farron and decided to test his theory. He told the other man everything he was thinking.

Farron nodded slowly. "That sounds plausible. And if he's taken Harper, too, he could be cleaning house entirely. She's the last link."

"Apart from his own father."

"That too." Farron sighed. "What a fucking mess."

"Have you any idea where he might have taken them?"

Farron looked lost. "He's a contractor—he could have access to any number of empty properties."

Milo called Halsey. "Already on it. We went to his apartment. It was cleaned out. Milo, if it is him—and it's looking increasingly likely—then I don't think he's planning on living through this."

"Which gives him nothing to lose by killing Romy and Harper."

"No. I'm sorry, man. Hang tight. We're on it."

"What do you want, Nico? What has all this been about?"

He had tied the two women up now, or rather he had held a gun on Harper while she tied Romy's hands in front of her with a zip tie and then bound Harper across the other side of the room. Romy stared at him, hatred in her eyes. Nico smiled at her.

"Cleaning house, Romy. Everyone who has ever *dismissed* me, or *cheated* me, or *ignored* me."

"Pathetic."

His smile faltered, and he cuffed her across the face. "Shut your filthy mouth."

Romy's head snapped back, and she groaned. *Don't make him mad while Harper is here...*

"Look, you have me. Just let Harper go, that's all I ask."

"I can't do that, Romy."

"Why? What has she ever done to you, Nico? What have any of us done to you?" She stared at him. "Did you kill my parents?"

"Yes."

The immediate response floored her, and she felt a sob rising in her throat. "Why?"

"They were just collateral, Romy. You were the one I wanted dead."

"Why?"

"Because you chose *him*. Because you chose everyone over me."

"What about Jae?"

"Just a warning. Do you honestly think I give a fuck about your cousin and his boyfriend?"

"It doesn't make sense."

"I wanted you scared, frightened. And then I would swoop in and protect you. But, as always, you chose someone else. Like my father did." He waved the gun in Harper's direction. "You've met my dear half-sister, of course."

Romy wasn't shocked. "So, it is true. And Sarah Keys?"

"A bastard like me. I like to think of Sarah as my practice run. I hadn't intended to kill her, I just wanted to be in her life, be a brother, but she wouldn't believe me. She didn't want to hear that Keith was her father. So..." He shrugged. "I'd already killed once. It took nothing to stick that knife into her."

"But how the hell did you get away with it? Why didn't the police investigate Sarah's death as a murder?"

Nico smirked. "Ah, there's the rub. Not quite ready to tell you that yet."

"I don't get it. Why didn't you just kill me in the car? Why bring us here?"

"Because I fucked it up last time. I wanted to take my time

killing you. Stabbing you was such a rush, but I had so little time to do it. I won't make that mistake again."

"You're fucking insane. You'll never get away with this."

"I don't intend to live to find out."

And that was the line that finally scared Romy into shutting up.

FORTY-FOUR

WHEN JAE AND MOON arrived, Milo went to them and wrapped his arms around them both. They both—even Jae—hugged him back, the three of them standing in a shocked, silent vigil for a few moments.

When Milo released them, Moon's face was wet with tears, and Jae looked drawn and thin. "I'm so sorry, Jae."

"It's not your fault. Do the police have any clues where she's been taken yet?"

Milo shook his head and filled them in on what he knew so far.

"Halsey promised to get in touch as soon as they know anything more."

"Talk of the devil," Farron spoke up behind them, and they turned to see Detective Halsey walking into the gallery.

"Milo. Hey, Jae, Moon. Mr. Lee."

Milo stared him. "Jim?"

"There's been a development. A significant one." Halsey drew in a long breath. "Forensics were doing their preliminary examination of the car. We found that the driver's seat belt had been cut through. However, the passenger's side... wasn't. It had been released or had never been worn. Which is why I need to ask you, Milo, would there be any reason Romy wouldn't wear her seatbelt?"

Milo shook his head. "No, and she was wearing it this morning, because I fastened it myself." He smiled wanly. "She was kind of mad about it, telling me she could 'fix the damn thing' herself."

"Then it was released sometime after they set off. Milo, we took some fingerprints from the fastening. Would you mind? We just need to eliminate yours."

"Not at all. Should I come to the station?"

"Please." Halsey looked around at the rest of them. "It might be an idea for you all to come, just so we can keep you informed."

"And safe. Yes, guys, you all need to come."

The car ride to the station was silent. After Milo had given his prints, they were shown to a room and offered coffee. Then it was hours of waiting, of frustration, of terror, thinking that any moment Halsey would come to say they had found Romy and Harper dead.

When Halsey came to see them, it was with a grim expression. "No news on their whereabouts, but we do have an idea who Nico's accomplice is… and you're not going to believe it."

"Are you okay?" Romy asked Harper, who shook her head.

"No."

"Where does it hurt?"

Harper chuckled to herself. "Everywhere, but I'm not the one recovering from a stabbing."

"But you were in the accident, too."

"I had my seatbelt on."

Romy frowned. "I thought I had mine on… I did have mine

on. It must have failed, somehow." She fell silent again, bringing the plastic tie that bound her hands to her mouth and trying to gnaw through it.

Harper was silent for a long moment, watching her, as they heard Nico approaching the door.

"Harper, where do you think we are?" Romy whispered, but the door opened before Harper could reply.

Nico came in. "Okay, you can get up now, Harper."

Romy was confused. "What?"

Nico grinned at her. "God, I never took you as dumb, Romy. How do you think I knew where you'd be today?" He looked over at Harper, who smiled back at him and pulled her unbound hands from behind her back.

She smirked at Romy. "Surprise, bitch."

The shock was icy cold and constricting—every truth Romy had known shattered.

"Harper... I don't understand."

Both Harper and Nico laughed while Harper rubbed her wrists. "I'm his accomplice, you moron. How do you think he found it so easy to get to us? How he knew we would be travelling together along that road at that time?"

Romy hardly recognized her friend. "Why? Why are you doing this?"

Harper was across the room in a flash, pinching Romy's face hard in her fingers.

"Why? Because Connor loved *you*, Romy. He *always* loved you. *Everyone* fucking *loves* Romy Park. Just like everyone fucking *loved* Sarah Keys." She looked back at Nico. "My *brother* here is right. We got screwed over by everyone. My parents, his parents, you. So, like he said, we're cleaning house."

Romy couldn't breathe. Harper? No, she had to be dreaming... but she knew she wasn't.

"I can't believe this."

Nether of her captors said anything, and Romy closed her eyes. There was no hope. The police, Milo, no one would never think to suspect Harper of helping Nico. Romy retched then and threw up, spattering Harper's expensive pumps.

"Jesus." Harper backed off in disgust. "Why don't you just fucking kill her already? What are you waiting for?"

She moved to the other side of the room and took her shoes off. Nico didn't take his eyes off Romy.

"Because we're going to have some fun, first, aren't we Romy? By the time I've finished with you, you'll be begging me to kill you."

Romy's head pounded, and dark spots swam in her vision. "Where are we? If you're going to kill me, does it matter if you tell me?"

"Don't tell her."

Nico gave a heavy sigh. "Harper, when did I put you in charge?"

"What?"

Nico turned to smile at her. "You've served your purpose, Harper. You gave me access and alibis. You got me into her condo, her gallery... Milo's place. You brought her to me today. Thank you."

"What?" Harper frowned at him.

"I don't need you anymore."

Romy cringed back against the wall as Nico reached for her, but he easily pulled Romy up into his arms. She made herself a deadweight, and he grimaced. Harper hovered near the door.

"What do you mean, you don't need me? We're in this *together*, asshole. We made a deal."

"Harper, if you still want Milo Keys, then you need to not be here when I kill the love of his life."

Romy, to the surprise of all of them, suddenly laughed. "So that's what this is really about, Harper? You wanted Milo?"

Harper narrowed her eyes at her. "And I would have had him, too, he was primed and ready, but…"

"*If it wasn't for you pesky kids.*" Romy quoted at her. "I think they call that the Scooby Doo motive."

"Fuck you."

"Milo already does that." Romy had nothing left to lose now, but the look in Nico's eyes told her something—he had no loyalty to Harper, and if Harper pissed him off enough… maybe she could distract him. It was just a case of riling Harper up enough… "That gets to you, doesn't it? Thinking of me and him making love… and it's so good, Harper. The best ever… I can see why you hate me… I always get them first, don't I? When I'm dead, do you really want my sloppy seconds?"

Harper lost it then, darting over to her and slapping Romy hard across the face. Screaming profanities, Harper clawed her fingernails down Romy's face, drawing blood, before Nico, letting go of Romy, grabbed Harper's shoulders.

"Get a fucking grip or I'll—"

Romy, freed from his grip, whirled around and grabbed the metal bucket of water. Swinging around, she brought the edge of it down on Nico's temple as hard as she could.

He went down, not knocked out but shocked by the sudden blow. Harper recovered first, running at Romy, but Romy put her head down and rammed it hard into Harper's stomach.

The other woman went down, and Romy ducked away from them and ran for the door. The first bullet pinged off the door frame as Nico shot at her, but Romy didn't care. She was going to die anyway, and she was damned if she wasn't going to try and get as far away from her killers as possible, if only to make it harder for them to escape justice.

The second bullet grazed her shoulder as she got through the door… and found herself in some kind of hunting lodge. Where the hell were they?

In the divorce, I got the mansion and the hunting lodge in the woods…

The middle of nowhere. But Romy knew she didn't have time to waste.

"Romy, look! I'll kill her."

Romy stopped and turned, her heart thudding wildly. Nico had Harper in his arms, and the gun pressed to her ex-friend's temple. Nico smiled as Harper whimpered.

"Now, she may have betrayed you, but I know you don't want her to die. Not like this. Now, get back here, and I'll let her go."

Romy's eyes met Harper's. *It's my life or yours, she thought… and you have blood on your hands.*

"I'm sorry."

Harper screamed as Romy darted through the lodge and yanked open the door. It was dark outside, and she plunged into what looked like thick forest. She heard a muffled shot and gave a sob… Nico had gone through with it. He'd killed Harper, and now he was coming after her.

Branches whipped against her face and skin as she ran as fast as she could, not caring that her battered body was screaming at her to stop, to take a breath. Fear, terror, pain—it all crazed her mind, but all she could think of was to run.

The sudden bright light in her eyes and the sound of men shouting made her scream, tripping over and slamming to the hard ground beneath her. The air was whipped into a frenzy around her, and the noise was deafening.

What was going on?

*Schwoop schwoop…*The rhythm above her was familiar…

A helicopter.

What the hell....

"Romy!"

Through her madness, she heard him, and it was like a breath of heaven to her fevered mind.

"Milo?"

There was noise, shouting, lights, and she was being lifted. Panic was her first reaction, but then she felt herself being held tightly, a familiar voice murmuring that he loved her over and over, and that it was all okay now.

EPILOGUE

Seven months later...

ROMY FELT HIS ARMS go around her, and she leaned back into Milo's big body. "Is it time?"

"It is."

She turned in his arms and smiled up at him. "I love you, Mr. Keys."

"I love you, Mrs. Keys."

"That sounds so grown up."

Milo chuckled, then sighed. "Come on. Let's get this over and done with."

They walked hand in hand back to the courtroom and took their places. The judge came in, and they all stood. Romy looked over at the defense table.

Harper Van Warren stood in her black dress with a white pilgrim collar. She half-turned to look at Romy, but at the last minute looked away.

You had me fooled, lady. Romy could feel nothing but sadness. All that potential thrown away because of jealousy.

Nico had turned the gun on himself, not Harper, obviously.

At first, Romy had thought that finally he'd done the right thing, but Milo had argued, "He was a coward. He was equally to blame, but he left her to deal with the consequences. Fuck them both."

Romy felt Milo squeeze her hand now. She was glad Jae and Moon hadn't come today—it was more affecting than she had expected, and when, a few moments later, the jury found Harper guilty on every count, Romy felt only a deep sadness.

They didn't speak in the car on the way home, but Romy kept her hand in Milo's. Sailor greeted them joyfully, and they both hugged the dog before going upstairs to change.

As Romy pulled off her jacket, she gave a sigh and looked over to her husband of three weeks. "It's done."

"It's over." Milo drew her close and kissed her. "Finally. And we made it."

"We did. And our family is safe at last." Romy leaned into him, and he tightened his arms around her.

"You bet it is. *Our* family."

Romy brushed her lips against his. "Do you know how much I love you?"

"I've got a pretty good idea." He chuckled as she grinned at him. "But I'd probably be more convinced if you were naked right now."

"Such a pervert." But she was already unbuttoning his shirt and soon, she was naked, too, as they tumbled onto the bed.

There was a lightness to their lovemaking this time, something that hadn't been there before. Their nightmare was truly over. Romy giggled as Milo tickled her until she was breathless, then as he hitched her legs around his waist and thrust his ramrod hard cock deep into her, she gasped and writhed beneath him until fireworks exploded in her vision and every cell in her body ignited.

Milo buried his face in her neck and gave a long, shuddering groan as he came inside her, and Romy clenched her muscles around his spasming cock. "Jesus, Romy... Romy..."

As they recovered their breath, Romy smiled up at him. "You know, we get to do that whenever we want for the rest of our lives."

Milo chuckled. "Hell, yes. Even when I'm old and grey..."

"*When?*"

Romy shrieked with laughter as he tickled her as punishment for her teasing. "Okay, okay, I'm sorry..."

He gathered her to him. "You're forgiven. Are you excited about tomorrow?"

"We're meeting the newest member of our family. Of course, I'm excited."

"We'll be a family of four."

"Six. You're forgetting the kids."

Milo laughed. "Moon and Jae *hate* it when you call them that."

"Which is why I do it." Romy stuck her tongue out at him, then sighed happily. "But yes, I cannot wait for tomorrow."

The next day, Romy had tears in her eyes as she gazed at her 'daughter.'

"Oh, she's so beautiful."

The small Cavalier King Charles Spaniel, a rich ruby red color, looked up at Romy and Milo with big brown eyes, her little wiggly body a blur as she wagged her tail. Romy scooped her up in her arms.

The rescue center staff member smiled at her. "Have you chosen a name yet?"

Milo stroked the puppy's silky head. "Nova. Her name is Nova."

"New beginnings," Romy whispered, and Milo kissed her temple.

"A new life for all of us. Happy, forever."

Romy's eyes filled with tears, and she nodded.

"Forever," she agreed, and kissed him again.

DARK HEARTS BOOK 2

SAY HER NAME

COMING SOON

AFTER THE LOSS OF her infant daughter and the subsequent breakdown of her marriage, New York radio producer Autumn Riley is struggling to get her life back on track.

Burying herself in work, she returns from a break in California to find that her radio station has scored the biggest coup in recent years—an exclusive series with Noah Larsen, a Danish-American writer and Nobel Prize winner who has just written a book that is causing scandal amongst the Manhattan elite.

But then Autumn begins to receive photographs of a child who resembles her dead daughter, and her inner demons come back to haunt her.

Will her new love Noah help her to overcome the terrible loss and find out who is threatening her?

Or will Autumn give in to the overwhelming grief and let her tormentor win?

ABOUT THE AUTHOR

MIA O'SULLIVAN

Mia O'Sullivan enjoys travelling and theatre when not creating her next suspenseful thriller romance or contemporary sexy and passionate paranormal love affair novels. However, wherever the location or backdrop of her next genre's plot, the readers can always expect her novels to be fantastically, shockingly, steamy and a little prohibitive.

STAY CONNECTED

Like my Facebook page to get updates, fun, and prizes!

Other books from Chestnut Treehouse Publishers
www.chestnutpublishers.com

ALSO BY MIA O'SULLIVAN

DARK HEARTS SERIES

Book 1: Tell Me Why
https://buy.bookfunnel.com/m5biaoth34

Book 2: Say Her Name
https://buy.bookfunnel.com/s4cn7x2jng

Book 3: His Beautiful Liar
(upcoming in 2020)

THE MONTGOMERY CHRONICLES

Book 1: Finding Alexandra
(upcoming in 2020)

Book 2: Enemies of Mine
https://buy.bookfunnel.com/8gs0j3o4q3

Book 3: Betrayals
(upcoming in 2020)

VENETIAN VAMPIRES SERIES

Book 1: Blood Innocente
https://buy.bookfunnel.com/ab27tiqzau

Book 2: Blood Primativa
(upcoming in 2020)

www.ingramcontent.com/pod-product-compliance
Lightning Source LLC
Chambersburg PA
CBHW05202424 0626
47153CB00006B/1950